THE DUKE'S AMULET

THE DUKE'S AMULET

A Novel

Phyllis Martino-Nugent

iUniverse, Inc.

New York Lincoln Shanghai

The Duke's Amulet

iUniverse books may be ordered through booksellers or by contacting:

iUniverse
2021 Pine Lake Road, Suite 100
Lincoln, NE 68512
www.iuniverse.com
1-800-Authors (1-800-288-4677)

Because of the dynamic nature of the Internet, any Web addresses or links contained in this book may have changed since publication and may no longer be valid.

This is a work of fiction. All of the characters, names, incidents, organizations, and dialogue in this novel are either the products of the author's imagination or are used fictitiously.

ISBN: 978-0-595-46217-9 (pbk)
ISBN: 978-0-595-70505-4 (cloth)
ISBN: 978-0-595-90518-8 (ebk)

Printed in the United States of America

For my husband, Thomas M. Nugent,
whose confidence and support never faltered

"For when all is said and done, the very fabric of the universe, which we can contemplate in the vast spaces of heaven, so resplendent with their shining stars, in the earth at its centre, girdled by the seas, … adorned with so many different varieties of trees, lovely flowers and grasses, can be said to be a great and noble painting, composed by Nature and the hand of God. And, in my opinion, whoever can imitate it deserves the highest praise."

The Book of the Courtier by Baldassare Castiglione
© George Bull, 1967 Penguin Books

PROLOGUE

▼

Firenze, 1490

The light is fading quickly. The gloom persisted all day, punctuated by sporadic rainfall, and despite the lamps I lit, little light remains. Still, I plod on at the desk by the window. I sense that my time on this earth grows short. So, I write my story, the story of how I came to be in this place and in this time. Even though my fingers are cramped and my tired eyes burn, I am determined to relate our story on these pages—the story of our love, which has bound us together. My love, the master of my heart, does not fret over my constant scribbling, although I expect he will soon come to fetch me. He understands my need to write this memoir. I trust him in all things, and I will trust him until I die. He promised that he will keep the memoir safe.

I write in my native language. It becomes more and more difficult to recall my own tongue so this is an exercise to remember my history as well, not only for myself, but perhaps one day for my children. There is much about my previous life I have forgotten after all my years here. The faces of my family are no more than faint shadows. I miss my brother most, but I try not to dwell on a past that is forever lost in the mists of time.

I read somewhere that in medieval times the great mystics and those gifted with visions were encouraged by their superiors in Orders to record their inward journeys. So now, I, too, make this record of my journey upon this earth, and I pray it may bring me a measure of peace. Some day, perhaps this memoir will be found and read. No doubt there will be cynics who will discount it as the ravings of a madwoman, but maybe too there will be believers.

Time, in the end, is the master of our fates, and fate has given me the greatest gift of all. This is my moment in time, and I have lived out my life in the here and now. While it is true that I am a prisoner here, it is a prison I welcome. For I am loved and love in return. I am held captive to a kiss.

CHAPTER 1

▼

Urbino, Italy, Modern Day

Liz Cummings opened one eye and squinted at the bright sunshine streaming into the room. The sound of church bells ringing from the towers of nearby churches roused her from a deep sleep. In that moment between sleep and wakefulness, the bells reached into her dream and became part of it. Seconds passed before she realized where she was and recalled why she had come to Italy in the first place.

The burial chamber. She would see it today.

She raised her head and looked around the unfamiliar room.

Throwing back the covers, she rose and quietly crossed the room to the window. She felt the soft, plush oriental carpet tickling her feet. She leaned against the sill and peered through the morning glare at the budding trees. Spring had come early to Italy.

"What's that ungodly racket?"

The muffled voice came from behind her. Liz turned to look at the source. Janet Conklin lay sprawled on her stomach in the twin bed next to her own. The pillow covering her head barely concealed her unruly mop of red hair.

"Church bells."

"I know," Janet groaned. "But why, and when will it stop?"

"It's Sunday, Janet, and I have no idea when they'll stop."

"Oh, God, my head hurts."

"I'm sorry to hear that," Liz tried unsuccessfully to sound sympathetic. She circled her bed to the nightstand and picked up her watch. "We'd better get moving. We're supposed to meet up downstairs with everyone for breakfast in less than an hour. Do you want to use the bathroom first?"

"No!"

The bells ceased pealing.

"Thank God," Janet mumbled.

Liz picked her way to the bathroom through their suitcases and belongings partially disgorged on the floor in piles and thrown on chairs and dresser tops. She washed hurriedly, thankful she had tossed her toiletries on the sink the night before. They had arrived hours overdue fit for nothing more than collapsing into bed. The quick shower perked her up and washed away the grime of more than nine and a half hours of travel.

Her inspection of their room and bath when they arrived had been brief and came as a pleasant surprise. Six months in this room would not be so bad, unless she considered too closely the prospect of sharing the bedroom and bath with Janet.

She glanced around the large tiled bathroom while she put on her underwear. The foreign bidet in the corner was the only item in the room to give her pause. She recalled Janet's crude comment at first catching sight of it.

"You wouldn't mind if I had a friend sleep over, would you?" Janet asked with a tilt of her head in the direction of the bidet. "It's what the French designed it for, you know, repairing long afternoons in the sack." Janet threw her head back and laughed when she observed the embarrassing rush of color on Liz's face. Liz had prayed her whole life for the ability to control her blushes. She turned away, pretending not to hear Janet's remark or her scornful laugh.

Liz desperately wanted to get along with her teammates, but Janet's teasing embarrassed Liz. It would have been so easy to point out that the University might frown on sleepovers or let the crudity of the remark set the tone for their relationship.

Since they would be working together on the same project and sharing the same living space, Liz bit her tongue. The last thing Liz wanted was to appear inexperienced or worse—prudish.

Liz pushed the incident out of her mind and slapped on some moisturizer, brushed her chin length bob, and applied a little lipstick before returning to the bedroom. A quick rummage through her suitcase produced a sweater and a pair of checked slacks. With a sideways look, Liz confirmed that Janet had not moved.

"Janet. You better get moving. The bathroom's yours."

Janet rose on all fours, climbed from the bed and staggered into the bathroom.

"I'm going downstairs to look around," Liz called as the bathroom door slammed shut.

She grabbed her purse and a jacket and left, taking a last look around.

The room in daylight showed that a good deal of care had been taken to provide them with comfortable, if not luxurious, accommodations. Both rooms had been freshly painted, and the handsome, though worn, oriental carpet on the bedroom floor, paired with the lofty ceilings, lent the room an air of old world elegance. Burgundy draperies, hung on wooden rings from decorative rods, coordinated perfectly with the wine-red color of the carpet. Lots of closet space and five drawers each in the two antique dressers assured that the roommates would not be cramped. On one dresser, a small microwave oven occupied a corner with an assortment of cups, glasses and bowls stacked neatly beside it.

Their room faced east on the second floor of a two story dormitory building of the *Università di Urbino*. In the morning light, the aged brick of the university buildings glowed warmly. Liz walked briskly along the landing and caught a glimpse over the railing of Steve Nelson, her supervisor, and Jack Schmitt, the fourth member of the team from the University Museum in Philadelphia. They were talking in the courtyard with Dr. Mariangela Grasso, their liaison, who had met them last night. Liz hurried down the stairs to join the little group.

As she approached them, Dr. Grasso greeted her with a cheerful, *"Buon giorno."*

"Good morning," Liz responded, her gaze resting momentarily on Dr. Grasso, and then, turning to the men, informed them, "Janet will be along in a few minutes, I think."

"I'm afraid, Dr. Grasso, that we're still a little jet lagged," Steve said.

"Please don't worry about it. The long delays you experienced were unfortunate. As soon as Janet joins us, we will walk to the dining hall; it is not far. And we will discuss what we have learned so far about our unknown nobleman before we join the rest of the group. There will be many introductions and so forth.

"Also, I would like to introduce our beautiful city to you this evening as my guests for dinner."

"That would be very nice, Doctor, thank you," Steve replied for the others.

Liz made a concerted effort not to notice the wolfish expression on Steve's face, but she could feel her throat tighten even as she smiled pleasantly. Both men wore identical expressions, and Liz longed to snap them out of it with a well-placed head-slam.

Dr. Grasso, a petite brunette, in stark contrast to Liz's own slightly taller, slim blondeness, had strong Roman features. Even when dressed conservatively in a gray skirt and pink twin set, she packed a sensual punch. Liz pegged her at early thirties. She wore her long hair off her face in a french braid. Too severe a hairstyle for one so young, nevertheless, it displayed to perfection her fine skin and delicate bone structure.

"Here she comes," Jack said. "Hurry up, Janet, I'm starving," he called out to her.

All he got in response from Janet was a scowl and an even slower pace.

They left the courtyard entrance on foot and turned right.

"*Eccolo*! There is the *Palazzo*," Dr. Grasso said, pointing up to the top of the hill.

Staring at the *Palazzo*, Liz felt a prickle of excitement that started in her fingertips and traveled up her arms until the hairs rose on the back of her neck.

The gray stone building, both grand and graceful in its proportions, dominated the hilltop like a queen on her throne.

Deep within the building, discovered only recently in a hidden burial chamber, was a mystery waiting to be solved. The skeleton of an early renaissance nobleman and the artifacts interred with him was what had brought her to Italy.

∗   ∗   ∗   ∗

Breakfast was noisy. All the members of the team were gathered for the "meet and greet," and the atmosphere soon turned festive.

"Dr. Grasso," Liz said, "I expected to hear only Italian, but I've lost count of all the languages being spoken, and some I don't even recognize."

"And now, we can add English to the mix," Steve interjected.

"Students come from all over Europe to study here in Urbino and Padua and throughout Italy," Dr. Grasso explained. "Help is here from the University of Padua and also students from Prague, Budapest, Krakow, Bratislava, Hamburg, Munich, so the unfamiliar languages you hear may be Polish, Czech or Slovak.

"In general, these students are studying our methods for conservation and restoration. Since the fall of communism, the governments of the former eastern bloc countries—whose antiquities were sorely neglected for fifty years or more—are engaged in an enormous undertaking to save their cultural treasures, and as part of that effort, are subsidizing the studies here of their brightest students."

"I know our country's private foundations are also involved in funding what they see as world heritage sites that face certain destruction without the vast sums of money needed to bring them back from the brink," Steve added.

"You are correct, Dr. Nelson. I know that large donations came to Italy from the United States to help with restoration after the earthquake in Assisi in 1997." Dr. Grasso looked up expectantly.

"And here is Dr. Bertolucci to greet you."

An elegantly dressed man who could have been a double for the actor Vittorio DeSica approached the table.

"Welcome, *benvenuti*. We are very happy you are here to help us."

Dr. Bertolucci circled the table, shaking hands with all four members of their team.

"Thank you, Doctor, we're certainly glad to help in any way we can. And thank you for the comfortable accommodations."

"If you need anything, please, you need only ask. My old friend, your director, would be upset with me if I did not take good care of you. Now, are you ready to see the burial chamber? Of course, you are. *Andiamo*."

Dr. Bertolucci, head of the project, and Dr. Grasso escorted them through the galleries to the chapel where Dr. Bertolucci, with expansive gestures, gave them a brief history about the *Palazzo* and it occupants.

"Now, this building is the National Gallery of the Marche, but it began as a fortress in the 1200s. In the 1400s, Duke Federico, the greatest *condottiero* or warlord of that age, expanded it into what you see today, as a home for his family, you understand, one to rival any of the great houses in Italy. Its galleries today hold some of the greatest art of the western world, and we are fortunate to have some fine Raphaels along with those of his father, Giovanni Sanzio, who was Duke Federico's court painter."

They walked the length of one gallery and turned into another. Countless paintings, portraits mostly, were arrayed along the walls in a double row like the ancestors of a lost race, which in fact they were. Liz walked along under the gaze of the faces that seemed to peer down at her with a sneering haughtiness. Some of the faces were quite beautiful, while the expressions of others were terrifying in their cruel features. The jewels and brocade in which they were painted to display their wealth and position could not hide their soullessness and lack of humanity.

"Raphael was born in Urbino as were many other great artists and architects, like Bramante," Dr. Bertolucci continued. "The list of artists who embellished this building is a litany to the precursors of the High Renaissance. Perugino, Ucello, Titian, Botticelli and the great Piero della Francesca, whose work also adorns the Church of San Bernardino here in Urbino. They are all here. Their hands and hearts were guided in great measure by Duke Federico. He was very demanding and had the most exquisite taste, as you see. And here we are at the chapel."

He hung back to allow them to enter.

Silence fell as they admired the colorful frescoes adorning the walls and ceiling of the massive chapel. Dr. Bertolucci did not rush them, but led them slowly to the back of the altar to a wide staircase.

"I wanted you to see the family crypt and the chamber before we went to the laboratories to view the artifacts and the remains of our nobleman, so that you will have a clearer picture of our discovery and the work you have traveled so far to do."

They descended the stone staircase into the crypt. The stairway, which was wide at the top in the chapel, narrowed slightly and then more as they went down into the subterranean depths of the *Palazzo*. Halogen lamps mounted on the walls ensured plenty of light to see their way down. The cool, dry air had a musty odor that was only mildly unpleasant.

Though the group spoke in whispers, their voices echoed off the stone walls.

When they had gone down about fifteen steps, dampness enveloped them and conversation ceased. The silence, interrupted only by a nervous cough or two, confirmed that the group marked the change. It grew darker, and the stone steps, a little slippery.

Liz reached out to steady herself; her hand came in contact with the cold, damp granite wall, sending a shiver along her spine.

When they at last entered the crypt, Liz counted eight stone sarcophagi lined up in a row down the center of the chamber. Faint light from above and the back of the crypt bathed the stone effigies with an eerie glow throwing the carving on the tombs into relief. One wall of the crypt had been cut directly from the rock face. Liz felt her chest grow tight with the weight of time pressing in on her. Voices echoed off the walls as if from a great distance.

"There are only eight tombs, Doctor," she heard Steve say. "Are there more in another chamber?"

"No. This is the only crypt. Unfortunately, the Duke had only one legitimate son, Guidobaldo, who married, but died young without issue. The line died out with him. There is some speculation about how many illegitimate sons the Duke may have had, but they would be entombed here only by the grace of the Duke's son and heir," Dr. Bertolucci answered.

"Even though Guidobaldo was quite young when he died, he accomplished a great deal," Dr. Grasso interjected. "He is the one responsible for the University here in Urbino."

"Guidobaldo married a young woman of the DellaRovere family," Dr. Bertolucci picked up the story. "They laid claim to the Duchy upon her death. Their claim was valid, and they held the Duchy until an avaricious Pope annexed the lands for the papacy. It remained part of the Papal States until the *Risorgimento*, when Italy united under one king."

Steve moved to the back of the crypt. "It looks like the repairs to the crypt are almost complete," he observed.

"Yes. Almost finished. The engineers think that an underground spring was responsible for the collapse of the foundation. Imagine! How lucky that the damage from the spring caused us to find the hidden chamber. Hidden for almost six hundred years. The testing we have done so far proves it is an intact burial from the mid-1400s, Duke Federico's time. When the workmen saw the inside of the chamber, all work immediately stopped, and our department was called. Once the chamber was inspected, photographed, and the artifacts along with the remains of the nobleman removed to the laboratory, they resumed work on the foundation. Now, please," Dr. Bertolucci gestured toward the stairway, "follow me, and we will proceed to the laboratory to see the artifacts and the remains of our unknown nobleman."

Liz eagerly left behind the dank crypt with its forbidding air. First one out of the crypt, she lingered in the chapel, mesmerized by the beauty of the frescoes. Something about them tugged at a cord anchored deep within her.

"Dr. Bertolucci," she blurted impulsively to that startled gentleman, "I would like to return to the chapel later to look at the frescoes more closely and make some sketches. Will I be able to get into the *Palazzo*?"

"When we get to the laboratories, the first thing we will do is distribute key-cards to all of you to permit access to the laboratories and buildings where you will be working, including the *Palazzo*."

*   *   *   *

The labs were located in a modern, block-like building that the University had made available to the team of researchers. Dr. Grasso led them into the first of the labs. Inside, she opened a cabinet and counted out four electronic keycards from a box and handed one to each of them.

"*Benvenuti* to Lab 4," she said, with a smile. "This is the computer hub of the project. All the state-of-the-art technology, like computer models and the research tools now so necessary in our work, are located here. The other labs are dedicated to different functions, photo lab, carbon-dating, et cetera. Remember, you will need your keycards to enter the labs as well. Here, we are cataloging the results of our testing of the artifacts. In another, the archives are on a database which is being searched for a clue as to the identity of our nobleman. We have a medical lab for blood analysis and for the mitochondrial DNA research we hope to do, but so far we have not been able to recover any from the skeleton.

"We will now go next door," she went on, "to see the artifacts and our nobleman."

They trailed after her into an identical lab marked with a large "3" on the door.

"Here in this case we have the bones of the one whose name and face are unknown to us. In the next several months, hopefully, we will learn everything there is to know about him."

Liz gazed down into a glass-topped case. Arranged in the case with unmistakable symmetry were the bones of the man found in the crypt.

"In the case with him is the amulet which he was wearing when he was discovered," Dr. Grasso continued, "and while it was not the only object interred in the chamber, it had been placed on the body over his armor. We thought it appropriate, if a trifle romantic, to permit this one object to remain with him. It must have held great significance for the people who placed him there. And, we are hopeful it may yet provide a clue to his identity."

"It's been determined he was a male?" Steve Nelson inquired.

"Yes, from the structure of the pelvis, our scientists have determined he was male, and we are still hopeful we can extract a viable sample for DNA from a tooth. Whether or not we can find a match and determine his blood line," Dr. Grasso shrugged, "who knows?"

Dr. Grasso opened the case while Liz stood by the counter with her hands resting lightly on its edge.

A feeling of profound sadness and loss overwhelmed her at the sight of this forlorn human being, who had once been as full of life as those standing in the room.

This collection of bones had once walked the streets of Urbino. What dreams had clouded his nights?

Did he have loved ones who had mourned him? What unexpressed dreams had he harbored? All these thoughts ran pell-mell through Liz's mind as she viewed the skeleton.

The voices of the living sounded far away, and she heard them like the distant buzzing of bees.

Abruptly lightheaded, spots formed in front of her eyes, and she broke out in a cold, clammy sweat. As her senses reeled, she feared she would pass out.

What's wrong with me? Liz asked herself, weak-kneed as she gripped the counter. Please, not a panic attack; if I give in, I could blow my chances here, she told herself.

With that thought foremost in her mind, she backed away from the case and took a couple of deep breaths.

She experienced a moment or two of anxiety that her panic attacks had returned, and then relief as her anxiety subsided.

Concentrating on what Steve was saying, Liz looked away from the skeleton.

"I notice that some of the ribs and the clavicle on the left side are badly damaged. Did that occur when you removed the skeleton from the crypt?"

"No, Dr. Nelson, we were extremely careful. At first, we surmised that the injuries occurred when the body was placed in the crypt. However, he was clothed, and an armor breastplate bearing the Montefeltro crest was on the body. We removed those artifacts in the crypt and concluded he was interred with great care. We discovered the injuries when we removed the armor and clothing, and so the conclusion was that the injuries were ante-mortem."

"I would agree with your conclusion."

Liz stepped up to the case again to get a better look. She turned her attention to the amulet.

A large sapphire of the darkest blue, mounted in a setting of gold engraved with what looked like "runes," rested on a square of velvet in the corner of the case. Curious as to its weight, Liz reached out to lift it from the case. She picked it up.

A surge of electricity coursed up her arm. She cried out and dropped the amulet back into the case where it landed over the fragile bones.

In response to her cry, all eyes turned toward her.

"What happened?" Steve asked.

Liz tried to respond, but coherent speech eluded her. She felt faint and looked down at her hands which were trembling.

The earlier lightheadedness rebounded, even as her right hand and arm tingled slightly and then went numb.

She groped for a chair. Helpful hands reached out to guide her.

"I'll be all right," she said, when she regained her speech, meant more to reassure herself than the others.

"What was it, Liz? Are you all right?" Steve inquired.

Everyone began to speak at once, trying to be helpful. But Liz's thoughts whirled around in her head like a carnival ride. A panic attack, something she hadn't experienced in two years, and now this.

"She's white as a sheet," Janet remarked.

"I felt a shock, an intense electrical shock," Liz managed to say.

"Impossible!" Dr. Grasso said. "There is nothing in the case that would hold a charge."

"Maybe so, Doctor," Steve cut in, "but something obviously happened. And if Liz said it felt like electricity, well, I believe her." He spoke with such finality in his voice, that speculation ceased.

"Why don't we go back to our room, Liz," Janet suggested, "and you can have a cup of tea or something and a little rest." Janet spoke to Liz, but looked pointedly at Steve.

"That's a good idea," Steve agreed.

"I'm sorry," Liz added.

"There's nothing to be sorry about," Dr. Bertolucci offered, concern etched on his handsome face.

Liz agreed to leave the tour and return to her room with Janet, who appeared unperturbed at having to leave early.

When they were outside, Liz breathed in deeply of the fresh air. They walked slowly back to their room, the lightheaded feeling leaving her to be replaced by a tiredness bordering on exhaustion.

"I'm sorry," she repeated to Janet, feeling the need to apologize again.

"It's all right, Liz. You look better already. To tell you the truth, I was getting a little bored, but you sure jazzed things up ... I know what you need. After you've had a little rest, what do you say to going out and exploring a little on our own. It would do you good."

"You mean that's what you need."

"You catch on fast, girlfriend."

"Whenever you're ready, you go on. I can take care of myself. I don't mean to be ungrateful, but I think I better stick around. Anyway, I want to call my brother."

"Suit yourself."

True to her word, not fifteen minutes after they returned to the room, Janet was out the door.

Glad for the time alone—to think about what had happened and try to analyze it—she tried to compose herself before she was ready to call her brother in California.

She made herself a cup of tea and unpacked, all the while turning over in her mind the scientific possibilities that would explain what had happened in the lab.

What Dr. Grasso said was true enough; there was no way that the amulet could have held an electrical charge sufficient to cause such a jolt. Static electricity could produce a shock, but there was no evidence that static electricity had built up in the case.

She checked the time and realized it was the middle of the night in California. The phone call to her brother would have to wait.

Lou worked as a project engineer in Silicon Valley, and in his spare time, just for fun, designed computer models. Typical engineer, she was certain he would have a simple explanation for what had happened that would allay her fears.

He had been her rock and comfort during the dark days of her junior year in college. A whole semester had been lost while she grappled with depression after her breakup from her longtime boyfriend.

Lou would cheer her up and put a sensible face on the incident. It brought a smile to her face remembering him teasing her about her "tae kwon do" classes and facing off against Italian muggers.

✳   ✳   ✳   ✳

Fresh air and sunlight would do more good than all the medicine in the world, she decided. So, after a quick change into her U of P sweatshirt, a neat pair of jeans and sneakers, she was ready to go back to the *Palazzo* for a closer look at the frescoes. She grabbed a water bottle, her sketchpad and camera, and headed out the door.

She easily retraced her steps to the chapel and stopped still in the doorway. A low sigh, almost a moan, escaped her as she crossed the threshold.

I'm home. The unbidden thought entered her mind. She had not realized that she was holding her breath.

Breathtaking. The word echoed in her brain, and she struggled to shake off the feeling of melancholy homecoming, a poignancy that washed over her like a tide, a feeling at once of welcome and shattering loneliness.

She shook her head at her foolishness and opened her sketchpad.

Determined to make good use of her time, she moved along the right side of the nave, the cool silence beckoning her deeper into the chapel. She slowed her step and gazed reverently around at the walls and vaulted ceiling. The chapel was of a simple nave in design, as in many Romanesque churches, with an apse where the altar was situated.

To the left of the altar stood an ornately carved marble baptismal font. She wondered how many generations of Montefeltro babies had been christened there.

The right side of the altar was guarded by large ornate chairs. Behind them, the stairs led down to the crypt. Light flooded the chapel from above, mimicking a heavenly glow. Its source was a series of dormer windows cunningly hidden in the painted scenes of the vault.

In the stillness of the chapel, Liz heard the faint sound of church bells. The tolling penetrated her reverie and propelled her to action.

It's getting late; she thought, I must find something I want to sketch.

Midway up the nave, she dropped her sketchpad and picked up her camera to take a few photos. It was easy to move from one side to the other since no pews blocked her movement. She zipped back and forth snapping away, energized for the first time all day. Then, she resumed her circuit of the chapel, carefully inspecting each figure as she went, marveling at the artistry of the painter and the vibrant color—color as fresh today as it must have been the day it was painted.

The frescoes behind the altar depicted the Crucifixion and Ascension. No surprise there.

She turned and inspected the door wall where she had entered the chapel. The Assumption was to the right, and St. Joseph leading a donkey with Mary and the infant Jesus—ah, yes, the flight into Egypt—to the left.

Over the door, John the Baptist with the River Jordan flowing serenely behind him. The blue of the river blended with the sky surrounding Mary and coloring the desert above the Holy Family. Very charming and certain to inspire devotion among the faithful.

The two side walls and the vaulted ceiling though were markedly devoid of any biblical scenes. No cavorting cherubs or heavenly hosts. The ceiling was a realistic representation of the night sky. In some places, it was midnight blue with stars peeking through the firmament. In others, lightning pierced the clouds, tearing across the heavens.

Fearsome depictions of battle covered the walls. Horses thrashed in their death throes. Men-at-arms battled with swords, in armor, on horseback and on foot. The scenes of carnage swirled, and blood dripped from lances and battleaxes wielded with ferocious intensity. Bodies were piled like grotesque lumber.

In the background, on a flat landscape, sat castles under siege. Liz noticed that the tents, helmets and armor in which the embattled were dressed were distinctly different. So distracted was she by the sheer carnage of the scenes, it took some study before she understood that she was seeing an epic battle of the Crusades.

But why portray such violence in a chapel? she wondered. She had always found it interesting that the adherents of Islam referred to the Christians as infidels, and the Christians referred to the Islamic peoples as infidels.

She read that the Duke was a warlord, so maybe he thought it fitting in his chapel. How strange! How pitiful!

Or was it possible that his ancestors had fought in the Crusades, and this display was meant in some way to commemorate or extol their noble sacrifice. Could she ever fathom his intent?

Sobered and intrigued, she continued her circuit around the nave. Almost to the end of her circuit, in an obscure corner away from the raging battle scenes, standing proudly in front of a glorious tent, Liz came face to face with a mirror image of herself.

Staring across the ages at her was the same cropped blond hair, the same straight nose, the same mouth and jaw, the same clear gray eyes.

Dressed unmistakably as a boy on the battlefield, 'he' was arrayed in a black tunic with an armored breast plate and armor covering 'his' calves. 'He' wore no helmet and held the reins of a horse, as if he were a page.

Blind, unyielding fear gripped her. Her pulse pounded in her head and air was sucked from her chest. Bile rose in her throat with the realization from some frozen corner of her brain that she was indeed looking at herself pictured on the wall.

How could this be?

Her breathing stopped, strangling her as if a giant hand had reached into her to squeeze the life from her.

She swallowed hard and pushed the fear down into a deep well where its tentacles could not reach her constricted throat. Her body gratefully responded by filling her lungs with a blast of cold air that helped to clear her mind.

Two tentative steps found her inches from the wall. She clenched her jaw, unconsciously biting down on her tongue. She tasted blood.

She reached out her hand. As her fingertips neared the image, she heard voices, lots of voices, speaking in rapid Italian.

She withdrew her hand and turned to see who had entered the chapel, but she was alone. She looked and waited, but no one showed himself. No visitors. No guard.

Her pulse had slowed and her breathing had returned almost to normal.

Facing the wall once again, she picked up her camera and took a photo.

She put the camera down near her sketchbook and approached the wall again.

She reached out her hand once more, this time daring herself to touch the captivating image.

As her hand made contact with the wall, she pitched headfirst into a whirlwind and hurtled dizzily down a shaft of blinding light until she hit something solid and blessed oblivion overtook her.

CHAPTER 2

▼

Liz awoke, disoriented and chilled to the bone at the end of a long freefall. The voices speaking rapid Italian returned. She opened her eyes and looked up at two dirty faces bent over her. Her head ached terribly, and when she tried to move, she groaned at the pain from a lump on the side of her head. She ignored the two men who were covered in white dust and looked around fearfully, her heart pounding in her chest. She lay in a crumpled heap on the same patterned marble floor of the chapel, but the chapel was somehow different. She propped herself up against a bright white wall to await her fate.

Good, she thought, making a quick survey of her sprawled body, two legs, two arms and what felt like two heads.

One of the men knelt down beside her and said something. *"Da dove vieni, giovanetto?"*

He spoke Italian to her—nothing so unusual about that. But, amazingly, she understood him.

She stared blankly back at him. He had asked where she had come from. She had to come up with an answer, and quickly. Then she heard herself utter, *"Come vuoi che lo sappia."*

As the unfamiliar words tumbled from her mouth, she thought, My God, I'm speaking Italian.

She told him she had no idea how she had gotten there. That much was true.

Fighting the urge to get up and run, she instinctively knew that she couldn't get far in her condition. Her head ached so badly, it was difficult to think, and even the slightest movement caused violent dizziness. What had happened? The last thing she remembered was taking a photo in the chapel.

Her best course of action, she decided, would be to play dumb. Luckily, that wasn't difficult.

But why had this fool addressed her as "young man?"

Her head down, she watched two feet approach and stop inches from her right leg. The other two men moved aside deferentially. She looked up slowly at a man who towered over her, covered in the same white dust as the first two. He stood with his hands on his hips surveying the sorry state of affairs, namely, her. He stared at her from the most amazing pair of green eyes Liz had ever seen.

The other two men started talking at once and gesticulating wildly. The tall man held up a hand to silence them.

"*Basta!*" he barked.

He looked as though he expected her to say something, so she complied, "*Non sono da questo luogo. Un viaggiatore. Scusi tanto se la disturbo.*"

Her apology for interrupting them and her lost traveler story started the two other men babbling again, but the tall man was strangely silent, just staring at Liz. She felt extremely vulnerable under that emerald gaze that pinned her to the wall like a specimen of some exotic butterfly.

Finally, he broke the spell, "*Non ti muove.*"

All right, Liz thought, I won't move a muscle.

The three of them turned back to resume whatever she had interrupted by her unexpected arrival.

She shrank back further against the wall and tried to draw as little attention to herself as possible.

Every now and then, the first two threw suspicious looks in her direction, but not the green-eyed man. She may as well have become part of the wall for all the attention he paid her.

One careful look around confirmed that she was still in the chapel. The altar was exactly where it should be, and the floor was undoubtedly the same, but the walls were only partially frescoed.

Some scenes gave way to unfinished plaster, like the area where the men were now working.

The vaulted ceiling too was partly finished, and most of her view of that was blocked by scaffolding.

It was then she noticed other men moving about carrying buckets of water and tubs of the white powder that floated over everything, making them look like medieval gargoyles. All of them were clad in dust-covered rags, and the air was dense with the smell of unwashed bodies.

From her vantage point on the floor, Liz watched as the green-eyed man transformed a section of the wet, freshly-plastered wall into a most imaginably lifelike depiction of a dying horse. She sat immobile for what seemed like hours watching the transformation take place. During this time, her head began to clear, but she acquired a sore bottom and stiff joints from the cold marble floor.

While sitting there, Liz assessed her situation—calmly, rationally. From the evidence at hand, she was forced to accept that she had somehow for some reason—or the possibility existed, for no reason at all—traveled back in time. Bizarre it may be, but no matter, she could not allow herself to give in to fear or panic.

It would do no good to lose her head or waste time thinking about the whys and hows. For the moment, she decided, it was vital for her survival to concentrate instead on what to do about it. What she did or failed to do over the next few hours could determine whether she lived or died.

To find the way home—the doorway or portal through which she came—yes, that was important; and to remain alive to do just that, she needed to keep her wits about her.

As daylight faded, some of the workmen lit lanterns and hung them from brass standards. Soon it was too dark to continue, and they began to pack up their tools. The green-eyed man covered up pots of paint and handed brushes to young boys—probably so they could clean them, Liz surmised—and prepared to leave the chapel.

Observing the young boys, the germ of an idea formed in her brain.

She rose clumsily to her feet and coughed to attract the attention of the green-eyed man. He had evidently forgotten all about her, for he wore a surprised expression when he turned to look at her.

He said something to one of the two workmen who had first found her—a beetle-browed fellow with bushy eyebrows—but Liz was too far away to hear what was said. When the two workmen walked over to her, gripped her by her arms, and attempted to haul her off to who knew where, she protested loudly to the green-eyed man.

"*Per piacere, Maestro,*" Liz howled out indignantly, at the same time casting an imploring look at him.

He gazed back at her impassively and then beckoned her. The two goons released her, and she trotted up beside him on unsteady legs like a newborn colt.

The hint of a smile hovered at the corners of his mouth under his cheek stubble. He turned and resumed his exit from the chapel. She stuck close to him, her long legs easily keeping pace with his stride as they left the chapel and entered the *Palazzo*.

The long gallery, instead of being furnished with works of art as before, was bare. Only a few feet from the chapel doorway there was a makeshift opening onto an exterior wooden stairway that the workmen were using to carry their tools and equipment in and out of the chapel. An oiled canvas curtain was tied back, and it was through this doorway that the green-eyed man led her down to a cobbled courtyard.

At the foot of the stairway, he muttered, "stay here," more at her, than to her.

The sun was setting, and the workmen hurried to carry the last of their equipment down the wooden stairway for the night into a lean-to beside the chapel.

Liz squatted on her haunches beside the stairway and surveyed the courtyard. The chapel appeared to be an extension of the *Palazzo*, and beyond the courtyard, the ground sloped gently.

She stood up and peered down the hill. In the fading light, she still could make out the outbuildings, orchards of fruit trees beyond, and a pasture with horses grazing. The view was serenely beautiful, reminiscent of a daVinci landscape. Fading into the distance, a ring of tall cypresses, of a green so dark they looked black, stood erect and motionless like lonely sentinels against an evening sky that turned from burnished copper and gold to violet.

Real soldiers in scarlet tunics and caps, swords at their sides came walking up the hill. Liz gaped, recovered herself, and quickly sat back down when she saw the green-eyed man stop the soldiers and say something to them.

Whatever their response, it caused the green-eyed man to return and enter the lean-to. Her blood pounded in her throat. Will they come to throw me into some dark dungeon at any moment? Merely contemplating the thought made her have to gulp back the tears that sprung up in her eyes.

The man soon emerged from the lean-to wearing a clean pair of breeches and carrying a fresh white shirt and a pair of boots. He sat on the bottom step of the stairway and shed his dusty boots and put on the fresh ones. Then he stood and removed his shirt, sending a cloud of white dust into the air.

"We must speak to Captain San Martini," he addressed Liz at last, "and I am told he is in the *Palazzo*."

Liz wondered if it was this Captain San Martini who would decide her fate.

"I cannot walk through the *Palazzo* covered with lime dust or Mistress Isabella will have my head," he continued.

"Who is Mistress Isabella?" Liz inquired.

"She oversees the household and reports directly to the Duchess. Captain San Martini is in charge of the *Guardia del Palazzo Ducale*. You will become familiar with them if they decide to let you stay. You do want to stay, don't you?"

"Oh yes, Master," Liz answered emphatically. I've got to stay near the chapel, Liz thought, and this is working out better than I could have hoped.

She never once took her eyes from the green-eyed man as he changed his shirt. Broad-shouldered and well muscled, with a trim waist that tapered to slim hips, he had the look of an outdoorsman or athlete rather than a painter. In spite of his physique, it was his striking eyes—deep set and flecked with gold—that held her attention. She caught herself staring and felt a warm blush suffuse her neck and throat. She reluctantly tore her gaze away.

He shook his head, ran his hands through his hair, and laughed as more lime dust flew around.

"Well then, *Piccolino*, let me see to it. Do not be afraid of the Captain when you meet him. And Mistress Isabella is softhearted and will deny you nothing. Just remember to look hungry and pathetic," he said with an indulgent smile.

"Master, you have not told me your name. What am I to call you?"

"I am Piero della Francesca. You may call me Master Piero."

When she heard his name, it confirmed her suspicion and caused her heart to flutter ever so slightly.

She was in the presence of an early Renaissance master. She could do much worse than to have a friend like him in the household.

They climbed back up the wooden stairway and turned into the *Palazzo*. The long hallways were beautifully furnished with chairs, tables and braziers burning coal that emitted a lovely heat. Servants were lighting bronze lamps suspended from the ceilings, and, as they passed by doorways, Liz could see lush Turkish carpets and more carved tables.

After walking down several passageways, they stopped in front of a large tapestry.

Her companion moved the tapestry aside to reveal mammoth double-doors. He pulled at a cord with a ring attached to it that was mounted in the wall to the right of the door. In a moment, Liz heard footsteps approaching.

The door was flung open by a large, barrel-chested man whose face was marred by a jagged scar running down the right side from his temple to his jaw.

Liz recoiled in shock at the sight of this ugly mountain of a man. He stood well over six feet tall—even taller and much broader than her companion. His bulk, the scar and the menacing expression on his face set Liz to trembling.

"Piero, my friend, what have you there?" he asked.

In light of this new and fearsome threat, Liz drew closer to Master Piero, her benefactor. She heard Piero answer in a leisurely drawl.

"I'm not sure, Luca, I found him in the chapel. The poor fellow was dazed."

"And hungry," Liz interjected.

"And hungry," Piero confirmed, with a laugh.

"We cannot feed every fool who comes to our door, young one," the giant said to Liz.

"This is Captain San Martini of whom I spoke," Piero said to Liz, and she executed a clumsy bow in greeting.

"I'm sure the Duchess would not begrudge him a hot meal," Piero continued. His posture was non-threatening, almost languid, and Liz got the impression that this verbal sparring was a favorite game in which the two men often engaged and enjoyed.

Captain San Martini crossed his arms over his chest and scowled.

He was clad from head to toe in black. On his upper body, he wore a velvet tunic or doublet that ended just below his hips. The solid black was broken by bits of snowy white fabric gathered at his throat and spilling through slits on the sleeves that were joined to the doublet at the shoulders by pieces of silver cording. The same silver cord decorated a black sash at his waist from which dangled a sword in a beautifully jeweled scabbard. His long muscular legs were clad in black hose, and he wore black leather boots.

"Maybe we should ask her," Captain San Martini said finally, rocking back and forth on the balls of his feet.

"Now, Luca, you and I should not disagree over something as trivial as giving this young boy something to eat. You and I both know a decision like that is up to you."

"So, I have the authority to make only trivial decisions, is that what you are saying?"

"Luca, what is it now?" an unmistakably peeved feminine voice called out from within.

"There's the Duchess, Luca. Why not let her decide this little argument for us?" Piero teased.

The scar on Captain San Martini's face blazed fiery red, but before another retort could escape his lips, a woman stepped into the hallway.

There was no mistaking her for anyone other than Battista Sforza da Montefeltro, the Duchess of Urbino, for Liz had seen her likeness plastered on posters all over the exterior of the *Palazzo* announcing an upcoming exhibit—or rather the *Palazzo* Liz had left scant hours ago.

Liz dropped spontaneously to one knee and bowed her head.

"Master Piero," the Duchess inquired, ignoring Liz. "What is it I must decide?"

"This young lad turned up in the chapel. He's hungry, and Luca here has refused to feed him before we send him on his way."

"I did not," Captain San Martini replied petulantly.

Piero threw up his hands in disgust.

"Enough of this foolishness," the Duchess said. "Which would you prefer, Luca, that I order him to be killed? You see spies everywhere. Well, we cannot kill everybody you would like to kill or we would not have time for anything else."

This exchange caused Liz's heart to drop with a thud into her stomach until she caught sight of Piero's broad smile and the twinkle in his green eyes.

"Stand up, boy—for heaven's sake, Luca," the Duchess admonished him. "Help him up. Can't you see the lad is terrified?"

Captain San Martini pulled Liz roughly to her feet, and this treatment provoked in her a burst of righteous anger. She stifled words of her newfound Italian vernacular, filthy words forming in her mind for which she didn't even know the English equivalent.

If she was ever to find a way out of this predicament, she would have to wrest control of the situation.

"Please, Your Grace, may I speak to you, in private?" Liz asked, hoping a tender heart beat under her splendid velvet gown.

"No!" Captain San Martini bellowed.

"Unless I am mistaken, I still make decisions here," the Duchess countered haughtily.

The Duchess led Liz into a small, comfortably appointed sitting room holding several delicate chairs. A fire burned in a marble fireplace, sending flickering light over the warm gleam of a lady's inlaid fruitwood desk.

"You will have to forgive Luca," the Duchess continued, "He comes with a long history of service to the family and takes liberties. But for all of that, he has never failed to protect me, so I forgive him much."

"Your Grace, he need fear nothing from me. I have come at great cost, after a perilous journey to serve Your Grace and the Duke."

Liz's idea—if she could swing it, and she had nothing to lose—just might keep her head on her shoulders. She might be able to secure a position within the household to give herself the chance she needed to find a way back to her own time.

"*È vero*? And where have you come from?" she asked, eyeing Liz's clothing and wrinkling her nose in distaste.

Liz had hoped she wouldn't ask that. But since the *Palazzo* would offer protection from all the unknown peril that lurked outside and give her access to the chapel, she dived headlong into a whopper of a lie.

"From *Arezzo*, Your Grace," she lied. "I wish to apprentice with the great master, Piero della Francesca. It is well known throughout Tuscany and Umbria that he is working here. I have great admiration for his work in the Church of St. Francis in *Arezzo*."

"Then you are indeed fortunate for two reasons that occur to me: he is just returned from the mountains to the north, arriving only last night, and you seem to have him on your side."

Liz shot a glance through the open doorway at Piero. He was regarding them intently, and she prayed that her instinct about him was correct.

"We will let him decide whether he wants to keep you. But meanwhile, go with them, and they will see to getting you something to eat."

Confirming Liz's long-held notion that passing the buck was a very old art form, Liz bowed to the Duchess and followed her out to the two men waiting in the hallway.

"Your Grace, what have you decided?" Piero asked.

"Feed him, to be sure, but he wants more from you, Master Piero," she answered.

"I want to be an artist," Liz ventured to say. "I have traveled far to offer my services to you as your apprentice. One night, on my way here, a driving rainstorm sent me to seek shelter in a barn. When I awoke, all my belongings had been stolen, and I was left with only these clothes which I made myself."

Piero glanced from the Duchess to Captain San Martini.

"I see," Piero responded. "We shall talk of this on the way to our evening meal."

"What are you called, my lad?" Captain San Martini asked.

"Cosimo," Liz lied, the name popping into her head and instantaneously out of her mouth.

"Like the great Medici," the Duchess said.

"I know, Your Grace. My grandfather is also named Cosimo."

"There, you see, Luca, he is a fine boy, and we will leave him in Master Piero's capable hands. I think it would be well, Master Piero, if you would take him on."

"Your Grace," Piero said, making a courtly bow. He nodded to Captain San Martini before taking his leave.

Liz followed him. By the rigid set of his shoulders and the frown he was wearing, Liz knew there was trouble brewing. They had descended two flights of stairs before he whirled on her. In spite of being on her guard, he was too quick for her.

He grabbed her right ear and yanked her into an alcove.

"Ow!" Liz cried out.

"What did I say to you? Didn't I tell you that I would handle this. But you saw fit to insinuate yourself."

"I'm sorry, Master."

"Oh, no you're not, but you will be. In exchange for your apprenticeship, you will serve as my personal servant. After our meal, you will assist me in my bath. I will sleep in the garrison tonight so that you may rise very early tomorrow to clean my quarters. If you perform your duties to my satisfaction, I will then, and only then, decide whether I will apprentice you. Do you understand, *Piccolino*?"

"Yes, Master."

Out of the frying pan, into the fire, Liz thought, rubbing her sore ear.

CHAPTER 3

▼

Piero led the way to the lowest level of the great house. Not one word passed between them since the ear pulling incident. As they marched along a wide stone-flagged corridor, Liz seesawed between despair and hope, fear and anger.

Her ear still throbbed, and she was cold, tired and hungry. Her eyes burned as she blinked back tears of frustration. Totally alone—her fate resting in the hands of these people—she looked forlornly around for a way out. Servants scurried about, but there was no one in that quarter to help her. No hope of rescue.

She took a deep breath and concentrated on her surroundings. The place was like a rabbit warren. How would she ever find her way out, and where would she go if she did? Blasts of icy air rattled through the corridor from intersecting hall-ways. Her teeth chattered from a mixture of cold and fear.

"I will not be your nursemaid when we get to the kitchens," Piero said at last. "You will go to Mistress Isabella who will get something for you to eat and some clothes for you to wear."

Tears gathered in the corners of her eyes, but she turned away so he would not see them.

"I have business to attend to, *Piccolino*. Mistress Isabella will see to you, and then you may help me with the bath before you retire."

"Yes, Master," Liz replied, with a catch in her voice that stopped Piero in his tracks.

"Are you all right? I am sorry I hurt you, but you must learn to do as you are told. Your last master may have indulged you, but I will not."

Liz refused to make direct eye contact, but that didn't seem to trouble Piero in the least. She was somewhat mollified by his apology. He is after all, she thought, laboring under the assumption I'm a boy. Nevertheless, she vowed to herself, next time, she would be on her guard, and he might find himself with a little more than he could handle.

As they entered the kitchen, delicious aromas assailed her nostrils, and her stomach rumbled loudly in response. Warm air from the cookfires and ovens responsible for those wonderful smells dispelled the chill at the doorway to the noisy, cavernous kitchen.

"Venison! Mistress Isabella is roasting the game I brought back from the mountains. Are you hungry, *Piccolino*? What am I saying; of course, you are. Young boys are always hungry. You will find this the best venison you have ever eaten."

She trailed after him through the maze of tables, chairs, and basket-toting servants where he halted in front of two large doors.

"These doors lead out to the courtyard. Across the courtyard are the artisans' quarters where you will sleep," he said, opening the massive oak doors. Blazing torches lit a path to two outdoor pumps. While they washed their hands in the cold water, several people passed by, greeted Piero, and stopped to chat.

When they returned to the kitchen, Piero was approached by a short, stout matron.

"Master Piero," she exclaimed, as he took both her hands in his and stooped to plant a kiss on both cheeks.

"You have outdone yourself," he said.

"Come, eat your fill," the matron said, a blush suffusing her face.

"I will. And will you take care of this young one? Feed him. And if you can, find something fit for him to wear? I am deciding whether or not to make him my apprentice."

"Of course. Leave him to me." With a critical eye, she scrutinized Liz, taking in her clothes and shoes.

At that moment, Captain Luca walked up and took Piero's arm.

"Captain Luca," Mistress Isabella snapped, "Where have you been all day?"

Two bright spots of color appeared on his cheeks, turning to crimson along his cruel-looking scar.

"What concern is it of yours, Mistress?" he responded, his gravelly voice betraying his irritation. "If you must know, I've been about my duties among the Guard and following the Duke's orders."

"Indeed? I heard you were called to task by the Duchess for carrying out the Duke's orders a little too ... enthusiastically." Mistress Isabella—and Liz concluded that this formidable woman was the housekeeper—smiled devilishly at the

Captain even as her words antagonized him. At least ten servants milled about trying to look busy while eavesdropping shamelessly.

The Captain ignored her remark and turned his attention again to Piero.

"Piero, we must speak … now."

Mistress Isabella laughed heartily which caused her to jiggle all over. The two men walked to one of the tables in a far corner and seated themselves. A young boy rushed to do their bidding.

Liz stood by as Mistress Isabella recovered from her laughing fit. She basked in the attention of her staff.

"My, my, Captain Luca is displeased. He hates it so when I'm quickly made aware of everything that happens in the *Palazzo*," she sputtered between chuckles.

Then she looked at Liz, recalling that she had another duty to perform. Liz got the distinct impression that very little escaped the scrutiny of her black, beady eyes. The servants too examined Liz. She must have seemed an oddity to them, but they in turn sparked her interest as well.

Mistress Isabella was dressed like a sober housekeeper should, head to toe in practical, unornamented black. It may be true that black is slimming, but not in this poor lady's case. Her dark hair was streaked with gray and was pulled back and pinned at the nape, and she wore what looked like a turban. It sat plopped on the top of her head like a gigantic mushroom. Liz couldn't help staring, then caught herself and prudently assumed a deferential attitude.

When Mistress Isabella completed her inspection, she quizzed Liz, "So, you will be working for Master Piero?"

"I hope to be apprenticed to him, Mistress," Liz replied, adopting her most angelic expression in an effort to appear as non-threatening as possible.

"You would be fortunate indeed to have such a master. Come along then. Sit over there and warm yourself for you look chilled to the bone. One of the maids will bring you some *minestra* and meat and bread."

She directed Liz to a large settle beside one of the hearths, and she sat down and waited expectantly for her food. Despite the precarious situation in which she found herself, she had passed unscathed through the interview with the Duchess and was being allowed to remain. This little success encouraged and consoled her, but she forestalled congratulating herself prematurely. Each moment, a new test seemed to present itself so she would be wise to keep up her guard.

True, she was completely out of her element and had to rely totally on her native instincts, which had never before been so severely tested; but so far, her head was still attached to the rest of her, and she firmly intended to keep it right where it was by whatever means necessary.

The fact that no one asked her for identity papers or interrogated her was hard to believe, but maybe it simply meant that no such things as identity papers existed in this time. Or it may have merely been characteristic of the age. Her story was found believable, and so she was accepted at face value.

She reminded herself that her one advantage was that only she knew what she knew. Surely, no one else could possibly guess the truth. And the truth was that she would have to pull this off if she were to find a way to get back. With her brains and some luck, she could gain their confidence along with access to the chapel. The portal was there. The door to the future was there, and it was her future she meant to reclaim.

A young girl—a child really—brought the soup, a chunk of the venison, bread and a cup of wine to one of the rustic dining tables and motioned to Liz, who hastened to the table to dig into the food.

Everything was delicious, and she ate ravenously from a bowl made of a pewter-like metal. She noted all the utensils were made of the same metal.

While servants lit rows of candles mounted in chandeliers, she concentrated on the food on her plate. The hot soup eased her hunger. She finished it quickly and reached for the bread while sneaking furtive peeks at the people around her.

She noticed that Captain Luca and Piero had their heads together, engrossed in conversation.

I wonder what they're cooking up, Liz asked herself.

The food actually helped her brain to function more clearly.

She strongly suspected that the amulet held the key to her predicament—that it was in some way responsible for transporting her back in time to the mid to late 1400s. Maybe, she mused, some unknown cosmic force had combined with the energy emanating from the amulet to thrust her back in time.

Good Lord, that's what I get for watching too much science fiction on TV, she nearly laughed out loud at her thoughts. That's one bad habit I won't have to worry about anymore. Sounding pretty lame even to herself, she continued with her hypothesis. None of this made any sense, but neither did the fact that she was sitting in this kitchen eating this delicious meal. It was not a dream, of that she was certain.

Perhaps it would be necessary to find the amulet in order to return to her own time.

For all intents and purposes—if indeed there was a purpose behind it, and it was mere speculation at this point—she was a refugee in a land of strangers and even stranger customs.

There was no one with whom she could share this secret, no one she could trust with this knowledge. If she tried, they would think her a sorcerer or a fool. Despite frightening herself silly with these thoughts, she was determined to remain confident that she would be able to make her way back to the chapel and find the spot where she had tumbled into the past.

She finished her meal, and the young girl returned and removed the utensils. Liz smiled at her and tried to engage her in conversation, but she didn't answer.

"She's deaf," said a voice at her elbow. Liz turned and beheld a colorfully dressed, pale, rather plump young man of about twenty years or so.

"I'm sorry, I didn't realize," Liz replied.

She stood and held out her hand. "I'm Cosimo," she said, immediately realizing her mistake. Shaking hands might be a modern custom, not common in the 15th century. She dropped her hand awkwardly to her side.

The young man looked at her quizzically and bowed slightly, a handkerchief pressed to his nose.

"I am Raffaello Sanzio. My father, Giovanni, is court painter here. I understand you have come to apprentice to Master Piero."

"Word spreads quickly."

"Of course, it is like a family here and we thrive on gossip."

Liz smiled pleasantly and nodded, thinking to herself, can this really be the great Raphael—Renaissance master. He reminded her of the Pillsbury Dough Boy.

Instead of the sober, day wear worn by Captain Luca, the Duchess, and Mistress Isabella, Signor Raffaello sported a gold and burgundy brocade doublet with a turban and dark gold hose.

He leaned closer to share a confidence, and Liz detected a whiff of stale sweat and garlic.

"You will find Master Piero to be a difficult man to work for. If he refuses you, I could certainly use some help in *Lo Studiolo*, presuming you possess any talent and are willing to work hard."

"Thank you, Master Raffaello, I will certainly keep your kind offer in mind." Liz backed away and bowed as she had seen him do. She took an instant dislike to him, but gave him her most sincere-phony smile.

He turned and ambled off, the personification of *ennui*.

After waiting for some time for Mistress Isabella to return, Liz grew impatient. She rose from the settle and took a walk around the large kitchen. Two immense walk-in fireplaces, one at either end, were going full tilt, and loaves of bread were being removed from several brick ovens by bakers. Pots and pans hung from the ceiling. A large stone sink topped by a row of windows ran the length of an outer wall.

Additional kitchen staff busily prepared vegetables and meat at two wooden tables which stood in the middle of the room, and more servants were bringing in buckets of fresh water for the sink and removing the scraps.

In spite of the noise level and amount of work going on, the kitchen was spotlessly clean. Beyond the work space, the room opened up to the dining area for the servants where Liz had eaten her meal, next to the fireplace seat.

She endeavored to keep out of everyone's way by wandering off beyond the dining area, where she came upon a separate windowless room. It appeared to be a storage area or larder which was as cold as ice. An amazing variety of food was stored there. Liz took it to be a room-sized cooler.

Bunches of dried herbs were piled in a corner. There were tubs and barrels filled with every variety of foodstuffs. Round glass jars with wax-covered cork tops, filled with what looked like pickled vegetables, crammed the shelves.

There was a barrel filled with salted fish. Liz lifted the lid of one of the other barrels to find it filled with rice. Other tubs contained flour. A barrel with a scrawled "*Venezia*" on its front revealed loose tea when she lifted its lid.

Many of the tubs and barrels were labeled with their point of origin. Here was proof that a lively trade existed between Urbino and the neighboring provinces along with Venice and its eastern trade routes.

Through an arched doorway in the rear of the larder, a stone stairway led down a flight of steps, but Liz avoided going down and instead returned to the kitchen.

Captain Luca and Piero had left their corner. Liz surveyed the kitchen, but they were nowhere to be seen.

In a few moments, Mistress Isabella entered the kitchen with an armload of clothing.

"*Andiamo*, young Cosimo, let us go into the artisans' quarters to find you some place to sleep," she said cheerily.

Liz followed her out taking the clothes from her as they went. Mistress Isabella acknowledged Liz's gesture with a friendly smile.

"These things are much too fine for me," Liz commented, feeling the soft cotton lisle and velvet of the garments. "There is hardly any wear."

"They belonged to young Lord Leo, the Duke's nephew. There are more things he has outgrown that I think will fit you and that you may have, but I couldn't carry them all. When we get you settled, you can fetch them. It is good you arrived today, for tomorrow I will be very busy with the preparations for the young Lord Guidobaldo's birthday party. It will take two whole days to put the food in readiness."

"Lord Guidobaldo?"

"The first birthday of the Duke's young son."

"From the looks of the kitchen, the preparations have already begun."

"Oh no, tomorrow we will be stumbling over each other. The Lady Battista and I have been preparing the house all week for the *festa*. The staff has been working very hard, but food preparation must wait until tomorrow. What you saw was the everyday work to feed the household. Tomorrow, at daybreak, everything of the freshest will begin to arrive from the countryside, and by early evening, much of it will be ready. The following day the celebration will begin, and it will last until well after nightfall."

As she talked, they walked across the well-lit courtyard to the artisans' building. Bright moonlight beamed down on a sheltered patch next to the kitchen where a neat herb garden thrived.

"You will find we have many young people who want to be in service here. The Lady Battista is generous and rewards her staff well. Remember, she insists on cleanliness. While at first some may balk, they soon come to see the wisdom of doing things her way. While sickness is all around, we here in Urbino have been free of it. Here we are."

They had come to the doorway of a two-story, stone building, with long narrow double-hung windows along the first floor and palladian-style windows on the second. Off to the left of the courtyard, the stone-paved roadway widened in front of more buildings.

"What are those buildings?" Liz asked.

"Those are for storage. There are dozens of out-buildings here in the *Palazzo*. Down there is the barracks for the garrison, and the stables, and the kennels for the hunting dogs. The Duke, when he is in residence, likes to hunt for boar and all manner of animals in the hills. He keeps a hunting lodge in the mountains near San Leo as well. But now, he is away leading an army against the Sienese for the Florentines. He will return soon, but not, I fear, in time for his son's birthday party. Your master, Master Piero, has been at the hunting lodge and brought back game, which is hanging in that stone building to the left. To the right is the garrison. The game will be put to good use for the *festa*. Of course, he also brought back the plants he needs for his paints to continue his work on the chapel. You understand?"

Liz nodded in assent. Thanks to Mistress Isabella's talkative nature, Liz was able to learn things it might have otherwise taken her days to find out.

The doors of the artisans' building opened directly into a large dormitory room which stood empty. Clothing was strewn about between the rows of cots.

They lit two candles in wall sconces by the door and carried them to the rear of the room to a flight of stairs. They climbed the flight slowly, but still had to stop on the landing for Mistress Isabella to catch her breath.

"That room is a mess down there," she remarked between gasps. "After saying how clean we insist on keeping things here, how can I justify that mess, I ask you?" She wagged her head and clucked in dismay.

Her exertions had caused her turban to slip precariously to one side. She straightened it and gathered up her skirts as they picked their way along the upstairs hallway.

"It's dirty up here too. Though in the dark, it's difficult to tell. It may just need a good sweeping up," Liz said.

"The privies are out back when you need to use them, but Master Piero also has a private privy chamber next to his room. I hate to think what those privies are like. I'll inspect them at first light. With guests coming ..." She shook her head and left the thought unspoken.

She stopped before a door.

"Master Piero's quarters are here. I am certain he will want you close by. There is another smaller outside room on the other side of the privy chamber that should serve you well, I think, so tomorrow, clean that one up as well."

Mistress Isabella pushed the door open, and they entered a large room which resembled the study of a scientist rather than an artist's bedroom. The door wall was lined with bookshelves, and the opposite wall was comprised of two lovely palladian-style windows with a large *armadio* or wardrobe between them. The generously proportioned windows would let in a tremendous amount of light, Liz thought, as she crossed the room to look at the view.

The luminous moonglow dwarfed the light thrown by the little candle she held. Even so, deep shadows persuaded her there was nothing to see, and she would have to wait until morning.

Disappointed, she turned back to examine the room. She heard Mistress Isabella complaining anew at the mess.

"*È uno di quei porci!*"

Liz jumped to Piero's defense.

"I'm sure he had a lot on his mind, and besides he has just returned, as you said. Please let me start in the morning to clean. It does look like a pigsty, I admit, but it's too late to start tonight, and he said he wanted me to help with his bath. I can gather up the dirty linen tonight and leave the sweeping and dusting until tomorrow."

Taking a dirty shirt from the outstretched arm of a clay model, Liz began picking up dirty clothes from every part of the room.

"Very well. I will send some of the young ones up with brooms and cloths after breakfast to help you. Let them assist you with the windows. *Guarda quelle finestre*! Look how dirty they are. I will have the linen washed and returned. And I'll have a word with Master Sanzio and Master Piero about the workers' quarters, you can depend on that. I wouldn't worry about his bath tonight. Once he gets to the garrison with Captain Luca, and they start drinking and talking, he won't be back here. That's what they do, drink and talk, except when they talk and drink."

Liz chuckled at her little joke, and they exchanged a knowing look.

"Check in the privy chamber there."

Liz opened the door that Mistress Isabella indicated and went into the privy chamber where a washstand with mirror stood near another smaller window. There was a door on the opposite wall. A hip bath sat in the corner. It was relatively clean. The chamber pot in the privy seat had been emptied, but it looked like it hadn't been washed in some time.

"It's not too bad, Mistress Isabella," Liz called from the privy.

Back in the bedroom, Mistress Isabella was stripping the large four-poster bed. Liz opened up the bottom sections of both windows and gathered up all the dirty clothes. Then she spread the sheets Mistress Isabella had stripped out on the floor and threw the dirty linen down on top of the sheets.

"What are you doing?" Mistress Isabella asked, watching with her hands on her hips.

Liz smiled. "We don't have a basket so we will improvise." She tied the sheets up and threw the bundle over her shoulder.

"Hah! What a clever young fellow you are."

"I know. I'll fetch the other clothes you set aside for me and come back up to sleep."

They hadn't taken three steps toward the door when a little gray mouse ran across the floor, and Mistress Isabella let out a shriek loud enough to wake the dead. She went running from the room. Liz was hampered by the bundle, but managed to catch up.

Mistress Isabella ranted at the top of her voice, "I'll bring in two cats. They will soon rid this place of vermin—there's probably all kinds because of these pigs. It serves them right. Bah! Men—they love to live in dirt. I hope you see what comes of living like a pig. Sickness and death, that's what."

The way she went through the dormitory would set speed records. Her eyes darted all around looking for any more signs of mice while mumbling something about "coming out at night" which did nothing to calm Liz's fears.

Liz tossed down her bundle near one of the pumps in the courtyard. Mistress Isabella's shouts brought servants running from the kitchen.

Liz pointed at Mistress Isabella's turban which was in serious danger of falling off, and she quickly righted it. She rattled off detailed instructions to the servants before beckoning Liz to follow her into the kitchen.

Mistress Isabella indicated the small pile of clothing on a bench. "Don't forget your things."

Liz scooped up the pile and bowed her thanks.

"Thank you, Mistress," she continued. "I promise to get an early start in the morning."

"Good. Go to bed now. I doubt you will see Master Piero in his rooms this night."

As she trudged back across the courtyard toting her bundle, she prayed Mistress Isabella was right.

She lit a taper at the door of the artisans' quarters and stopped dead in her tracks. In only a few minutes, some of the workmen had tumbled into their beds, fully clothed, with cups and plates left on the floor. To reach the back staircase, she would have to weave her way through the cots with the sleeping men in them. Some others were preparing to join their fellows. Snoring like the hum of a hundred airplanes filled the room.

Instinctively, she turned on her heel and walked rapidly around the outside of the building. Near the privies, she found the back entrance. Mounting the stairs at a run, she dashed into Piero's room and threw the bolt on the door.

With legs like lead from exhaustion, she stumbled to the bed, dropped the armload of clothing, and collapsed onto the bed.

She looked up at the moon, perfectly framed by the beautiful window, now streaked with dirt. Sobs wracked her body as she gave in to her fears. Throughout this long, horrible day, she had held herself in check because she knew with unyielding certainty that her tears would do more harm than good. Now, at last, alone in the room, she could let go.

In a perverse way, the sobs cleansed her of the anxiety and fear that had all but consumed her over the course of the day.

She glared through her tears at the mocking smile of the man in the moon before falling into a deep, dreamless sleep.

CHAPTER 4

▼

While Liz was being fed, clothed and generally cosseted by Mistress Isabella, Piero and Captain San Martini finished their meal and then adjourned to Captain San Martini's rooms in the barracks to continue their discussion in absolute privacy.

This was their first opportunity since Piero's return to delve in earnest into what Piero had seen and heard on his mission into the mountains. The Duke's fortified stronghold at San Leo provided the perfect base of operations on the Duke's northern border. It was well provisioned throughout the last two months of winter by Piero's hunting expeditions. Under the guise of a hunter, he moved unobtrusively through the mountains to the border of the lands of Duke Malatesta of Mantua. Quietly observing movements of Duke Malatesta's men-at-arms and picking up snippets of information from local farmers, he was able to return to Captain San Martini with a fairly concise picture of Duke Malatesta's plans for the spring. Piero knew that Captain San Martini would not be pleased with the picture painted for him.

After they cracked open a bottle of the Duke's best red wine, they settled themselves comfortably by the fire. Piero was anxious to recount what he had learned over the last months, but Captain San Martini instigated the conversation with a word of welcome.

"I'm happy to see you returned safely, Piero. I sense you are eager to recount the adventures you had on your travels."

"I'm sorry to say I saw no sign of Guelph forces at all, Luca. If, as you suspect, Malatesta is in league with the Guelphs, I could find no evidence of it."

Captain San Martini crossed the room to a table with scrolled maps stacked on the shelf above it. He took one of the maps down and flattened it out onto the table and tacked it down.

Summoning Piero to join him, he said, "Show me the route you took."

"First," Piero said, stabbing the map with his finger, "I went east to the seacoast and headed north and then back to the west into the mountains. Each hunting trip took me further west. I stopped at the hunting lodge on Monte Titano and then skirted some of the towns in the westernmost part of the province. I saw nothing suspicious. The country people huddled in their homes for warmth, but I did speak to a few of the Duke's loyalists. And I asked some questions in the marketplaces. I crisscrossed the countryside on one particular trip that took me three nights' journey out and two nights' back to the lodge."

Moving his finger along the map, a somber expression on his handsome face, he continued with his report.

"On my last trip out, I stopped several times to exchange news with farmers gathering kindling and such, and they mentioned a small band of armed men sporting Malatesta colors that had passed through their village only the night before. It prompted me to investigate further, but I saw nothing, no armed men or any suspicious activity, but the hunting was good." His third glass of wine was taking effect since this last remark was accompanied by a sloppy grin.

"So, if he is planning to move in the spring, he has kept it well hidden."

"Luca, there were no redoubts, no breastwork, no bulwarks, no men moving about building any storage huts. This would have been the time his men would be engaged in such pursuits. The people would have seen it, and some word would have reached me."

Luca nodded thoughtfully, but Piero could tell he was still unconvinced. Luca rolled up the map and put it back on the shelf.

He sat down and poured them more wine. He tilted his head and looked sideways at Piero as if coming to terms with what Piero had told him.

"Word has come from the Duke that the campaign he is waging against the Sienese for the Florentines has been bogged down for over a month," he confided to Piero. "The siege has dragged on." He stopped to drink from his cup. "The Duke had hoped to be done with it and be home by now, but it appears the stalemate will keep him away at least another three weeks."

"I may not be a *condottiero* like His Grace or a man-at-arms like you," Piero countered, "but I would think that with the spring rains coming on, three weeks may be too optimistic."

"You may well be right, Piero, but what it means is that I am stuck here guarding the *Palazzo* for the Duke because, first and foremost, I have a sworn duty to protect the Duchess and the young Lord Guidobaldo, as well as this city until the Duke's return. You have been my eyes and ears most of this winter, and for that I am grateful. Maybe," he continued with a sigh, "I am becoming too old for this, like a spinster who hears a little noise and looks under her bed, expecting to find a man lurking there to jump out and deflower her."

"Or hoping to find a man there ready to deflower her," Piero corrected him.

Luca laughed heartily at that one, and agreed that the long winter had taken its toll.

"I need to feel my blood moving again, Piero, I need a horse under me and the smell of battle. There's nothing like it."

"If you say so. When I agreed to help you, my friend, I told you my reasons. I am no warrior, but I am the Duke's man and his loyal servant …"

"And you have no great love for the Pope," Luca finished the sentence for him.

"The Guelphs and their misguided devotion to the Pope will be the end for all of us. Our freedoms are at stake, Luca. You know it as well as I do. The Holy Father would swallow all of Italy if given a chance, and they are helping him gobble it up bit by bit … the fools."

They fell silent for a few moments, both men lost in their own thoughts. Piero broke the silence.

"I know Duke Frederico found it difficult to take his stand with the Ghibellines because the Pope favored him in the past for his service to the Papacy …"

"Yes, it's true, but with Malatesta poised to make his move against us, under the pretext of doing the Pope's bidding, when everyone knows he has been waiting for just such an excuse to make war on Urbino, the choice was made for him," Captain San Martini added.

Piero asked, "Are the patrols still going out?"

"Yes, every day. We cannot let down our guard for even a moment."

"Has the Duchess said anything to you about Malatesta?"

"No, she has not confided her feelings to me. Doubtless, it is hard on her. He is her kinsman, after all. To know one of her own seeks to bring her world crashing down around her must cause her great distress. So, she hears daily Mass at the Church of San Bernardino, under my watchful eye, of course."

"Surely you don't attend with her."

"No, I wait outside."

The laughter they shared at this remark was in direct proportion to the amount of wine they had consumed. When they recovered sufficiently, Captain San Martini picked up the thread of conversation.

"What of this young Cosimo who appeared in the chapel as if out of nowhere? Where did he come from? He says he comes from *Arezzo*, at least that's what he told the Duchess."

"But you don't believe him. Do you think he's harmless?" Piero asked.

"He seems so, but he bears watching until we know for sure."

"Don't worry. I'll keep a careful eye on him," Piero reassured his friend.

Piero's expression turned serious, and his companion asked, "What is it my friend? Surely, the boy does not worry you so."

"No, of course not. In the mountains, Luca, I had a lot of time to think. It has probably already occurred to you, but ..." he hesitated, uncertain how to express his misgivings, "what about some hidden, potential danger from inside the *Palazzo*."

Captain San Martini barked out a derisive laugh. "Indeed, I have already thought of it, my friend. And, if you were to pick someone out from everyone in the *Palazzo*, who would be your choice as the pawn of Malatesta? Eh?"

"It's not for me to name names, Luca. I wouldn't want to be responsible for bringing suspicion upon anyone."

"Come now, my friend, you brought it up. For a good reason, I presume."

"No, no, there's nothing. It was merely a thought that entered my head."

"My friend, you are young. You will always have thoughts enter your head. Some of them will be good thoughts, and others will be unkind. In my life, I have learned it is healthy to be suspicious. There will always be men who are ready to dishonor themselves if it would advance them in this world. Desperate men. Like your Judas."

"He's not my Judas, Luca."

Piero looked away and pretended to scan the wall as if some interesting pattern had suddenly materialized to attract his attention, but both men knew the doubts that hung unspoken in the air between them.

Captain San Martini at last gave voice to that doubt.

"Which do you think it is, then? The father or the son?"

"I cannot accuse the Sanzios of anything, save an overabundance of pomposity."

"Aha! How did you know which father and son I meant? I could have meant Serafino and his boy."

"The blacksmith? Don't be ridiculous!"

"We both know the Sanzios favor the Guelphs in this conflict, and they have been unable to convince the Duke to confirm that Raffaello will succeed the old man. They hide behind pleasant masks, but it would not surprise me to learn that they conspire against His Grace."

"They make no effort to conceal their bitterness," Piero objected in their defense. "For that reason alone, I don't think they're involved in any conspiracy to usurp the Duke's lands for Malatesta. Surely, if they were involved, they would try to deflect suspicion by covering up their feelings. But they have not. Whatever you may think of them, I have found them to be honorable men."

"Especially Giovanni," Captain San Martini concurred with a nod. "He has served the Duke and the old Duke before him with distinction. The son, on the other hand."

He banged his palm onto the table, and the sound resonated like a pistol shot in the quiet room.

"The old man is unwell, and is easily swayed by his son," Piero noted.

Captain San Martini impulsively put an arm around the younger man and grinned broadly at him.

"I'll tell you one thing of which I am sure, Piero, it's a good thing you are a painter and not a politician."

"*È vero.* I had better go now. It is late, and I told my newest apprentice he would help with my bath. I'm sorry my work took so long today, but I could not lose the light. You were riding about the countryside early this morning when I returned."

"I was checking the outposts. You make it sound as if I took out a blanket and a picnic lunch."

"I'm sorry," Piero said with a smile.

"Stay here tonight. It is late, and we will find you a comfortable bed."

"All right. I won't decline your invitation for I'm dead tired."

Luca led him down a short passageway into the main garrison, and Piero quickly found himself in a small room with a freshly made bed.

Before he pitched face down on the bed, Piero turned a vacant gaze on his friend.

"Be careful, Luca."

"Don't worry about me. I'm like Mistress Isabella's favorite rooster. I have survived this long because I am too tough to kill."

Luca closed the door softly. Piero's last conscious thought before he fell asleep was of his new apprentice. Let him wait next to a bath gone cold.

CHAPTER 5

▼

Liz slept huddled in a blanket in the middle of Piero's bed. The raucous crowing of a rooster popped her eyes open, and she sat bolt upright. In the faint light of dawn, she looked around the room and breathed a sigh of relief. She was alone. Piero had never returned and the door was closed.

She got up and padded groggily to the door. The key was still in the lock, and she tried the knob to make sure. She removed the key and tossed it on the bed before entering the privy.

While she washed from a basin of cold water, she made a mental note to bring up a bucket of fresh water and then turned her brain to the list of possible pitfalls the day could bring.

Her stomach started to churn so she forced herself to stop fretting about what could go wrong and instead think positive thoughts, like the possibility of finding the portal. The thought of finding the portal and putting an end to her lonely sojourn in this strange land lifted her spirits.

What good could come of worrying over all the mistakes she might make. She reminded herself that customs could vary greatly from, say, Rome to Venice, in this time period. She could always chalk up her inevitable *faux pas* to her youth and the fact that she supposedly hailed from a different part of the country.

No doubt about it, she would make mistakes. But if she was careful, prepared with a ready excuse, she would find she was her own best friend.

The bundle of clothing was still at the foot of the bed. She looked through it and selected a baggy pair of woolen tights, a shirt, a worn leather belt and a pair of scuffed suede boots. There was another pair of soft black leather boots in the pile as well as shirts, two doublets and more tights. She took off all of her clothes except her underwear and stuffed them with her shoes under the bed. Then she took the toweling she had found in the privy and ripped it to make a binding for her breasts before putting on the clothes she had gotten from Mistress Isabella.

The sky was growing brighter, and the view from the window drew her like a magnet. The cock was still crowing as she looked out over the red rooftops of the town, the jumble of buildings stopped by the remnant of an ancient wall, probably Roman. Beyond, the sun filled the glorious Italian countryside with soft light. No longer marked by the winter's harshness, the early spring vista of farms, vineyards, rolling hills, and cypress gave way to the distant sea. It was a landscape reminiscent of many a Renaissance painting.

She tore herself away from the view for a closer inspection of Master Piero's room. Maybe she could learn something about this man who held her future within his grasp. Two storage chests under the bed attracted her attention and she tugged them out, but they were padlocked. So much for prying into them, she thought. The wardrobe was not locked, but going through that revealed nothing more than that he favored cut velvet over brocade. In one of the drawers in the wardrobe, though, she found a key-ring with two keys. She eyed the storage chests, but returned the key-ring to its drawer for a later inspection. He might return at any moment, and it wouldn't do to be caught snooping. If I'm patient, she thought, he may open them for me.

The books and objects strewn about his bedchamber, especially on a large round table in the center of the room that served as workspace-cum-desk, revealed much more about the man. They showed the master painter to be the possessor of an extremely inquisitive mind.

His bookshelves overflowed with texts on mathematics and perspective, Latin texts on diverse subjects like mythology and philosophy, books holding designs for telescopes, and the science of astronomy. A rudimentary telescope sat on a small table by the window. She pictured him using it, scanning the night sky. There was a small notebook next to the telescope filled with calculations and exquisite drawings of the constellations.

Sketchbooks were stacked in a haphazard pile on the table. She opened first one and then another. Every inch of paper was taken up with all manner of drawings, each with detailed measurements to capture perspective.

Even though these were rough sketches done mostly in charcoal, Liz saw the hand of true genius. Several of the sketchbooks contained drawings of female nudes, and another, detailed anatomical drawings of parts of the body, displaying bone and sinew.

Liz sat on the edge of the bed engrossed in the drawings until sounds from the first floor reminded her that the rest of the world was preparing for the day.

She closed the sketchbook she was leafing through and returned it to the table, dividing the pile in two neat stacks. She checked her reflection one last time in the dingy mirror in the privy chamber. The binding and the full shirt disguised her curves just as the sweatshirt had done. Pulling the shirt down in the back as an added precaution, she started off for breakfast, confident she could pass muster.

Her stomach rumbled in anticipation as she unlocked the door and started down the hallway.

At the bottom of the staircase, she came upon one of Mistress Isabella's cats—a big handsome tabby—making short shrift of a mouse.

"Good job," Liz said, as she hurried by, not looking too carefully at his handiwork and thankful she hadn't yet had her breakfast.

She ran around the outside of the artisans' building toward the courtyard and almost collided with Captain San Martini coming up from the barracks.

"How are you, young Cosimo?" he said in greeting, slapping her sharply on the back.

"I'm fine, thank you, sir," she replied, catching her breath.

They walked side by side to the kitchen door. "Would it be all right if I came to the stables to see the horses?" Liz blurted out the request.

"Certainly. Any time, but I imagine Master Piero will keep you busy."

"Is he coming to breakfast?"

"He went to the chapel to give the workmen their orders, but I'm sure we'll see him at breakfast when he's through."

The kitchen smelled invitingly of warm fresh-baked bread and roasting meat.

When they entered, heads turned in their direction, and faces registered surprise at seeing them together. Dressed befitting a young man of the artisan class, she spotted Mistress Isabella right away and strode purposefully in her direction to present herself for inspection. She bowed low. Liz completed her obeisance and stood erect with shoulders back and chin high.

She was rewarded with a broad smile from Mistress Isabella.

"I thank you for my clothes and for this food, good Mistress, and please convey my humble thanks to our good mistress, *La Duchessa*," Liz murmured.

"Well said, young man, but it is to God we must give thanks for all things. Eat your fill now, for I know you have your work cut out for you today. I can only spare a couple of young lads to help you, but I will send them with you when you finish breakfast."

Liz squeezed into a place at table with some of the servants. Breakfast was a *frittata* and a slice of cold Parma ham, bread, fruit, and wine mixed with water or weak tea.

She longed for a strong cup of coffee, but it would be some time before New World coffee would make any impact on the diet of Italians. By the time of the Renaissance, tea had been introduced at many of the courts of northern Italy—thanks to Marco Polo. And Liz had seen the evidence—the barrels of tea in the storage room. The court of Urbino, through trade with Venice, could easily secure luxury items such as silks, spices and tea from the Orient.

Liz gave herself a mental hug to think she was here doing the practical work in archeology she had been trained to do. Not cataloging the finds of others, not studying, but living it. If she was able to find her way back to her own time, would anyone believe that she witnessed firsthand what life was like in Renaissance Italy?

Liz gobbled down her breakfast and found Mistress Isabella in the larder.

"I'm going back upstairs to clean now, Mistress."

"Very well. The linens will be sent up shortly. And the young lads will bring up brooms and cleaning cloths with them. Make them do the windows and fetch what you need. I'm relying on you to supervise."

Liz left the kitchen encouraged by Mistress Isabella's confidence.

Out in the courtyard, she was transfixed by the commotion. Heavily laden carts were lumbering up the hill, and servants were lined up to unload them.

While she was indoors having breakfast, a steady light spring rain had begun to fall. She made a dash to the pumps and grabbed two buckets and started pumping frantically.

A hand reached down and covered hers on the pump handle. Liz looked up into emerald green eyes and straightened. His hand on hers was strong and warm, and she could feel the heat of him melting into her, claiming her.

"Master Piero!" she exclaimed breathlessly, "You startled me. I was just going up to clean. I'm afraid last night I fell asleep and got no work done."

"No matter, *Piccolino*. Truth to tell, so did I," he said with an engaging smile, displaying straight, extremely white teeth.

Liz hefted the buckets and staggered awkwardly with her load toward the door of the artisans' building. She stopped in the doorway. She looked back and smiled as she caught a glimpse of Piero entering the kitchen.

Slowly crossing the first floor to the back staircase, she tried not to slosh the water out of the buckets.

When she reached his room, she was panting and had to rest.

She picked up her bundle of clothes and the ones she had stored under the bed and took them through the privy to the small room beyond. She used the fresh water to refill the pitcher and wash the chamber pot in the privy, surprising herself with how quickly she had overcome her initial distaste for this task. Besides, she asked herself, what choice do I have?

Then she got down to serious work.

The young servants brought up the linens and brooms and more buckets of water. They also brought up cakes of brown soap made from lye and animal fat.

Liz opened windows and swept and scrubbed the privy first and then made up Piero's bed, the mattress of which she inspected carefully and found to be clean.

She wiped down the table and straightened up his bookshelves. The young boys washed all the windows while she dusted the rest of the furniture and swept the floor.

When she finished, she stood back and admired her work in Master Piero's room and the privy.

Next, she attacked the room down the hall for her own. She turned the small mattress and pounded it. She sent one of the boys down for more sheets and a clean blanket.

She inspected the interior rooms off the hall. They were small and filled with cast off bits and pieces of furniture. Her search through the jumble turned up a few things she could use in her room—oil lamps and candlesticks, several coal-burning braziers for the closest thing to heat she would get, along with the odd chair and table. She would need to scare up some of the dried moss and wood chips she saw the servants using for tinder to get the coals to catch fire.

She grappled with a heavy, free-standing *etagère* and dragged it across the hall to the privy chamber. She polished it, stocked it with the clean towels and perched a brass candlestick on top.

A small chest made a great storage cabinet for her room, and she stowed all of her clothing and the spare pair of black leather boots in it. Several ceiling hooks in each of the rooms puzzled her. She wondered what they were for.

By the time she was satisfied with the condition of the rooms, she had to wash herself again.

The twigs she found in the privy, she realized, were used like toothbrushes to scrape teeth clean. She tried one. It had a pleasant, minty taste and actually did a passable job. What good would it do to long for toothpaste, shampoo, a hot shower or moisturizer, she lamented to herself.

In the course of the morning, to fetch various items she needed, she had climbed the stairs no less than three times. This was growing old real fast, and Liz understood why she had seen so few fat servants.

The boys left Liz when they finished, and she was in her room making up her bed when she heard sounds coming from the hall. She peeked out into the hall and saw Mistress Isabella shuffling up the hall with armloads of greenery. She entered Liz's room and looked around.

"Good. Good." She dropped one bundle on the chair next to Liz's bed and walked into the privy, left another bundle. She proceeded into Piero's room, Liz trailing after her. The scent of fresh lavender hit her nostrils.

"You have done well. Everything seems in order," she remarked to Liz, who said nothing for fear of displaying her ignorance. "Hang those bundles of lavender in the rooms. Their pleasant fragrance will last for some time as they dry."

Liz rushed to comply. So that was what the hooks were for, she thought, and smiled involuntarily as she looped the first cord and tied it to the hook.

"Now come and have something to eat."

They went downstairs and walked through the ground floor dormitory. Mistress Isabella's eyes darting around looking for signs of vermin.

"I'm going to inspect the privies first."

"Shall I accompany you?" Liz inquired.

"If you wish."

While Liz wisely kept vigil outside, being totally disinterested in the condition of the outdoor privies, Mistress Isabella checked to make sure her orders had been carried out. Satisfied with the results, they rounded the building and crossed the courtyard.

"Now those privies will not disgrace us," Mistress Isabella commented. "I would have no visiting servants using them tomorrow and reporting to their masters the poor state of my privies. My good Lady Battista would be mortified."

Liz entered the kitchen in Mistress Isabella's wake and filled a plate with a wonderful dinner of *pasta con ceci* in an herbed chicken broth with butter, roast pork and steamed vegetables. At each table, there was a large round loaf of coarse bread or *pane rustico*, a green glass bottle of olive oil and an earthenware jug of good red wine. She saw the workmen who had discovered her in the chapel and exchanged pleasantries with them. After the main meal, cheese and pears poached in wine were brought out for dessert.

Amidst all the banter and laughter, Liz managed to overhear some conversation about Master Piero's return, and the tenor of the conversation led her to believe that he was held in high esteem by his workmen. By the time the meal ended, it was late afternoon. Possibly two hours of daylight remained, enough time for Liz to explore the chapel for the time portal.

She found the outside stairway and climbed up into the makeshift entry to the chapel. About twenty workmen with various helpers bustled about.

The eye in the storm of activity was perched on scaffolding midway up one wall. She watched Piero for a few moments and then strolled nonchalantly toward the wall where she had come through the portal. She felt along the wall in spots as she made her way around the chapel. If the portal was open anywhere in the chapel, she couldn't find it.

A momentary feeling of despair washed over her.

There must be something I'm missing, she thought, some way to make the portal open, some key I don't have.

Determined to think it through, she stood tapping her fingers to her lips, trying to come up with a rational plan for something by nature so irrational that she felt like kicking the wall.

She gazed up at Piero on the scaffolding where he was working. White dust covered him from head to foot. He stood legs apart in total concentration as he finished a section of *fresco*.

The section with the dying horse that Liz had seen emerge from the wall was now fully alive. Wild-eyed with flaring nostrils, Piero's brush had executed the perfect image of a magnificent warhorse. From the tip of his tail to his flailing forelegs, with the rider now pinned beneath him, he was complete. Piero stopped his brush in midair and stepped back to eye his creation, much as Liz had done inspecting her handiwork in cleaning his room.

Life for him was so simple, so pure. She envied him.

"Master," Liz shook off her mood and called up to him, "it would be better to come down here and look at him. He's magnificent!"

Piero turned and looked down at Liz, and she was appalled at the sight of him. His hair and beard were disheveled and matted. His green eyes were lusterless and red-rimmed. His arms hung at his side, and he was stooped with exhaustion. She watched him climb slowly down the scaffolding astounded by the transformation. He stood beside her and looked up at the horse, but was too weak to smile or utter a word.

"Master, I think you need that bath and a hot meal—and right now. Have you eaten at all today or stopped to rest?"

He shook his head. Liz took control. She turned to the head workman standing nearby whom she recognized from the dining room.

"The Master is finished for today. Please clean up the tools and put things right for tomorrow."

She took Piero's arm and led him away. He allowed himself to be led meekly from the chapel.

On their way to his rooms, Liz poked her head in at the kitchen and saw one of the young servants who had helped her earlier in the day.

"Please have buckets of hot water brought up to Master Piero's rooms for his bath."

Liz entered his room and sat Piero down on a chair next to the table. She removed his boots and put them out in the hallway.

"I don't know what's wrong with me or when I've been so tired," he mumbled.

"There's nothing wrong with you, Master, that a warm bath, a hot meal, and a good night's sleep in a clean bed won't cure."

This remark elicited a warm smile from him, but no comment.

Two boys entered the room with two buckets each of steaming hot water. She indicated the privy chamber. She followed them in and pulled the hipbath to the center of the room and, they poured the water into the tub.

"Go get more," she told them when the buckets were empty, "and some cool water too. And please ask Mistress Isabella to have a tray of hot food prepared and sent up for Master Piero."

Liz returned to Piero and began to strip off his clothes. He looked ready to fall asleep at the table.

"Your bath is ready, Master, let's get you in there."

She helped him into the privy chamber and closed the door. She took a moment to light the brazier in his room and approached the door to the privy with a lit taper. The sound of a splash signaled he had climbed into the tub.

Feeling like a tightrope walker at the circus—intense excitement mixed with the fear of falling—Liz took a deep breath and tapped on the door.

CHAPTER 6

▼

Liz heard a grunt in reply to her knock. She opened the door. Instead of seeing Piero sitting immersed in the tub as she expected, he stood by the washstand. Stripped to the waist, he was hacking off his beard. Water ran down his back making his skin glisten in the candlelight.

Liz ran to him. "Master, let me help you."

"I got most of it off." He waved her away like a little boy determined to do it himself.

She reached up with the taper to light the brazier. The tinder caught quickly and a shimmer of warmth rose from the coals' heat. How, she wondered, have I become his keeper? Next I'll be getting him to eat his veggies.

Piero turned, and Liz's breath caught in her throat. While the rear view of her new master was most pleasant, her senses were unprepared for a frontal assault.

The man was definitely not what she thought a Renaissance painter should look like. Brandishing the knife, he looked like a pirate or highwayman, all sinewy muscle and lithe grace. His muscular legs were still encased in his breeches, now drenched by his efforts to wet his beard. Liz concentrated on refilling the basin with hot water and averting her gaze from the wet fabric clinging to him in all the wrong places.

"It might be easier if you got in the bath, Master," she suggested, as she busied herself with towels and soap and readying his shaving things.

From the corner of her eye, she saw Piero strip off the rest of his clothing and squat down in the hip bath.

"Ah!" he sighed contentedly, sinking back in the warm water.

He lathered up with the cake of soap and bath sponge she handed him. She watched as he scrubbed at his arms and chest, and the water ran white from the plaster dust. He thrust the soap and sponge at her offhandedly.

"Here, do my back for me, there's a good lad."

The aroma of damp lavender filled the room. Liz rolled up her sleeves and plunged her hands holding the soap and sponge into the hot water. She worked a rich lather into the soft sponge. As she did so, her eye was caught by a solitary bead of water. Mesmerized and motionless, she watched it trickle slowly down Piero's spine.

"What's wrong? Don't be afraid to scrub," he said, glancing over his shoulder.

"I just wanted to get a good lather," she responded.

With an effort of will, she blotted every conscious thought from her mind and concentrated on the task at hand.

And so, for the first time in her life, she scrubbed a man's back.

"Shall I soap up your hair, Master?"

"Yes, if we have enough water for rinsing."

While she shampooed his hair, wild emotions fluttered in her breast, causing her heart to thump so loudly she was certain he could hear it. Even though circumstances compelled her to act a part, she could not avoid the feeling that she was in way over her head. She carried on with the charade, feeling guilty at the pretense. She wished she could confide in him, but that would be weak and foolhardy of her. Her survival justified any action she took. She steeled herself from these disturbing thoughts—and the even more disturbing sight of the naked and very attractive man whose hair she was washing—by making a weak attempt at acceptable conversation.

"The game you brought back tasted wonderful."

"The hunting was good. The Duke keeps five falcons up at the lodge, and I had my two as well. They kept me busy. They love to hunt almost as much as I do."

"Are there many servants up at the lodge?"

"Only a married couple—caretakers, really. I left some game for them as well. I didn't bother to bathe while I was there. It was cold as a witch's tit in the mountains and just too much trouble. This is so wonderful, I'm glad I waited."

He had his eyes closed and his head tilted back, so Liz was able to look at him all she wanted. She massaged his scalp and let her hands drift to the back of his neck. Gently, she guided his head forward and massaged his neck and shoulders and was rewarded with hearing his groans of pleasure.

"I think we're ready to rinse you off, Master, so close your eyes."

She poured one ewer of warm water and then another over his head. He raised his arms and combed through his wet hair with long elegant fingers. With his eyes still closed, she enjoyed an unfettered view of the movement of his muscles and the way the water clung to his eyelashes.

She had a towel ready when he rose from the bath—like Neptune rising from the sea. Liz quickly wrapped the towel around his middle and handed him another. He leaned one forearm on her shoulder as he stepped from the tub.

"I'll fetch a robe," she stammered and ran to the *armadio* in his room.

Liz mopped up and emptied the bath water, bucket by bucket, while he shaved himself.

"The celebration for young Lord Guidobaldo's birthday is tomorrow, Cosimo. I'll be glad to have a day of rest and society before I go back to the scaffold. Sometimes I dream of the scaffold." He paused, and their eyes met in the mirror, before she knelt to finish the mopping up. "It waits for me in my dream, and I walk toward it as if to my execution. What would you make of that, *Piccolino*?"

She peered up at him from the floor, where she was gathering up the cloths and buckets, and got her first look at his clean-shaven face. His unmarked skin glowed rosy bronze in the candlelight. The sharp planes of his face, the deep cleft in his chin, the straight nose and full mouth could not conceal the forthright character beneath the perfect features.

"I'm sure I couldn't say, Master," Liz responded quietly. To herself, she thought, even if I can't tear my eyes away, I refuse to fall under his spell, and I'll be damned if I'm going to analyze his dreams.

"Are you as able a barber? Maybe before tomorrow's celebration you could give my hair a trim."

"Oh, yes, Master," she replied, another lie on her conscience. "I'd be happy to."

"Good."

Liz carried the last of the buckets of water to the hallway and lit more candles in Piero's room. A knock at the door signaled the arrival of Piero's food. Liz took the tray and instructed the young serving boy to take the buckets down and to have Piero's boots cleaned.

Piero sat at the table and ate from the tray that Mistress Isabella had sent up to him. It was the same dinner that Liz had eaten earlier with the addition of a small bowl of soup. Piero finished the soup and wine and ate most of the meal.

"Before I take the tray down to the kitchen, Master, let me help you into bed."

Piero rose like an old man from the table and stumbled toward the bed, already half asleep.

"Thank you, *Piccolino*, for taking such good care of me," he said, as Liz tucked him in.

She placed a small candlestick on the tray and took the tray out, closing the door gently behind her.

The night had grown cool, and a brisk breeze snuffed out her lonely candle. She cursed herself for not bringing the lantern instead.

Stars in such numbers and with such clarity as she had never seen filled the sky. The wind threatened to whip the tray out of her hands as she hurried to the kitchen where the hearths glowed. Outside the warm circle of light, night reigned.

She went back outside and gazed up at the night sky. No street lights or light of any kind pierced the inky blackness. Though she wore no outer garment and the night was cool, she remained spellbound, face turned heavenward to the constellations.

When she returned to the room, Piero was snoring softly. Liz doused the candles and went to her room. She locked her doors and lit the brazier and a lantern on a stand near her bed. She closed the windows against the chill of the night before undressing.

When finished washing her face and hands, she climbed into her bed.

Her room was small, and before long, warm and toasty. She was weary clear through to her bones and soon dreamed of wet skin and starlit skies.

＊　　　＊　　　＊　　　＊

Liz woke early in the morning. Dawn had barely shown her face on the horizon when noises of rumbling carts and shouts roused her from a delicious slumber.

She tiptoed through the privy and listened at the connecting door to Piero's room. The sound of slow, deliberate breathing convinced her that it was safe to use the privy chamber. She locked the door to Piero's room and used the chamber pot. Then she washed her body thoroughly.

Every trace of her use was removed to her room before she unlocked Piero's door and relocked her own. She dressed hurriedly and carried the chamber pot down the stairs and out the back of the artisans' building to the privies.

Dodging carts laden with provisions from the country, she rinsed the chamber pot at the outdoor kitchen pumps, and re-washed her hands before going back up to her room.

She stashed her pot in her room and went into the hall. Piero was stirring so she tapped at the door.

"Master, are you up?" she called through the closed door.

"Yes, *Piccolino*, I'm awake."

"Shall I fetch you a cup of tea?"

"Yes. And by the time you return, I'll be ready for that haircut you promised me."

Minutes later she stood outside his door with a tray holding two pewter cups filled with tea, two slabs of *polenta* on a plate and some fruit. She knocked and entered to find him in his robe rummaging through his *armadio*. He took the tray from her and sat at the table.

"You seem to be continually feeding me, *Piccolino*."

"You work too hard and need nourishment. I must say, though, that you look much better this morning."

Piero only smiled up at her as he reached for his tea.

"This may be the only food we'll get until tonight," she continued, "it's getting really busy down in the kitchen."

"Don't worry. If you get hungry, just go to the kitchen and help yourself. Mistress Isabella always keeps a pot of soup on the stove."

They finished their meal in companionable silence and then set to work cutting Piero's hair.

She fussed about the room, stalling as long as she could. When she could stall no longer, she approached him apprehensively from behind, scissors in hand. She plucked up her courage, thinking to herself that it couldn't be that difficult to cut hair. She had watched countless times as her hair had been cut.

She combed his hair back off his forehead revealing a widow's peak and a natural part. His thick hair was quick to respond, and Liz gained more and more confidence as she took his dampened hair section by section and trimmed inches off all around. By the time she finished, his hair was almost dry and fell in soft waves to his earlobes.

A definite improvement, she decided, hoping he would be pleased with the result. The color was not black as she first thought, but a warm mahogany brown with ash highlights. Liz disposed of the clippings while Piero checked his reflection in the mirror.

"Very good, indeed, *Piccolino*. Thank you." He swallowed the last of his tea.

"Now to get to Mass. And what to wear? I already have the small clothes, but what doublet?"

Liz hunted around for his boots in the bottom of the *armadio*, and came up with a black pair. A freshly laundered shirt was already on the bed.

"How about the dark green cut velvet?" Liz suggested.

"Hm. No, I think the lapis blue and dark blue hose."

Outwardly, she remained the perfect servant—unnoticed and unobjectionable—anticipating what Piero needed before he knew he needed it. This necessitated her watching his every move and gesture. When Piero finished, he turned toward Liz.

"Am I now presentable?" he asked turning around.

"Yes, Master."

The blue doublet—even though not a match for those striking green eyes—fit him perfectly. Very presentable indeed, she thought, keeping her expression bland.

"Are you ready to go to Mass, *Piccolino*?"

"Yes."

"Let's go then. We mustn't be late."

As they started from the room, Piero outlined for her what activities awaited them.

"The partying will go on most of the day and into the evening when there will be fireworks, a big treat. We'll remain in the chapel after Mass to see the work, and tomorrow the scaffolding will go back up, and we will start in with your first assignments."

They had reached the lower landing when he stopped short.

"Wait. I forgot the Duke's gift. I always try to wear it when I know I'll be in the company of Her Grace or the Duke."

When they returned to his room, he pulled one of the chests from under the bed and opened the drawer in the *armadio* that held the keys. He fitted one of the keys into the padlock on the chest and lifted from it a small case. When he opened the case, Liz could not suppress a gasp of shock and surprise. Laying on a piece of satin brocade was the amulet she had seen in the display case in the Science Building scant days ago.

"Bello, no?"

He took her reaction for admiration. She was stunned and involuntarily retreated two steps from the cursed object. There was no way he could know the effect the presence of the amulet here in his room had on her.

She bit down hard on her bottom lip as the realization hit her full force that the man standing before her carefully draping the amulet over his head would one day be a prize specimen in a science laboratory. A cry of despair died on her lips as her throat filled with unshed tears.

"This is why I wanted the blue doublet. And then I almost forgot to wear it. It was a gift to me from the two Graces we serve."

Liz recovered her wits, knowing he expected her to say something.

"It's very beautiful," she managed to say, swallowing back tears.

He gave her an odd look and went on, "On the occasion of their marriage, I painted their portraits. In addition to the commission—which was a very handsome one, I might add—they presented me with this gift. I'm very proud of it. It's a sign of their patronage."

"That's understandable, Master. It looks very old. Do you know where it came from?"

"No, even the Duke doesn't know for certain. It was in the family's collection. Quick, we must hurry."

He locked the chest and returned the keys to the small drawer in the *armadio*.

Intent on learning more about the amulet if she could, she hurried along beside him.

A sobering thought occurred to her, one dire enough to halt her step at the top of the stairs. Suppose there was a reason for her being transported to his side. Suppose his life depended on her being here. Maybe someone, even now, was laying in wait to kill him, and she was meant to be here. The amulet belonged to him. Doubtless he was the abandoned man in the burial chamber. The Duke would have buried his favorite painter and friend near his family, but not with them. Looking at him, she could see how he would inspire envy. Maybe someone wanted him dead, and she was meant to be here to save him. It all made perfect, perverse sense.

With a sense of foreboding and thoughts of death and doom that descended on her as surely as she descended the stairs to catch up with him, she understood that he was no longer her source of protection, but rather one who needed her protection. She resolved not to let him out of her sight.

Liz caught up with him outside the building and attempted to get more information from him about the amulet.

"Master, do you have any idea what those symbols on the amulet signify?"

"No. His Grace told me he thinks it might be Etruscan, but he admits it's a mystery. He also said that it could also be ancient writing from the East."

"Maybe it was brought back by one of his ancestors from the Crusades," she guessed.

Her mind jumped from one conclusion to another, but her chance of learning more dwindled the closer they drew to the chapel doorway. A noisy crowd of courtiers were gathered there. Servants and merchants hung back to permit the courtiers to file into the chapel first.

"You could be right, *Piccolino.*"

"Master Piero, may I stay with you after Mass when you inspect the work in the chapel?"

"Of course."

"And when you present yourself to the Duchess to offer your congratulations, may I accompany you? You see, she has been most kind in taking me in, and I never had the opportunity to thank her properly."

"I don't see why not, *Piccolino.* I think she would be pleased."

CHAPTER 7

▼

The incense fumes caught in Liz's throat as they entered the chapel. Moments later, she understood why the incense was used so liberally. It helped to mask the foul odors of so many warm, unwashed bodies crammed into a relatively small space.

The chapel had been cleared of the scaffolding and equipment from the day before. Instead, people filled it to capacity creating an awful din.

Piero left Liz at the back of the chapel where she squeezed herself into a little space among the servants leaning against the rear wall.

Piero seated himself in front near the family on one of the makeshift benches brought in for the occasion.

Members of the nobility were seated near the altar on some of the ornately carved chairs she remembered from her previous life. Was it really only a few days ago? she asked herself. It seemed as though an age had passed.

The remainder of the crush—a mix of soldiers, servants and some who looked to be of the merchant class—squatted or stood shoulder to shoulder, waiting for the Mass to begin.

When the Mass finally commenced, the devout followed along with the white-clad priest, attentive and silent, while others conversed and all but ignored the worship service being conducted a few feet away.

The Mass was a celebration of thanksgiving for the first birthday of the young Lord Guidobaldo. People moved back and forth in front of Liz blocking her view so she only caught glimpses of the infant being held by his nursemaid directly behind the Duchess's chair.

Today, only the second time Liz had seen her, the Duchess was splendidly dressed in a burgundy velvet and brocade gown with every attention paid to her appearance.

She sat on an ornate chair elevated above the throng. The dark hue of her gown accentuated the fairness of her skin and hair and heightened her youthful grace and dignity. She wore her hair braided and pinned up under a veil with a simple burgundy velvet cap edged with pearls. From her neck hung a magnificent pearl necklace, and matching pearl drops hung heavily from her earlobes.

Her child favored his mother, fair-haired, with delicate, pretty features, and from his appearance, seemed far from robust.

Other young children sat with their nursemaids behind the nobles, but Liz had no clue as to their identity. One of the young gentlemen present could have been the nephew, young Lord Leo, for he was about the right size. She knew the Duke had sired some illegitimate children, and she wondered if some of these young people were the Duke's bastards.

Since the priest was the only one to partake of the host and cup, she was spared having to decide what to do about communion.

When the Mass ended, the buzz of conversation swelled to a roar as the congregation filed out. Liz hovered near the door to wait for Piero. She spotted Mistress Isabella walking with Captain San Martini. Deep in conversation, they did not see her.

One who did see her and approached was Master Raffaello, accompanied by an older gentleman Liz took to be his father because of their marked resemblance.

Raffaello, if possible, was dressed even more ostentatiously than before, with every furbelow one could imagine adorning his pudginess, including a slim bejeweled dagger tucked into his waistband. His father, though an older version of the son, was dressed somberly in black. Emaciation and a waxy pallor betrayed his poor health. His face also bore the deep scarring of the smallpox survivor, a fate his more fortunate son had escaped.

"*Buon giorno,* good Maestro Raffaello," she said, bowing from the waist.

"*Buon giorno* to you, young man," Raffaello replied, puffed up with the same *arroganza* he displayed at their first meeting. "Father, may I present to you young Cosimo, Maestro Piero's new apprentice. And this is my father, Giovanni Sanzio, court painter to the Duke."

"It is my great honor to make your acquaintance, Maestro Giovanni," Liz said, executing another courtly bow. She congratulated herself mentally on how good she was getting at boot licking.

The old man inclined his head slightly in her direction. She forced herself to make eye contact. His pockmarked face repulsed her, but the kindly expression in his eyes belied his countenance, overshadowing the awful pallor and the scars. To the heavy burden of being saddled with a pompous little twerp for a son must be added the awareness of his imminent demise and the sincere desire to see to it that his son followed in his footsteps as court painter.

Liz speculated as to what lengths he would go to secure Raphael's position at Court. Piero would likely present a considerable threat to his plans. Might Giovanni find it worthwhile to remove Piero from consideration? Would the Duke then turn to his faithful retainer and his young son, Raffaello, already here, and a genius well on his way to surpassing his father?

Liz recalled her evening meal the night before. While her mouth was busy chewing, her ears had picked up multiple conversations. One of those conversations, overheard at another table while she waited for their wine jug to come around within her reach, spoke volumes. It centered on Raffaello and his father. Two artisans grumbled in heated whispers about what would happen to them when the old man died if Raffaello was named to the position of painter-to-the-court. The tone of their conversation conveyed their opinion in no uncertain terms. They didn't hesitate to recount recent incidents of his arrogance and summed up in vulgar language the general disdain in which he was held by most of the artisans.

According to them, his reputation continued to decline with each passing day. As they left the table, they voiced the hope that Master Piero would be the next permanent court-appointed painter to oversee all of the work thereby "freeing us to pursue our craft like grown men, not like children or old women."

This conversation was foremost in her mind as she greeted the old father and son.

"Father, shall we go into the *Palazzo* to breakfast with the Duchess?" Raffaello asked.

"*Sì, certo*," the old man replied in a barely audible whisper. "I hope to see more of you, young man." Raphael had already totally dismissed Liz, but the old man's manners were impeccable.

"Thank you, sir." Liz bowed again in acknowledgement of his thoughtfulness and wondered again about them as they sauntered off to join the departing throng.

Liz wondered if a gentlemanly manner could fool her so easily. She reminded herself that a malevolent nature could be concealed beneath a thin veneer of courtliness. She debated back and forth in her mind. Well on her way to convincing herself that the old gentleman could never countenance the murder of his son's rival, no matter how badly he desired his position to pass into his son's hands, she failed to notice Piero appear beside her.

"Are you ready to help me?" he whispered at her shoulder.

Liz started visibly and turned to answer him, relieved to put disturbing thoughts from her mind.

"Yes, Master. What do we do first?"

"First, we find Leonardo and give him the orders for tomorrow. No one works today. I can only hope and pray that the workmen will be on their feet in the morning to carry them out." He said this with a rueful smile and a shake of his head.

"I'm sure the workmen and just about everyone else will do their best to recover and get back to work tomorrow."

Piero beckoned to Leonardo as Liz spoke.

"We shall wait and see, but I think you are too optimistic. It is most likely impossible."

It took only a couple of minutes to walk around the chapel and point out to Leonardo what preparations had to be made for the next day's work. Piero pointed where he wanted the scaffolding reassembled and spent a couple of minutes more studying the ceiling.

"So, the ceiling looks good, and tomorrow we begin the *intonaco* on the remaining walls."

Leonardo bowed to Piero and left them, and Piero walked around the chapel checking the plaster and the condition of the *frescoes* already completed before his trip.

"They have done well. Most of the ceiling is finished, and every star is just as I placed it. The color is good."

"You drew each and every star where you wanted them before you left?" Liz asked as he strolled toward her.

"Every one," he answered, "and they have done well mixing the blue and the gold colors and the touches of white for the clouds. I will have to heap praise on them tomorrow for they deserve it. When you begin in the morning, color will be the start of your lessons. That is the most important technique to master."

Piero stopped at the door of the chapel and gripped Liz's shoulders tightly with both hands. Liz's chest tightened with foreboding as she raised her eyes to his. Every gesture or word was like a sword hanging over her head. Never knowing if she had somehow given herself away constantly wore on her nerves.

"And now, let us go to the Duchess to add our congratulations," he said, releasing his grip.

Liz laughed nervously and breathed a sigh of relief. "Yes, master, and thank you for giving me the opportunity to thank the Duchess."

They sauntered along the passageway. A servant would occasionally block their path, rushing past with some last minute chore for the *festa*—a bundle or a basket of flowers, or a handy scuttle of coal to place beside a fireplace.

"Are you also ready for the *festa* tonight?" Piero asked with a mischievous grin.

"As ready as I'm going to be. Will you attend, as well?"

"I wouldn't miss it. I'll tell you a secret, Cosimo, I'm much more comfortable with the artisans and the servants than I am with the merchants and nobility. After all, my father was a tanner and bootmaker. He died before I was born, and my mother and her family did their best for me. They apprenticed me at an early age. Still, I cannot change who I am, and have no desire to do so. There are those who aspire to another station in life, but not me. I am a tanner's son and happy to be so."

"And you have your work."

"Yes. I have my work."

He slowed his pace and glanced at his apprentice. With a slow smile and a shake of his head, he said, "You are a strange one, *Piccolino,* so wise for one so young."

Liz felt the blood rush to her face causing her to turn her head away in confusion. They continued on their way, but she was reluctant to let the moment go.

"It's just that ..." she hesitated, afraid now to reveal too much to this man whose proximity made her tingle.

"*Chè cosa?* What is it? Tell me."

"I can understand how you can get so caught up in your work that everything else fades away, becomes meaningless somehow."

"Exactly!"

Her reaction to the sheer power of his physical presence confounded her. His potent smile and the fascinating curve of his lower lip held her as surely as if his hand gripped her wrist. The openness in his expression also confounded her. Used to dealing with the modern male—all closed attitude and subtle complexity—this meeting of minds that admitted her so readily to his central core as artist, she found immensely attractive.

And of what use is my discovery? she wondered, as she cast sidelong glances at his profile.

She longed to reach out to him, to touch his mouth and stroke his hair. To stop him and scream that she was not a boy and not a girl, but a woman, and more than willing to prove it. But he was oblivious to the effect he had on her. Every cell in her body quivered with aching need. She could feel her breasts tighten and her nipples harden at the memory of his hands on her shoulders. Her skin was still warm from his touch.

"There'll be dancing tonight, *Piccolino*. You do know how to dance?"

The teasing tone in his voice was loaded with promise—if she had been other to him than a young boy.

"No. I don't know how to dance," she replied sullenly.

"I will teach you then. After I spend some time with the gentry upstairs, I will be ready for a frolic with my friends in the courtyard."

"Am I your friend?"

"Of course you are. And there will be many young maidens who will long to be in your arms. I look on it as my duty to teach you all the arts. Not just the painting of superb *frescoes*, but the courting of young women too, which must be accomplished with gallantry and grace."

"And you know how to do this?" she inquired skeptically.

"Of course I do," he responded, followed by a dazzling smile.

If he didn't stop smiling at her, Liz thought, he'd soon charm her into getting a lot more than he bargained for. She could imagine his surprise.

"We're here," he said.

Jolted from her reverie by the lovely music wafting through the open doorway, she peered inside and saw the Duchess royally seated among a gathering paying court to her.

They joined a queue of courtiers in the middle of the grand salon to wait their turn to pay homage to the first lady of Urbino. As the line moved along, Liz picked up snippets of conversation.

Piero smiled graciously and bowed to several people. He seemed to know just about everybody. Finally, they stood in front of the Duchess. In unison, Piero and Liz executed perfect courtly bows to Her Grace.

"Welcome to court, Piero della Francesca, it is good to see you. We have had so little time to speak since your return. Perhaps we will make up for that today," the Duchess said, a note of tender gaiety in her voice.

"Many thanks, Your Grace. It is good to be home."

Giovanni Sanzio, a grave expression on his face, had positioned himself behind and to the right of the Duchess's chair.

"I value your opinion, Maestro Piero. What do you think of these musicians? Shall they come back this evening to play for my guests, do you think?" she asked, but Liz had the feeling his answer would hold no weight with her.

"Yes, Your Grace, they are very pleasing."

"There, Maestro Giovanni, he agrees with us. Luca seems to think they will put everyone to sleep."

"If there is any danger of that, Your Grace, you can bring your guests into the courtyard. I can guarantee you no one will fall asleep." Piero smiled his devilish smile and received a delighted chuckle from the Duchess in return.

"Yes," she agreed, "sometimes it's difficult to resist. But, alas, I am stuck."

Everyone twittered at her wit. However, there were two glum faces in the group around the Duchess who did not seem to find any humor in her remark.

While everyone within hearing distance closely followed the exchange between Piero and the Duchess, Liz had pinned her gaze on Giovanni. Giovanni's eyes never left Piero's face. She saw an odd expression play across the old man's face. The tenderness that she had noted to herself earlier had faded away, to be replaced by an expression of such malevolence that she gasped involuntarily.

Giovanni had been joined by his son, Raffaello, and together they stood glowering at Piero. The animosity emanating from these men was palpable. Liz was tempted to pull Piero from the room, out of harm's way.

A sinister looking fellow, who had detached himself from a small group to listen to the conversation, stood at Raffaello's elbow. Raffaello placed his hand on the fellow's arm in a possessive gesture.

"And I see you have kept your young apprentice," the Duchess continued, waving a languid hand in Liz's direction.

Liz forced a wan smile, all the while wishing she could close her eyes and reopen them to find herself back in her own world—hundreds of years in the future.

"Yes, Your Grace," Piero pronounced, "young Cosimo is a veritable firebrand. He is taking very good care of me, and tomorrow he will start work in the chapel. Though, I fear soon he will replace me. In the meantime, he has something to say to you."

Liz went down on one knee in obeisance and bowed her head. Then she rose up and addressed the Duchess.

"Gracious Lady, I thank you from the bottom of my heart for your hospitality and for the opportunity you have given me to work with the great Piero della Francesca."

Liz looked at the Duchess and then shifted her gaze to the Sanzios. Their stony expressions were mute evidence of the rancor her words provoked.

"I will strive my best to please him and to offer you no cause to regret allowing me to serve you and His Grace."

"Very nicely said," the Duchess commented.

Not soon enough for Liz, Piero withdrew then with Liz right behind him to return below stairs where they belonged.

When they were clear of the salon and a fair distance down the passageway, Piero stopped and spun her around by the arm.

"What could you be thinking? Did you think I missed the way you challenged them with your remark, the tone in your voice, and the way you glared at them? You were very foolish. You don't want to make enemies in that quarter."

"I only said what I believe."

"They are dangerous men!"

"I can handle myself."

"Per l'amore di Dio! You are just a boy."

He gave an exasperated sigh, and Liz realized how much she had upset him with her remarks.

"I'm so sorry, Master. I would not have caused you distress for the world." Her words were true enough, she thought, but how to account for the thrill she felt at his words of concern?

"What's done is done. But hear me, Cosimo, stay close to me. Do not wander off by yourself. Is that clear? Do you understand?" Sparks of green fire flashed from his eyes.

"Yes, Master," she replied, suddenly frightened.

What a wretched mess she had made of things with her big mouth. Life here had become a roller coaster, one moment on cloud nine, and next, plunged into deep despair. And all because she had become too sure of herself. She could kick herself for getting careless. She had to believe, in spite of how angry he was, that he would get over his anger, and call her *Piccolino* once more. She desperately wanted to feel that happy again.

CHAPTER 8

▼

Liz stumbled along behind Piero and swiped surreptitiously at unshed tears. By the time they reached the kitchen, she had recovered sufficiently to manage a smile when Mistress Isabella greeted them.

It didn't matter that the kitchen was abuzz with preparations for the feast; Mistress Isabella good naturedly set aside her duties to ladle soup for them. Liz ate greedily of the comfort food, a meaty, rich stock thick with vegetables and barley, and took a cup of wine with a hunk of bread for good measure.

As soon as Mistress Isabella saw to their needs, she left them to shuttle back and forth among the servants, directing and supervising the food preparation, not only for the party outside in the courtyard, but the far more important entertaining that would go on in the grand dining room upstairs.

She reappeared at their table, refilling their cups and pouring wine for herself. Her expression was fraught with worry and fatigue. Liz thought that she resembled a roman candle that had shed its final spark.

"These parties will be the death of me," Mistress Isabella lamented, as she plopped into a seat and raised her wine cup to her lips.

Piero took the matron's workworn hand in his and held it gently. Liz looked down at his long, slender fingers cradling Mistress Isabella's hand and wished with all her heart that it was her hand he held so tenderly.

"With the Duke so often away, it is fortunate that the Duchess seldom entertains," he said, patting her hand, "though I suspect there will be another party when the Duke returns."

"Oh, praise God, he comes home to us safe and sound. That would be a celebration I would welcome. And you, Piero, it is well you are back. We need you here. The Duchess needs your kind heart and good sense."

"I'm glad to be home," he said, standing and finishing the last of his wine. Liz noted the change in his expression, as though a cloud passed over the sun darkening the sky. She realized, with a start that discerning the shift in his mood was becoming like second nature.

"Cosimo and I have some things to attend to. But we'll be back later for the *festa*. Thank you for the food and wine."

Mistress Isabella nodded wearily.

"When will the guests begin arriving?" he asked as an afterthought.

"Just before Vespers are rung."

The worried crease on her forehead eased, and her eyes suddenly lit up with mischief.

"I am certain the young ladies will be glad to see you have returned. You know," she said, taking a sip of her wine, letting the pause underline the effect of her words, "there are worse things in life than settling down with the daughter of a prosperous merchant. Don't you agree?"

"You never give up!"

He shook his head and laughed before he bent and placed a kiss on her cheek. She tried to grab hold of him, but he was too quick and moved out of her reach.

"You're wasting your time."

"We shall see," she nodded sagely. "We shall see."

During their conversation, Liz remained in her seat. Finally, the teasing at an end, Piero appeared ready to leave. Liz jumped up and bowed quickly to Mistress Isabella and followed after his receding form.

"What was that all about?" Liz asked, giving free rein to her curiosity.

"Mistress Isabella decided some time ago that it is important I be married off to a proper—as in rich—young lady. But between you and me, *Piccolino*, it won't happen. I can't tie myself down; I'm already tied to my work. And, I can't afford a wife. I'm supporting my mother who lives in *Borgo San Sepolcro*. I'm overdue for a visit with her too, which probably has her worried."

They stopped to look at the game that was being carved up and carted outside for roasting. Next to the meat preparation, Liz saw servants at a table making what looked like filled pasta.

Liz recalled pictures she had seen of stucco wall decorations depicting pasta making on the Etruscan Tomb of the Reliefs. She watched as the servants filled squares of pasta with meat or cheese. Here was proof that *pastasciutta* or *macaroni* was being made in Italy long before Marco Polo's epic voyage to the court of Kublai Khan. True, she mused, it would take another two hundred years before the introduction of the tomato from the new world dressed the spaghetti that would be known and loved all over the world, but meanwhile, Italians were cooking up their pasta—both *maccheroni and raviuoli*—in chicken broth or slathered in butter.

"And besides," Liz resumed the conversation with Piero, "if you marry one woman, all the rest must suffer their loss."

His answering bark of laughter cheered her, and she clung hopefully to that single sign that their easy camaraderie of earlier in the day had returned.

They followed the servants carting the haunches of game into the courtyard. A few spits were already turning with whole sides of venison and beef roasting for the coming *festa*. The fires were being tended by young men standing next to stacked piles of firewood.

The afternoon sunshine poured into the courtyard and glinted off the colored specks running through the granite paving stones. A soft breeze ruffled the blossoms on the flowering trees distilling the air with the scent of rosemary and lemon. Birds trilled their spring melodies and butterflies flitted among the tubs of colorful flowers.

She followed their movement and song, feeling as one with this idyllic world where no frenzy as in the hectic modern world intruded to mar the scene.

There was a hollow feeling in her chest when she contemplated leaving this world and the man walking at her side. She told herself that no good would come from brooding about Piero's aversion to marriage. As if it had anything to do with her.

She would do better to put him out of her thoughts and concentrate on ways to get home. But while he stood at her elbow exuding masculine warmth, it was difficult to concentrate on anything at all.

Putting some distance between herself and Piero, she wandered over to watch the servants setting up tables and benches for the revelers. Tuns of wine were stacked in readiness next to a large open area where torches were being placed in the wall mounts and in free standing *torcheres*. Even such a little distance between them was enough to ease the pounding of blood in her ears.

How would she get through the night's events? she asked herself. She took two deep breaths, vainly trying to dispel her thoughts and the glum mood descending in a wave on her. Coming this far and blowing it tonight would be downright stupid.

"Over there is where the musicians will be and where the dancing will take place," she heard his voice behind her. She looked around to where Piero pointed.

Three servants were slowly unpacking straw-filled wooden crates.

"What are those things the servants are unpacking?"

"Lanterns made of glass. They'll be strung around the dancing area to hold lit candles for this evening's dancing. The Duchess purchased them from the Venetian glass makers."

While Liz stood admiring the bright, jewel-like colors of the lanterns and watched the servants string them like so many dangling stars along a silken cord, she heard the raucous shrieks of a group of children and turned to see Leonardo with a passel of children skipping along beside him. He carried one child piggyback and two were jumping up and down and swinging on his arms as he struggled to walk. He called out when he spotted Piero and Liz.

"Help, Maestro!"

"Leonardo, you look overwhelmed, old friend."

Piero scooped up the littlest one into his arms and tickled him, which caused the other youngsters to abandon Leonardo and turn with relish on Piero. Their gleeful squeals pierced the air scattering hundreds of birds from the trees into the clear blue sky.

In seconds, Piero was overrun by the shrieking children, who were delighted to have found a new victim.

Leonardo called out to the children, promising each one a sweet if they quieted down. Like magic, they immediately ceased their shrieking and stood like a row of expectant little soldiers. The smallest followed the example of the older children. Except for the stray giggle or two, serenity reigned.

Liz counted eight children. The clothing on the older children was carefully made and new looking, while the younger ones were clad in oft-mended hand-me-downs from the older children, but all of them appeared clean and well-fed.

As they scampered off after Leonardo, Piero ran his hands through his hair, straightened his sleeves and smiled.

"There," Piero nodded in Leonardo's direction, "is a perfect example of what comes of marriage. Leonardo is a master *intonacatore*. The best plasterer there is. He most probably could have been a fine painter, but there it is, you see, he has a family to rear and many mouths to feed."

"They're all his?"

"Of course. To whom else would they belong? And do you like the way I cleverly drew them away from their beleaguered father? I think he needed my help, don't you?"

Liz looked after the departing parade of little children, trailing like ducklings after Father Goose. They were a handsome brood with precious little of the beetle-browed features of their father.

Liz shook her head in amazement.

"They must favor their mother," she remarked, almost to herself.

Piero laughed and clapped a hand on her shoulder.

"Learn this as your first lesson, Cosimo. Always, but always, maintain a good relationship with the plasterers, especially the master. There is a strong partnership between the *intonacatori* and the artist. One is useless without the other."

"I'll remember, Master."

Piero could not fail to miss the small smile hovering wistfully at the corner of Liz's mouth.

"What is it that stirs in that fertile mind of yours?"

Liz glanced after Leonardo and his brood.

"I was just thinking. He found me when I first arrived here. I was frightened of him, but seeing him with his children, well, I don't think I can ever be frightened of him again."

"You will have to tell me all about how you came to be here, *Piccolino*," he remarked as they stopped to observe more of the activity in the courtyard.

"It was quite an adventure, and one day, Master, I promise to tell you all about it."

"I will hold you to that promise, *Piccolino*."

"Watching Leonardo with his children made me think of something you said earlier."

"What was that?"

"How you would not trade your work for married life and a family."

"Exactly right."

"Leonardo seems happy. His family life contributes to his happiness, don't you agree?"

"Yes."

"And what if you could have both? What would you do?"

Piero waited a long moment before replying. He seemed to weigh his response very carefully.

"I don't think Leonardo wanted to be a great painter. I think he was easily satisfied. I, unfortunately, would not be."

"Maybe you're right. Maybe he didn't want to paint pictures of life badly enough to give up real life."

Piero's head spun around, and he leveled his gaze at her. For once, she failed to read his expression. Like cold fingers gripping her heart, he continued to look at her, but did not speak.

"Tomorrow, we will begin our lessons with color," he said walking toward the artisans' building. "And not only how to mix the colors, but how to use them. How they blend to make up the whole."

"So it is esthetically pleasing," she responded, not permitting herself to be rattled by the sudden change of subject. She realized her remark must have struck a nerve.

"*Esattamente*! My master, Domenico Veneziano, started me out by teaching me how to mix the colors when I was but a small boy, so that is what I have done with every apprentice I train. First, the colors."

They continued walking through the courtyard, the preparations a marvel of organization.

"I think I'd like to go up to my room and rest a little before the party. Would that be all right?" Liz asked.

"I think that's a good idea. But first, let's go take a look at the chapel."

"You can't be away from it for long, can you?"

"No, it's true," he replied with a sardonic grin.

"I'm sorry if my remark upset you."

"It's forgotten. You made a valid point."

"Being in the mountains for so long away from your work must have been a strain. Why was it necessary?"

They climbed the exterior wooden steps and entered the chapel. She realized he wasn't going to answer her question, and she didn't press him further.

They reached the chapel, and he moved through the quiet and deserted space as though he was alone.

The door wall of the chapel was complete. And so was the wall behind the altar and the ceiling would soon be finished. Piero stopped before one of the blank areas on the side of the nave. The scenes of raging battle worked up from the back of the church and stopped little more than half way. The rest of the side walls were unornamented white plaster, waiting for the final coat of plaster and *fresco*. Liz warily eyed the spot where she knew she had come through the portal. Then, she ran her hand tentatively along that section of wall. It was as solid as granite beneath her touch.

Believing there might possibly be a clue to be discovered, she inquired, "Master, how long has the work taken thus far?"

"Almost three years. And between you and me, I have run out of ideas. If I finish the walls with more battle scenes, which would probably gratify the Duke, I think the work would lack balance. The theme would be overworked and lose its impact. As to what I want to do, I am at a loss. I sketched a few ideas and thought on it while I was in the lodge at San Leo, and I have some ideas, but nothing that pleases me, or more importantly, that will please the Duke. I want to add symmetry and, of course, perspective, but to show what?"

"May I make a suggestion?"

"Of course, *Piccolino*, you have a fresh eye. Tell me, what does it lack?"

"In my opinion, as exceptional as it is," she hesitated, taking a deep breath before plunging ahead, "it lacks background. A battle doesn't just happen; there is planning, strategy and preparation involved—just as in a painting or any work of art. What of the reserves of men and horses? Is no one observing the progress of the battle? Where are they? Could you not show tents and campfires? The men waiting for their chance to fight. The horses and pages, squires and lookouts. The forward observers. All those things that comprise a battleground. And the use of perspective is not only necessary, it is essential."

He stood with his arms crossed in front of him, an intense look of deep concentration in his eyes, as he listened.

"You could array the camp of the Muslim forces on one side of the chapel and the Crusaders on the other," she continued. Liz had his undivided attention, and his look of utter surprise and measured appraisal made her blush to the roots of her hair.

"I like it! I like it very much! *Piccolino*, you are a genius. Wait! I must not call you *Piccolino* any longer, but Maestro Cosimo."

"No, please, Master, you must not."

He gathered her up in his arms and spun her around. Then he dropped her just as suddenly and took to muttering to himself and pacing excitedly back and forth.

He ran down the wooden staircase and returned almost immediately brandishing a piece of charcoal. With feverish excitement, he quickly traced outlines onto the wall. Under his flying hand, tents and people took shape. She saw his back muscles go taut under his shirt as he worked.

The moment spent whirling in his arms when she had clung to him produced a pool of wet warmth between her legs letting her know she was getting in far too deep for her own good.

She leaned back against the wall and enjoyed the view. God, he was gorgeous, every long, lean inch of him.

She had helped a genius, she thought, as she followed his progress. Transfixed by his passion and her own, bitter tears sprang to her eyes as she contemplated the poignancy of her position.

She would learn art from the hands, heart, and mind of a genius, and in helping him complete his *fresco*, she would be instrumental in creating the portal that would send her away from him forever. Back to her own time.

One burning question battered at her brain—what if she couldn't bring herself to go back? Everything hinged on this man whose excitement at the prospect of finishing his work in a spectacular way had him nearly levitating off the ground.

He whirled back to her like a dervish in a fanatical dance.

"Certainly, *Piccolino*, you must now be part of this work. I have used many of the workers and plasterers, assistants, and even the servants as models for the combatants, and now you too shall be immortalized in *fresco*."

His words confirmed what she knew must happen. "I am honored that you would choose me, Master. I fancy being a page holding my master's charger, waiting to serve, as I wait to serve you," she said in a quiet, somber tone.

The admiration in his look caused a lump to form in her throat.

"What is it? You look as if you are about to cry?"

"The work, Master, it moves me," she lied and turned her head toward the sketch on the wall to stifle a sob.

He put his arm around her shoulders in a comforting gesture, but she pulled away from him lest her control shatter like glass at his touch.

"It's decided then," he continued, still attempting to comfort her. "I know what we will do tomorrow to finish this damn commission. What we must do right now, though, is to rest before the party, for you have need of some food and wine and music. No more tears now. Let's go."

CHAPTER 9

▼

With the party only a few hours away, Liz lay in her cot and tried to empty her mind of the jumble of thoughts that kept her eyes pinned to the ceiling. I need to be calm, cool, and collected tonight, not frightened and nervous, she thought. Occasional sounds from Piero's room told her that he was close and in no danger. As she tossed and turned, she took satisfaction in the fact that sleep proved just as elusive for him as it was for her.

After what seemed like hours of quiet, interrupted only by muffled voices from below, Liz finally dozed off.

The sun had set when she woke to the rumble of carriages, the jingle of harness and the shouts of the hostlers. Realizing she must have slept through the vespers bell, she heaved herself up from the comfortable cot and went into the privy chamber.

She pictured the courtyard bustling with the arrival of the guests as she poured water into the bowl on the washstand. Taking it back into her room, she made quick work of repairing sleep-dulled eyes. Combed hair and fresh clothes made her feel almost presentable before going through the privy to tap on Piero's door.

Hearing no answer, she tried the knob. She turned it gently and she peeked into his room.

He lay asleep on his back with his head turned slightly to the right, away from her, his left arm atop the blanket. She crossed the room on tiptoe and stopped at the foot of the bed. The sound of his breathing was slow and steady. In the shadowy room, his features appeared boyish and free of worry.

Liz admired the high cheekbones overlaid by feathery lashes, eyebrows like a raven's wings, and dark hair disheveled by sleep. His lips were parted slightly, and she longed to bend down and gently kiss his mouth. He took a deep breath, a sound which carried in the quiet room, causing Liz to start. Almost in the same instant, he opened his eyes. They locked on hers.

"Master," Liz whispered, "the guests have begun arriving. It's past vespers."

Piero threw aside the blanket, swung his legs to the side and sat up in one fluid movement. He leaned his elbows on his knees and dropped his head into his hands.

"Are you all right?" Liz could see he wore only a breechcloth.

"Yes," he answered, as he stood and stretched.

Liz's eyes never left him as the muscles of his back and arms lengthened and grew taut. He faced the window, and the soft light cast a golden glow on his skin, like an aura that flowed around him to draw her like a moth to a flame. Helpless in the grip of a strange hunger that took control of her will, she moved toward him.

"Past vespers, you say. I never heard the bell. I must have slept soundly."

"I didn't hear it either," she said sheepishly, "but I think it must be just after dusk. What a wonderful rest."

She stood motionless, remembering her damned charade and wondering what his reaction would be if she dared to reach out and stroke that golden skin.

Telltale sounds from below told them that the *festa* was beginning without them. Piero freshened up at the washstand while Liz, frightened anew by the prospect of navigating through the murky waters of court life laying in wait for her downstairs, distracted herself by folding the blanket on the bed and straightening the bedclothes. Gritting her teeth with apprehension, she fumbled inside the *armadio* for his clothes before turning to ask Piero about the people she saw earlier in the salon with the Duchess.

"Who were all those people with the Duchess? Are they all relations to her or the Duke?" she inquired, employing a casual tone despite the added distress of observing him in a state of near nakedness.

"Some are, but, I'm sorry to say, most are no more than parasites."

Liz looked at him in surprise, and he snorted derisively.

"Does what I say shock you?" he cocked a brow in amusement.

"No, Master, I suppose not," she replied. "I saw many of the same faces at Mass, and at the time, it struck me as odd that they would even be there since they seemed to have no interest in what the priest was doing."

Her offhand observation earned her a hearty chuckle from Piero. Even though the humor in her remark escaped her, his chuckle turned to laughter so strong he had to brace himself on the wall for support. Liz found herself laughing along with him. Then she started to hiccup, which set him off again. Like two simple-minded fools, they gripped their sides and wiped the tears from their cheeks until finally her hiccups abated, and their laughter subsided.

"Cosimo, you are wonderful, better than a tonic."

He took a moment to wipe his eyes with his sleeve before he continued. "What you said about those *bastardi* ..."

"I didn't mean anything by it. I was just ..."

"I know. I know. But your assessment of them is correct. You saw how they behaved, and you drew your own conclusion. It gave you a certain clear insight into their character. They are hypocrites, plain and simple. They placate the Duchess by feigning religious fervor, but they are too stupid to carry it through. They can't help behaving as they are naturally wont to do."

"Who was the gruesome fellow with Raffaello?"

"Ah, you refer to Ghirardino Ceva. He and his brother, Febus, would slit your throat without a moment's hesitation. Stay away from them. They strongly resemble one another, so you can easily recognize Febus. Rumor has it that Ghirardino has a soft spot for Raffaello, but no one knows for sure the exact nature of their relationship, if you know what I mean."

"I do." Liz swallowed hard. If she never saw the evil Ceva brothers again, her imagination would still be able to conjure up all sorts of unknown dangers.

"Good, you are not such a baby. There are others in that company who are not exactly harmless. You will come to know all of them over the course of time. While they are not as dangerous to your person as the Ceva brothers, they engage in an equally dangerous game. Do not let yourself be drawn into their circle of influence for they entertain themselves with plots and intrigue. They have no meaningful work, you see, and are greedy and lazy. A very dangerous combination."

"Then why are they here? What purpose do they serve?" Liz asked bending to help with his boots.

"None, I assure you. They have made themselves a comfortable nest, and they are content to live out their days as permanent guests of the Duke and Duchess."

"Surely, they are not all as you describe."

"True enough. There are some worthy fellows among them. There is Pietro Monte. He is an honorable fellow, and has served the Duke for some time, first as a soldier and now as master of the horse and in charge of tournaments. He's an old friend of Captain San Martini, so you will often see them together. Then there is Cesare Gonzaga and Morella da Ortona, both fine men, noble and trustworthy. They are the bulwarks of the Court and would give up their lives for the Duke or his son. As for the rest …" He shrugged his shoulders dismissively.

"Some fancy themselves musicians, and I am sure they will be called upon to add to the entertainment for the Duchess tonight," he continued, "for that is the main reason they are kept on. Others are scholars, dancers, mimics and talkers. Oh, Gesù, can they talk."

"It sounds as if it's a nest of vipers." A vision of Indiana Jones in the snake pit rose up in Liz's mind.

"That it is, *Piccolino*, and no one is immune from their venom. Stay close to me. And never, ever, turn your back."

"I promise to watch your back, Master, if you promise to watch mine."

He didn't speak, but only nodded and smiled. Maybe he was too overcome for speech, Liz thought, yet he conveyed all the eloquence of a Roman poet in that smile.

She took this conversation to heart and vowed to keep her promise.

       ✳   ✳   ✳   ✳

When they reached the courtyard, the *festa* was getting well underway. Tables were piled high with roasted meats, vegetables, fruit, honeyed sweets and nuts. Jugs of wine were filled as quickly as they were drained. She was jostled as people jockeyed for position at the tables, and with no orderly lines, there was a fair amount of pushing and shoving.

"The eating can go on for hours," Piero informed her.

Seating too was a haphazard affair, and the swell of voices almost drowned out the lively music coming from the far end of the courtyard where the musicians played. Torches winked on one by one as the shadows lengthened and night descended.

Everyone was dressed in their best clothes as befitted a grand *festa*. Liz estimated there were a couple hundred people in the courtyard with the number increasing each moment. The disorderly throng ebbed and flowed around the tables, where the food was being distributed by harried servants.

"*Attento*! Watch out!" Liz called out more than once after nearly losing her plate of food to the rudeness of her fellow diners.

At first, the loud shouting between groups around the tables alarmed Liz. Soon her unease lessened when she realized from the smiles on their faces that friendships were being renewed. The shouts and laughter rose to a crescendo and then fell, engulfing her like a tidal wave.

"Such a long winter, Giovanni, how is the Good Lord treating you?"

"I knew there would be so much food so I have not eaten all day."

"Praise God you will leave some for the rest of us."

This last remark was greeted with more loud laughter and slaps on the back.

The torchlight glinted off the jeweled hilts of the blades at the waists of just about every man there, a warning that the wearer was armed.

Piero steered Liz away from the hubbub to seats at one of the long tables set up for the diners. The rowdiness of the crowd astounded Liz. The way they were bumped and elbowed was far worse than Liz had seen at the monkey house in the zoo.

"*Piccolino*, I'm going to leave you here and go up to the Duchess for a while. Eat your fill and stay out of trouble. You see those two over there standing with Captain San Martini?" Piero pointed to two grizzled men who stood silently amid the partygoers. "That's Gonzaga and Morella da Ortona, the ones I mentioned to you. Stay close to one of the three. Listen to the music. Don't drink too much. Do you hear me?"

"*Sì, Babbo.*" She grinned at him, sly as a cat.

"Pàpa, is it? Don't take liberties with me, *Piccolino*," he responded sternly. "If I come back later and find you dead, I'll be very disappointed in you."

"Well then, Master, I will do my best not to disappoint you."

Powerless to prevent a wry smile from turning up the corners of her mouth, she remained seated with her plate of food growing cold before her. He stood over her, close enough for her to feel his warm breath on her face.

His emerald eyes flickered in the torchlight turning the gold flecks lurking in their depths to a burnished copper. She yearned to press her body close to his, to see his eyes gleam with desire, to set him afire as much as she burned for him. Instead, she sat numbly as he tapped his index finger twice to the center of her forehead. Then, he turned and was gone.

*   *   *   *

She ate heartily. His little speech before he left, demonstrating a genuine concern for her welfare as it did, consoled her, but still she worried for him now that he was out of her sight.

She finished eating and strolled idly toward the musicians past Captain San Martini and his fellow gargoyles. Their stony faces closely resembled the grotesque figures on the Cathedral at Notre Dame. Just maybe, she supposed, they assumed such expressions to intimidate everyone. It worked.

Nevertheless, she nodded pleasantly to Captain San Martini. Giving them a wide berth, she found a seat on a low wall where she could hear the music. She had a view of the kitchen which throbbed with activity.

The air this fine evening was warm and fragrant with the scent of flowers, the ever present citrus scent of bergamot overlaid with herbals and the sweet night blooming jasmine.

The music, the scented air, and the wonderful meal she devoured with relish, which consisted of a large piece of very tasty honey-roasted pheasant, with a helping of *patata di erbe* and roasted fennel, made her drowsy. The pheasant might have been some of the game that Piero had hunted, and knowing this, made it taste even more delicious. A fistful of bread, a cup of wine, grapes and cheese became dessert.

She washed her hands and face under the kitchen pump, the cold water helping to revive her. Liz's actions provoked an inordinate amount of interest from her fellow diners. They darted puzzled looks in her direction as they passed. Their sanitary habits were restricted to wiping greasy hands and mouths on various parts of their apparel.

Liz held her head high as she sauntered closer to the musicians, happy to put a little distance between her and the rude partygoers. The musicians played a lively air that reached clear down to her toes.

She peered intently at the different instruments being played by the musicians. Liz counted three lute players. Instead of using a *plectrum*, each plucked at his instrument with his fingers. Three recorders of different sizes produced a pleasant counterpoint in three different tones. The ensemble included two *tamburi* or drums, and two viols—one a *viola da gamba*—held between the legs, much like a modern *cello*. And lastly, two strange looking instruments she had never seen before that looked like small pump organs were being vigorously played. She asked a young fellow standing nearby what the instruments were called, and he told her they were, "*organetti.*"

Each of these odd-looking instruments was mounted on a stand, with a contraption like a bellows at the back that the musician pumped with one hand, while with his other hand, he played a keyboard on the opposite side. Despite being played in an awkward sideways position, it had a very charming sound that blended beautifully with the other instruments. The sound strongly resembled that of an accordion.

To Liz's untrained ear, the musicians sounded very professional. They were colorfully clad in coordinating red and yellow doublets over red hose with fanciful yellow caps on their heads. The partygoers seemed to recognize the tunes they played and would applaud and shout loudly when they began an air that was particularly popular—very much like a Renaissance "Top Forty."

Liz enjoyed the music which reminded her of a combination of chamber music and an early form of ethnic country music. She watched the dancers whirl around in a succession of different dances depending on which tunes were being played. Soon, she was able to differentiate some of the dances and applaud along with the rest of the bystanders for the best and liveliest of the dancers.

After a while spent lolling against the wall, she noticed the crowding around the tables of victuals had thinned so she returned for more to eat. She settled for another helping of the succulent grapes, the red flesh of which was cool and refreshing on her tongue. The juice ran down her chin leaving a sticky trail of deep red, like wine on her face and hands. She recalled that she had neglected to take fresh water up to their quarters for the morning, and soon it would be too dark to see her way.

She washed up at the pump and was looking around for a bucket in which to tote the water into the artisans' building when the mocking tone of a male voice spoke.

"Here is this little Ghibelline washing his hands like Pontius Pilate. What guilt can you expect to wash away with water, *bastardo*?"

Liz turned and the stench of body odor hit her in the face. The foul smelling Raffaello greeted her, but it was his friend, Ceva, standing beside him, who had spoken. Ceva's threatening posture caused the hair on the back of her neck to stand on end. She glanced around for Captain San Martini or one of the other gargoyles, but they were nowhere in sight. She faced her tormentor head on.

She needed only a moment to size up Ceva's intent. Despite the crowd around him, he appeared eager to provoke a fight. A hush fell over the crowd, and they parted, as the Red Sea parted for Moses.

Not about to cede control of the situation to Ceva, she looked past him, and with relief, saw Captain San Martini approaching from one direction, and Piero hurrying from the other direction.

She stood her ground and smiled disarmingly at both Raffaello and Ceva. They looked the worse for drink, and their faces had the smug expressions of those whose overconfidence would be their downfall.

As Captain San Martini approached to within earshot, Liz narrowed her gaze on Ceva's face.

Never letting her smile falter, she spoke softly to Ceva. "If, as you say I am a whore's son, then you, *fratello*, indeed are my brother."

Ceva froze, his face wearing a stunned expression, but in the next instant, his hand shot out.

Liz saw the flash of a blade.

Instinctively, her arm flew up, deflecting his thrust with a striking blow.

As his knife clattered to the pavement of the courtyard, the strong arms of Captain San Martini lifted him off his feet and swung him into the air.

It had happened so quickly, Raffaello had no time to get out of the way, so down he went, landing on his fat rump with a loud grunt.

The crowd roared their approval with shouts and hoots of laughter, followed by a sound like a collective sigh of relief.

Liz turned to Piero; and as she did so, she noticed that the smug look on Raffaello's face was gone.

"What happened? Can't I leave you for a moment?" Piero lashed out, each word penetrating her like a bullet hitting its mark. He grabbed her arm and pulled her aside, while she clutched awkwardly at his arm, trying to pry herself free of his grasp.

CHAPTER 10

▼

"Which question shall I answer first?" Liz retorted, succeeding at last in pulling away. Her voice sounded shrill. Liz felt the eyes of the crowd boring into her.

She reacted to their stares by unclenching her fists and shifting her weight to a less belligerent stance.

What was it with this guy? she asked herself. What did he have to be angry about? The confrontation with Ceva couldn't be laid at her door.

Piero opened his mouth as though he was about to argue further, but seemed to think better of it and said nothing.

Taking her cue from him, Liz softened her tone. "Please, Master," she cajoled, "let's take a walk where we can talk privately."

When they reached a quiet alcove, she turned on him.

"Let me correct your misapprehension. You were gone for hours, not a minute." She kept her voice menacingly low.

Piero took a step back but found himself hemmed in by a flight of stone steps.

"Are you sure you're all right?" he asked, reaching out to touch her.

"Of course, I am. I told you before. I can take care of myself. And I didn't start it. Ceva tried to pick a fight with me. That's all there was to it. He called me a name. He expected me to back down or run, which I think under the circumstances would have proved fatal."

"I have no doubt he would have stabbed you in the back. Rest assured Captain San Martini will take care of him. They'll be no further incidents. As long as there was no harm done, we'll do our best to forget the incident ever happened."

"I don't think so. He drew a knife on me. I want to bring charges against him."

Piero's puzzled expression tipped Liz to the fact that there probably was no such thing as charges or complaints.

"Anyway …" she said, turning away to hide her chagrin.

"As I said," Piero repeated, "Captain San Martini will deal with him."

Liz faced Piero and noticed the telltale tightness about his mouth and the worried crease on his brow, sure signs of concern. Verbally, he may have downplayed the incident, but the worry evident on his face betrayed him.

Liz was surprised he had backed down so easily when confronted with her show of temper. And she wondered if his concern would have been as great if it had been any of his other apprentices Ceva had attacked.

A calm, unshakable confidence came over her, quieting her dread. Ceva had wanted her dead. By rights, she should be lying lifeless on the courtyard cobbles, but she wasn't. She may have gotten lucky, but she showed her mettle. Maybe next time, she wouldn't be as lucky.

There would probably be talk. So many people had witnessed the way she disarmed Ceva. They might wonder how a young boy was able to survive an attack from a cutthroat like Ceva. All she had to do was claim she got lucky. And maybe, just maybe, there would be a way of turning this incident to her advantage.

She left Piero and sauntered over to where the wine was being dispensed. Her mouth had gone dry as the rush of adrenaline had subsided. She drew two tankards.

Walking carefully back toward Piero, she took a long gulp from one tankard on the way. She handed the other tankard to him and swung hers up to touch his in a toast. "Truce?"

His smile was constricted. "Truce."

Wine in hand, she led the way toward the musicians. They joined their fellow partygoers, enjoying the music and watching the dancers under the romantic glow cast by the torches and lanterns.

To turn the conversation to more pleasant topics, Liz inquired. "Master, what is this dance called? I have seen it a number of times. The dancers called out something to the musicians, but I couldn't understand what they said."

"It's *La Gagliarda*. It's very popular. I've been told it originated at the court of Venezia."

"So that's what they were shouting." Liz shook her head in disbelief. "It takes a lot of stamina."

Piero's expression softened as he elaborated on the dance, and the wine smoothed away the lines near his mouth. When the dance came to a dizzying conclusion, they laughed as the dancers staggered from the floor and collapsed into the arms of their companions.

Precisely at that moment, two simpering, giggling young women approached Piero and took him by each arm and dragged him onto the dance floor. He accepted their advances with good grace and smiled engagingly at them.

Liz, meanwhile, was rocked to her toes by a surge of intense jealousy. Her throat tightened, effectively locking out the air from her chest. She had the mad desire to smash her fist into the insipid faces of the two young women.

The elegantly garbed and coiffed young women simply walked up and stole Piero away.

How dare they!

*   *   *   *

Good Lord! She had to get control of herself. There was no doubt in her mind that he held a growing fascination for her, but she just couldn't admit to more than that. It just wouldn't do to fall in love with him. She must quell her feelings and concentrate on survival, not love.

This evening's encounter with Ceva proved to her the precariousness of her situation. She was just plain lucky tonight, but was she willing to take the chance that her luck would hold?

Since her attempts so far to find the portal had failed miserably, she conceded she needed help to get back home. The alternative could be deadly.

Her thoughts were diverted by the arrival of the Duchess and her entourage. She glided into the midst of the *festa* followed by her guests. Smiling graciously, she greeted many in the courtyard by name and good-naturedly accepted their best wishes for her son.

The Duchess moved among her subjects to shouts of *Vive Lunghi nostro Signore Grande e Sua Signora*! The laudatory shouts echoed, picked up and carried to the rear of the throng, which by now numbered well over 300, and surged forward again. Long Live our Great Lord and his Lady!

Liz sidled up to Piero and took his arm, easily coaxing him away from the two girls while all eyes were focused on the Duchess.

Liz clambered up onto a four-foot wall to get a better view. Piero stood in front of her, and she rested her hands on his shoulders for support. The feel of his strong muscles sent tremors coursing up her arms straight to her heart. Liz reluctantly removed her hands as the musicians took up a stately air. On cue, the first fireworks pierced the night sky.

I am witness to one of the grandest courts to exist in any age, Liz thought. Every manner of courtly grace and chivalry paraded before her eyes—a human tapestry so rich and complex, the sight of it caused a shiver to curl up her spine. But, as with all humanity, ugliness and depravity existed alongside the beauty.

So many poignant thoughts raced through her brain as she watched events unfold before her. Not even nearly losing her life could mar this night. She wished she could go back to her own time to bring her brother here to this moment, to experience this night. An intense wellspring of emotion caught her by surprise.

This age would reach the heights of human achievement at the same time that human rights—as interpreted in the 20th-21st centuries—were being trampled. In mankind's long history upon this earth, Liz asked herself, is it not always so? The great achievements failed to blind her to the poverty, disease and war.

The Duchess approached the spot where they stood. Liz jumped down and stood beside and slightly behind Piero. They bowed as the Duchess passed. As Liz straightened, she saw a wistful smile lingering on the Duchess's face. How easily she carried the mantle of a Duchess, the epitome of regal charm and grace, Liz thought, as she followed the Duchess's progress among her subjects.

$$* \qquad * \qquad * \qquad *$$

As soon as the Duchess retired into the *Palazzo*, Piero casually draped his arm around Liz's shoulder and wandered over to Captain San Martini and his friends. They stood with faces turned up to the heavens enjoying the fireworks display.

"*Piccolino*, you have no muscles," Piero teased. "We will need to build up your strength for the work you will be doing."

"You'll find I'm up to any task you give me, Master," Liz replied, feigning offense by shrugging off his arm.

The fireworks lit up the sky, and the crowd of revelers whooped and jumped with each volley, as though they could reach all the way up to the stars.

"Are you all right, lad?" Captain San Martini asked as they joined his group.

"Of course he is, Luca. Did you not see the way this boy defended himself?"

"Yes, I did. Very impressive, but if there is any more fighting …"

"Luca," Piero interrupted him, "Cosimo was unarmed. There was no bloodshed—no thanks to Ceva—and if Cosimo was dead or wounded at Ceva's hand …"

"I'm not saying …"

"But you are, old friend. If it is necessary to warn anyone, let it be that scoundrel, Ceva, who would attack an unarmed boy after hurling insults at him with the intention of goading him to fight. Cosimo did nothing but defend his honor and his person."

"All right, Piero, all right. Calm down. I concede that the boy had the right to defend himself, and that he did well. You don't have to attack me. You growl like a mother wolf when her cub is in danger. I will have plenty to say to Ceva in the morning for drawing his blade tonight."

Captain San Martini's agreeable manner softened his retort, but all heads swiveled toward Piero to observe his reaction. He looked sheepish, but held his own in the face of their mocking glances, for Captain San Martini had captured perfectly the way Piero leaped to Liz's defense. Piero shrugged off their stares as though they held little weight with him.

Now Liz leaped to his defense.

"He doesn't want me to be treated unfairly, that's all. Surely, you can understand."

"Yes, of course." The three men said almost in unison with much nodding of heads.

"Cosimo, it's getting late. Since I want to get an early start in the morning, perhaps we should turn in," Piero suggested.

"Can't we stay a little longer? Just until the fireworks end?"

"All right, but only for the rest of the fireworks."

They perched on an outer wall, dangling their legs over the side, affording a great view of the fireworks bursting above the valley. Others nearby included two of Piero's apprentices whom she had never met. They had been pointed out to her by Mistress Isabella when they inspected the privies, but there had been no time for introductions.

One was a dark fellow with a squint in his right eye, named Serafino; the other was his cousin, Emilio, who was as fair as Serafino was dark. They appeared to be in their late teens and close in age. After Piero introduced them, he told Liz *sotto voce* that they shared the same last name—Romano—because their fathers were brothers.

Both fellows stared glumly at the display of fireworks. After a couple of failed attempts to engage them in conversation, she concluded that they were slow-witted. They paid no attention to Piero after their initial greeting, and showed no interest in her, so she ignored them.

After a short while spent oohing and aahing over the fireworks, Piero stood and stretched.

"Have you had enough?"

"Sì, Master. I'm ready to turn in."

"Don't forget, we start early tomorrow," Piero said pointedly to the Romano brothers as they left. Their response was a mute nod.

As they trundled off through the thinning crowd—many had wearied of the festivities—the compline bells rang out, marking the end of the day.

The pealing of the bells that rose up to God like a prayer of the faithful fired Liz's resolve.

She admitted to herself that she might never get home without his help. But she needed to know where Piero stood on issues great and small. She could never bring herself to confide in him if she couldn't learn what he thought he knew of the world.

"Master?" Liz said, pulling at his sleeve to get his attention.

"What?"

"I think I understand now why it is that you like me so much," she said, weighing her initial words carefully.

"And why is that?" he asked with a mischievous smile.

"With such dull fellows as the two Romano cousins, you must have said a prayer of thanks when I came along."

"Indeed, I did," he agreed with a chuckle. "And when I go to my bed tonight, I will say another prayer of thanks and also a prayer that God protects you, *Piccolino*, for I cannot say why, but you have become very important to me."

Liz looked up into his face, so open and full of feeling, that hope—so elusive up to now—rose up in her breast. She decided to play her hand and find out what lurked inside his handsome head.

"Master, do you believe in fate? I mean …, do you believe that sometimes things happen and there is no explanation, and its effect is almost … magical?"

He gazed at her thoughtfully for a long moment before answering.

"If you mean, do I believe that the life of a man is ruled in great measure by chance, I guess I do. We take a chance every time we …"

"No, that's not entirely what I mean," she interrupted. "I mean, do you believe that in life there are things that happen that cannot be explained? That there are forces at work that make us confront the very nature of the universe?"

"I only know, *Piccolino*, that there are things of God and things of man. And what I know of both would fill a thimble. There is so much in the world and beyond that I don't know, that I must believe—unless it is proven to me to be untrue—that anything is possible."

"You'll never know how glad I am to hear you say that."

"What questions you ask, and on such a night?" He shook his head at this puzzling young man who wanted to know so many things, and who yet remained a complete mystery to him.

Liz hugged his answer to her chest like a warm blanket. The words he chose, and the way his eyes glowed when he looked at her promised much more than she could have dreamed.

*   *   *   *

When they parted for the night, Liz ran the scene over and over in her mind. They were hopeful words, she decided. He would be receptive, of that she could be certain. She pondered what to tell him first.

For pity's sake, she speculated, how difficult can it be?

Before she turned in, and for the first time since she was a child, Liz got down on her knees next to her bed and prayed. She prayed that he would not betray her, that her faith in him was not misplaced, for she would be putting her very life in his hands.

CHAPTER 11

▼

The cock crowed at first light, a job he took very seriously, prompting Liz to wish he would end up in tonight's stewpot. She rose on unsteady, wine-soaked legs and clutched her head, moaning softly all the while, and shuffled to the privy.

Tumultuous birdsong heralded the arrival of the sun, hinting that the day would be fine and sunny, but their song was lost on Liz.

I think I could kill for two aspirin and a cup of coffee, she said to herself, gripping the edge of the washstand and looking at her bleary-eyed reflection in the mirror. She was too sick to appreciate the beauty of the mirror—the Venetian artisan's workmanship with the exquisite silvering of the clear glass and its ornately carved frame.

She cleaned herself in slow motion, vowing to limit herself to one glass of wine per day, no matter how tempted she was to drown her woes and her pitiable self in its red depths.

Downstairs, not even the sound of snoring reached her ears. An abandoned graveyard would be livelier than the first floor of the artisan's building—an apt comparison since the workmen were sleeping as if dead to the world.

While she pumped water into a bucket at the kitchen pump, she filled her lungs with great gulps of the fresh morning air. She plunged her hands into the bucket and threw the cold spring water on her face. The shock jolted her fully awake. She drank directly from the pump and felt reasonably human.

Her memory of last night's *festa* was sketchy, and she hoped the amount of wine she consumed did not lead to any indiscriminate or compromising behavior on her part. With these thoughts foremost in her mind, she peeked into the kitchen.

The kitchen maids were up and reviving the hearth fires. She asked one of them to put the kettle on for tea. Then, she took up a bucket of water for Piero's use. She knew Piero was eager to begin in the chapel and would soon be stirring.

Morning sunlight streamed into their rooms. Her reflection in the privy mirror startled her. In only a few days, her face was thinner, her cheekbones higher, and her eyes seemed larger.

When she lifted her shirt, she peered at her arms and shoulders. Definitely leaner and more muscular. The transformation would aid in her continuing masquerade as a boy, but mother nature would not be so easily fooled. Unless the events of the last week conspired against nature, soon her period would come. There would be no disguise good enough. How will I manage it? she asked herself.

She filled the ewer with the clean water and used the rest to clean the privy.

She heard Piero moving around in the next room. Quickly pulling on a clean shirt and lacing up her doublet, she left the privy and sped back to the kitchen for their breakfast. She carried back a tray with two mugs of tea, fruit, and two big slices of toasted *polenta* smothered in some of the leftover roast fennel that she found so tasty the night before. The maids were breakfasting on the same thing; and while she hoped Piero found it tempting, she avoided looking at it. The aroma alone caused her stomach to do flip-flops.

*   *   *   *

Piero also awoke to the birdsong and the sunshine, but had lain in bed when he heard Cosimo in the privy. He had a vague recollection of a disquieting dream that had disturbed his night's sound sleep. He was able to recall the feeling the dream conveyed, but struggled to recall the dream itself.

Suddenly, like a point of flame across his conscious mind, his dream came back to him.

In the dream, he was dancing with a beautiful young maiden in a moonlit garden. The familiar scent of night-blooming jasmine hung in the air. The garden was surrounded by high, ivy-covered walls. Musicians perched on a ledge or balcony high above the garden, and the strains of their music drifted sweetly in the night. Piero and his partner were alone. Save for the musicians, they could have been all alone in the world. The maiden was heavily veiled and dressed in a flowing garment of gold cloth. Her arms and shoulders were bare. Her veils, however, floated over and around her permitting Piero a glimpse of her skin which shimmered with a pearly luster in the moonlight. The only ornament she wore was his amulet which hung around her neck and nestled between her breasts. He wanted the music to go on and on. Finally, the music ended. He reached down with eager anticipation to gently lift her veil. When he did, it was to see Cosimo's face smiling lovingly up at him.

Piero rose and shook off the remnants of the dream that left him awash with shame. He staggered into the privy still wondering what hidden meaning the dream held. He needed to clear his head of the disturbing image because a full day's work lay before him.

He washed and went back to his room to dress. His clothes were strewn about where he had carelessly dropped them the previous night. He stowed the amulet away in the chest, dressed, and began to pick up his clothes when there was a knock.

"*Entra.*"

"*Buon giorno, Maestro,*" his apprentice said, entering the bedchamber with the breakfast tray. "It's a glorious morning. It seems we are the first ones up," young Cosimo prattled, depositing the tray on the table. "I can't wait to get started in the chapel."

Piero could not bring himself to look at his young apprentice.

When Liz realized Piero was unresponsive, she ceased her chattering.

"Are you ill, Master?" she asked at last.

"No, Cosimo, I'm well," Piero answered taking his first sip of tea.

They finished their breakfast in silence.

Liz wondered what caused his dark mood and chalked it up to too much wine. She had no trouble understanding that.

*   *   *   *

When they reached the chapel, some of the workmen had already straggled in. Cosimo took up a position against the wall and waited along with the workmen while Piero studied the wall. Every few moments, Piero paced up and down, abruptly stopping to look at Cosimo. The look in his eye made her uneasy, as though he had some secret she was destined never to learn.

Finally, Piero beckoned to her, and together they looked over the section where the Christian encampment would be immortalized.

"Is something wrong?" Liz asked.

"No. I told you, nothing is wrong," he answered, and Liz could see the muscles in his jaw tighten.

"Could you put my likeness here, Master, in the foreground among the horses and tents?" Liz asked warily, hoping the change of subject would ease the tension.

"Yes, but first, I want you to bring the clay models down from my studio."

Liz hurried off to get the models, and Piero could feel his mood start to lift as he became engrossed in the work. The memory of his disturbing dream slowly faded away.

*   *   *   *

They worked nonstop until noon and then resumed until night fell.

Liz marveled as his chalk flew expertly over the wall. She spent her time watching, listening and fetching whatever he needed.

Piero's technique consisted of sketching in his ideas in *sinopia*, a red chalk, on the second coat of plaster. He talked to her as he worked, explaining that many artists use a different process, that of doing a cartoon, and then transferring a tracing from the cartoon onto the dry plaster.

"I find it much too confining and tedious. I think my method is superior because I work directly on the wall. I am free to change my mind. Nothing controls my hand but the idea in my mind. This way the pictures grow on the wall rather than on paper which then requires another step to get it on the wall. I never want to invest so much time in the preparation of a cartoon that I find myself reluctant to do something else that appeals to me more. Do you understand?"

Piero took pains to demonstrate to Liz that his way gives him far more control over perspective when he is able to see the figures emerge from the wall and begin to "live."

While Piero concentrated on the tricky positioning of a horse's hoof and fetlock, Liz strayed over to the portion of the wall where the portal was located and ran her hand over the wall, but as before, the wall was solid. The time might come—and soon—when she would feel the portal opening. She wondered what she would do when that happened.

By nightfall, most of the Christian side of the encampment was sketched. The following day he would do the same for the Muslim side.

At supper that evening, Piero was animated in his conversation, and his renewed confidence expressed itself in his expansive gestures.

"Master, I can tell how pleased you are with the progress of the work today." Liz commented.

"I'm very pleased, *Piccolino*. I feel an energy and purpose flowing through me that I have missed these past weeks. And you worked hard today too. Carrying down the models, learning about the colors. Every step is crucial, but the proper colors are what give life to *fresco*."

"I hope I am able to remember everything. It's a lot to learn, when all I want to do is watch you. And the sketch you did of me is wonderful."

He only nodded his agreement for he was dipping bread into his wine and dribbling it down his chin onto his hands and sleeve.

Gripped by an idea, she looked around the kitchen and spied Mistress Isabella. Excusing herself, she hurried over to the housekeeper.

Piero watched his apprentice talking and gesturing to the housekeeper. Mistress Isabella nodded several times. After a few minutes, their conversation ended and his apprentice returned to the table.

Liz sat across from Piero and cast down her eyes, lest he notice how taken with herself she was.

"What was that all about?" Piero asked still wiping wine from his chin with his sleeve.

"Well, Master, I got an idea, and Mistress Isabella thinks it's a good one. She is going to have squares of bleached linen cloth sewn to use at the table so you don't have that dribbling on your chin."

She saw the puzzled expression on his face and had to suppress a giggle. She wondered how a genius can be a genius and at the same time be so clueless.

"You keep the linen square across your lap to catch spills and instead of ruining your fine shirts, you swipe it across your mouth instead of your sleeve. What do you think?"

"*Che furba!* You are the clever one."

They finished their supper and walked outside to take the evening air, and she thought four napkins would do for her own use in a few days when she would need them for her period. She was clever indeed to introduce "serviettes" to the court. But how clever would she be in hiding her predicament from them?

She couldn't help but wonder if it was from her dire need that napkins would come into favor first in the most civilized court of Urbino and from there spread across Europe.

"I think, *Piccolino*, if the work goes as well the rest of the week as it has today, we deserve a reward," Piero said calling her back from her musings.

"What kind of reward, Master?"

"If the weather is fair, we could ride to the sea and spend the day there."

"*Meraviglioso!*" Liz exclaimed. "We could take food with us and eat on the beach."

Piero agreed that was a fine idea.

Liz knew at once that the outing was the chance she was waiting for. They would be alone; it would be the perfect opportunity to tell him that she was a woman.

Entranced by the vision of the amorous scene that would play out when she at last revealed her secret to him, she nearly stumbled beside him in the growing darkness. At last, he would know the real girl beneath the masquerade.

They strolled through the courtyard and found themselves at the entrance to the stables. Captain San Martini was talking with Gonzaga and Morella da Ortona as the stable hands bedded the horses down for the night.

After the usual stilted formal greetings were exchanged, Captain San Martini asked her why it took so long for her to visit the stables.

"I never had a chance. I'm sorry. But I'm here now. May I look around?" she asked shyly.

"Of course. I will show you some of the Duke's best mounts."

"Luca," Piero said, "we are planning a little outing on Saturday to the sea. I plan on riding *Zingaro*. Which mount would you suggest for Cosimo?"

"How well do you ride, Cosimo?" Captain San Martini asked with an indulgent smile.

Liz was nonplussed, both by the question and by the sympathetic expression on Captain San Martini's face, for she could not recall ever seeing him smile before. Because of the scar, his smile had a grotesque, lopsided appearance, but his dark eyes glowed warmly which more than made up for his marred countenance.

"Well, I am a fairly decent rider, I suppose. Is this "Gypsy" the horse you kept up at the hunting lodge? He would definitely be too much for me. Can it be it was only a few days ago? It seems like a lifetime," Liz said thoughtfully, all the while peering through the gloom at the horses.

"You're right, it does seem so," Piero said with a wistful smile. "I wish the work was finished, and I was returning to the coolness of the lodge for the summer."

"Come," Captain San Martini interrupted.

They walked through the stable where the horses were calmly eating. There was one, a handsome silvery young bay that drew Liz. He nickered softly to her when she spoke to him.

The stable hands fussed about with brooms and water buckets, and Liz noted the stables were clean and the horses in beautiful condition. Their coats shone, and there was little stable smell.

She watched the young bay eating his feed. As he chewed, he would turn around every few seconds to look at her with eyes that slanted up at the outside corners giving him an oriental look. She got Captain San Martini's attention.

"I think he likes me," she remarked proudly. "And I like him. Is he gentle?"

"Oh, yes, you can go into the stall and make friends with him."

She glanced at Piero, who was lounging against the gate. With a nod, he unlatched it, and she went cautiously into the stall with the young horse.

She stroked his neck and spoke softly to him, and with a good natured insouciance, he resumed eating.

As she turned to leave, the young horse looked at her once more with his soft brown eyes.

"What's his name?" she asked Captain San Martini, carefully latching the gate.

"His name? He doesn't have one yet. We just acquired him. But he already gets along well with *Zingaro*. Why don't you think of a name, Cosimo. It seems we have waited for you to come along to name him."

"*Argento*! To match his silver color. That's his name. May I come back and see him tomorrow?"

"Yes, of course," Captain San Martini replied.

"Let's get to bed, *Piccolino*. We have a lot of work to accomplish tomorrow. You can stop at mid-day tomorrow to see *Argento. Buona notte, Luca.*"

"*Buona notte*," Liz called out over her shoulder as they left.

They went immediately to their quarters; and true to his word, Piero turned in right away, but Liz had a few things she wanted to do.

She stashed the cloth napkins Mistress Isabella had sewn up and left in her room so they would be ready when she needed them. Then she moved the hip bath to her small room. For the first time since her arrival, she would have the luxury of a bath.

She made several trips to the kitchen-yard pump and then carefully locked both doors to her room. The night was warm, and she was hot and sticky from working all day. A cool bath was just what she needed.

She sank back in the bath with a sigh, and she felt herself relax as the water eased her tired muscles. She lay back and let her mind drift back, back to the first moment she had seen Piero. The recollection of the terror she had felt made her smile. How could I have ever been terrified of him? she asked herself. Even as terrified as she was, she noticed everything about him. Totally a male, from head to foot, that was the first thing she noticed. And then those incredible eyes. And he didn't have to swagger, or threaten or raise his voice. She knew he was capable of killing her in an instant, but instead he had taken her under his wing. Befriended her. Treated her—once he had put her in her place—almost like a friend.

What would happen when she told him the truth? Did she dare provoke his anger? She had never seen him truly angry. How did she know what he was capable of? She had deceived him. Possibly he would focus only on that and not give her a chance to explain.

She put these dark thoughts from her mind. He would understand. She had to make him understand.

She turned her thoughts instead to the morning and the completion of her image on the chapel wall.

While she cleaned up the bath, she thought about her new love, a horse called "Silver." The name would mean nothing to anyone here, but it harkened back to the days of her childhood. How many times had she sat in front of the TV and watched old reruns of "The Lone Ranger?" In the stories, The Lone Ranger always managed to sort things out in the end. She wished for the same sort of happy ending herself. She took small comfort in the sweet childhood memory of that show, for despite everyone's kindness, and the love that was growing in her moment by moment for the wonderful man in the next room, she missed her old life.

How was her absence being explained to her family and friends? They must be frantic with worry, she thought.

Despite the loss of her old life and the homesickness that wracked her, she had no more tears to shed. She felt like crying, but her eyes were dry.

CHAPTER 12

▼

"*Buon fresco* has to be perfect—I have to be perfect—so that when it is applied, it dries as part of the wall," Piero explained for the umpteenth time. "There is nothing else that comes close, and there is no second chance."

While Liz agonized about the upcoming outing to the beach, fearing she would lose her nerve and never be ready to confide her secret to Piero, he worked on the chapel like one possessed by a demon. She ran several scenarios over and over in her mind, what he might say or do, following every twist and turn she could imagine.

Immersed in the design and creation of the encampments, Piero spread his contagious enthusiasm to everyone else working on the project with him.

Liz tried to analyze the untemperamental approach he brought to his relations with the workers under him. He almost always maintained his cool in the face of any problem and dealt with each one quickly and sensibly. She came to the conclusion that his equanimity stemmed from his reluctance to waste time on incidentals, like useless displays of temper, which would serve no purpose at all except to cause him to lose his momentum.

Most of the time, the problem was with supplies running low for the plasterers or with the timing that was so crucial to completing the allotted painting before the plaster dried. He refused to go back and use the *secco* method to correct any error, for he considered this inferior and not *buon fresco*.

"No margin for error?" Liz responded, her daydreaming at an end.

"None. This technique, Cosimo, is the truest test of an artist's skill and vision. At the same time, it alone is enough to destroy a mediocre painter. I accept the challenge, but I fear it too each time I take up my brush."

"Sounds like a love-hate relationship," Liz remarked before catching herself.

Piero gave her an odd look.

"But surely, Master," she recovered, "you can't believe for a moment that you're mediocre!"

Piero laughed and reached out his hand toward her. Liz took it and bowed over it as she had so often seen Leonardo do in greeting Piero. His hand was stiff with dried plaster and streaks of paint. Instead of feeling revulsion at the work-worn symbol of his dedication, Liz was profoundly moved by the privilege she had been granted.

Liz released his hand, and the moment passed. They turned their attention to the pots of color that awaited Piero's decision.

"I understand what you said about colors—how important they are—but what I don't understand is … how do you decide which colors to use?" Liz asked, her hand still warm from his touch.

"Several factors help me decide. What is available, of course," he ticked them off on his long fingers. "My observations of the world around me, and, most importantly, what appeals to me. I am the final decision maker. If I am happy with the composition of color, that's what I use."

"Simple enough."

"You think so? Well, let's see what you would use then."

The *bravura*—of the apprentice who had yet to put brush to paint—seemed to amuse him, and he grinned at Liz, a grin that caused Liz's heart to dance.

As she selected each color for the task he assigned to her, he nodded his approval.

"*Bene!*" he exclaimed with a hint of pride at her choices. "You have a good eye, Cosimo."

The chapel hummed with activity like a swarm of demented bees. Often, the workmen would burst into spontaneous song. So it was that Liz heard folk songs that had probably not been heard for hundreds of years.

She learned a tremendous amount about painting from Piero. Her adjunct art courses at college were nothing compared to what she learned merely by watching him.

Liz learned to anticipate what he needed, no matter the task, ready at any given moment to fetch and carry or bound up the ladder to join him on the scaffolding. Despite the intensity of the work, Liz caught herself watching Piero as he stood with legs apart lost in concentration in front of the *fresco*. At these times, he was oblivious to everyone and everything except the work before him. Liz looked furtively at him from under lowered lids, the rush of blood pounding in her ears.

During the time she spent obsessing over the upcoming outing with Piero, her main source of diversion was the daily visits she made to the stable to see *Argento*. She made sure to get down there early in the morning to hand feed him. She took to stealing an apple or carrot from Mistress Isabella's larder to ingratiate herself even further with the young horse. By week's end, Mistress Isabella was leaving out a carrot or two or an apple especially for her to give to the horse.

If he was in the paddock socializing with *Zingaro* or one of the other horses and saw Liz approach, he would gambol over to her for his treat. She always made sure she shared the treat with *Zingaro* too.

Sometimes, Liz had the chance to stop by the pasture in the evening before the horses had been brought up to the stables. On those occasions, she would continue down the hill and out to the pasture to find him—not a strenuous walk going down, but a tough climb on the way back. Liz would call to him—"*Argento!*"—and his head would come up, maybe only at the sound of her voice, but she liked to think he recognized his name. When he ran to her, tossing his head in greeting, she thought she would die with pleasure.

Then, after he had his treat, and Liz stroked his silky mane, she would bridle him and walk him back up the hill. More than once, Piero sent someone looking for Liz, and when they reported back that they couldn't find her, he told them, "Check the stables."

*   *   *   *

Liz woke early on Friday morning to warm breezes and spring sunshine. She dressed quickly, splashed water on her face and rushed down to the stables. She led the young horse out to the warmth of the morning sun and led him down to the pasture. The earthy smell from the vineyard-studded hills caused her to linger with the horse far longer than she should have.

Wildflowers in varied shades of pink, red poppies, and yellow buttercups attracted her like a honeybee, so while the young horse watched, she clambered over the fence and picked a bouquet for her room. At long last, like two old friends who had been out for a stroll, they parted and she walked up the hill alone from the pasture.

In the little storage room off the hall, she found a dented pewter pitcher. Before she hurried down to a quick breakfast, she placed the arrangement on her windowsill and stepped back to admire it. Even though she knew she would have to make up the lost time, the touch-of-spring effect the colorful flowers had on her drab little room lifted her spirits.

With a light step, she entered the chapel to find Piero standing at the long refectory table filling the containers with his clean, dry brushes, a job usually reserved for her or one of the other apprentices. She watched him stand the brushes up like so many magic wands poised to perform wonderful tricks.

"I'm sorry I'm late, Master. I was dawdling with *Argento* and picking flowers," she confessed. "I guess I forgot the time."

Instead of answering her or looking in her direction, he shifted pots of color from a box and lined them up on the table.

"I hope the weather is like this tomorrow," she remarked in the lame hope she could steer the conversation away from her lateness.

He continued to ignore her and seconds passed, seconds in which she fretted that he had needed her for something important, and she was off picking wildflowers. He had a right to be annoyed, she thought to herself.

"I am sorry to be so late," she repeated her apology, but still elicited no response.

"Don't worry, it will be," he said, finally breaking his silence.

So much time had elapsed, Liz had trouble recalling her earlier remark.

"How can you be so sure?" Liz asked him after a moment or two.

"I think the gods wouldn't dare to disappoint us," he answered, finally turning to look at her.

"Master, you sound almost like a pagan."

"You were the one communing with nature, picking flowers and playing with that horse when you should have been working," he said with a chuckle from deep in his throat. "I know what it is to enjoy the spring morning."

"I couldn't help myself, and I said I was sorry."

"So you did."

The incident forgotten, they set to work, and not another word passed between them—except those related to the work on the chapel—until they broke for lunch.

They ate their noon meal outside in the courtyard beside Mistress Isabella's herb garden. Warmed by the sun and the wine, not to mention the hearty soup, bread and fruit, they talked only of the work, never once discussing their planned outing.

When they resumed work, both the urgency and the energy of the morning were missing.

Piero worked up on the scaffolding without stop for several hours. His meticulous application of color brought the scene of the Christian encampment vividly to life. Liz stood below to carry up whatever he needed that wouldn't fit on the already overloaded scaffolding. Up and down she went, removing things he no longer needed and bringing up those he did.

She started up the ladder on one of her trips when she saw Piero suddenly throw down his brush and walk to the ladder.

"I have had enough for today," he said.

Something in the tone of his voice caused her concern.

"I have a kink in my back," he called to her.

"Are you all right?"

"Don't come up. I'm coming down."

When he stepped onto the floor of the chapel, he gripped the ladder for support and rubbed his lower back, then his neck.

"Let me do that, Master."

Liz rubbed his back for several moments, noticing the grimace of pain on his face.

"You're one big knot."

"I know. I've finished all I can with the plaster anyway."

"I have an idea," he continued "let's take the horses out for a run. I need some exercise to loosen me up, and probably the horses do too. When we return, you can give me a proper rubdown."

"You'll be all right by tomorrow? I've been looking forward to our outing." And dreading it too, she thought to herself.

"I'm sure I'll be fine. This has happened before. Standing for so long in one position, trying to keep my balance and creating great art, all at the same time, can be very tiring," he said with a wry grin.

"I can believe it," Liz gamely agreed.

He called the Romanos over and told them to shut down the work for the rest of the day.

On their way from the chapel, Piero stopped again to speak briefly with Leonardo.

Liz could see Piero grow visibly paler by the moment, and she became impatient for him to go to his room to rest.

"Why don't you go up to your room," she suggested. "I'll stop by the kitchen for some oil."

"What for?"

"I think you should have the rub down first before we go riding, and then when we get back, a warm bath will make you feel much better," she explained. "And then a rubdown after your bath with warm oil again before bed."

"You are serious about getting me to the seaside tomorrow, aren't you?"

"You bet I am," she said, relaxing a little.

In the kitchen, Liz got a cruet of olive oil and picked a couple of carrots off the table for the horses.

When she entered his room, Piero had stripped to the waist and lay in bed on his back with his boots still on.

Liz removed them cautiously and massaged his feet. He let out a low moan.

"Turn over, Master."

He turned over slowly, and Liz could tell he was in considerable pain.

She poured a little of the oil into her hands and rubbed them together to warm the oil.

She massaged the oil into his shoulders. In a few minutes, she was rewarded as she felt his muscles relax. After working his back muscles from his shoulders down to his waist, she shifted her attention to his neck, arms and hands.

As she held his hand in hers, she inspected it, half-expecting to see the root of his talent hidden there.

She knew better, of course, but couldn't help speculating—was the mark of his genius to be found in his hands, his brain, his heart, or his soul?

As she soothed his tired muscles and warmed them with her touch, her hands roamed over his body, learning every hollow and contour. The feel of his skin was like sweet torture. Her breath quickened, and her pulse raced. She knew she tread dangerous ground, ground that in an instant would turn to a quagmire, pulling her down into its depths from which she could never free herself.

He seemed to have drifted off to sleep so she ceased her ministrations.

"I think it might be a good idea for you to rest a little while. I'll go down to the stables and have them get the horses ready and bring you back some tea. All right?" she asked.

All she got in response was a snore. Liz took that as agreement and hurried from the room, grateful to make her escape.

When Liz got back little more than a half hour later, Piero was sitting up in bed.

"How are you feeling?"

"Much better. You have magic hands, *Piccolino*."

"I brought you some tea," Liz said, smiling and turning away to hide the telltale blush spreading across her cheeks.

Minutes later, they rode out of the city into a countryside ablaze with spring color. Piero pointed out the sights, like the distant peak of Monte Titano in the Republic of San Marino, but Liz was entranced by the flowers—poppies covering the hillsides, wild yellow-blooming gorse. There were walnut trees and chestnut trees, umbrella pines and tall cypress reaching up into the cloudless blue sky.

As the city retreated in the distance, Liz listened intently to everything Piero said and followed his every gesture.

Liz was happy to be out in the afternoon sunshine. Piero's color returned, which eased her concern. Even the horses displayed a spirited exuberance by prancing and tossing their heads, as if they wanted to join in the fun.

"Master, how late will we stay out?" Liz asked. "I mentioned to Mistress Isabella we might be a little late, and she said she would save us some supper."

"We won't go too far. There's a small stream up ahead. We'll stop there to water the horses and give them a rest, and then we'll start back."

"Have you noticed how well the horses get along?" Liz asked, playfully tugging on *Argento's* right ear.

They rode along for a while in companionable silence, reveling in the glorious afternoon and enjoying the exercise.

When they reached the stream, they dismounted, and Liz gave the carrots to the horses. While Liz and Piero relaxed under the shade of a tree, the horses grazed and drank from the stream.

"How's your back feeling?"

Piero lay sprawled on his back with his hands behind his head, the picture of total contentment.

Not the slightest sign of discomfort showed on his face.

What if I tell him now? she debated with herself. Should I seize the moment and tell him the truth now? What a damn coward I am, she berated herself.

Her heart pounded in her chest, a sure sign that the time had come to cut her losses. She must let him know not only that she was a woman, but that she loved him.

Doubt lifted like a cloud. She could fool him—and herself—no longer. If not for the fact he was wonderful and dreamy to look at, she'd have spent her energy trying to get back to her previous life. Instead, she had been falling in love.

Even though she had thought and thought, she still didn't have a clue how to return to her own time. She had wasted precious time in the pursuit of a man who had not a speck of interest in her except as her friend and mentor. He had been kind, nothing more.

Would he understand or get angry? Everything—her happiness and possibly her life—hinged on his reaction. She had perpetrated a lie, not only on him, but on everyone. He could decide to preserve their relationship and the promise of much more, or forever alter her future.

"Master," Liz trembled but edged closer to him and leaned back against the tree. "Are you asleep?"

"No."

"There is something I must discuss with you—a confession." She paused, groping for the right words.

He didn't move or open his eyes.

"I am no priest, Cosimo."

"I know that." Liz took a deep breath and continued. "There is a lie between us. And it makes me unhappy."

Piero opened his eyes and sat up, but his posture remained relaxed. He began to pick absently at the grass.

"And what is this lie that causes you unhappiness?" he asked tenderly.

"Master, I am not what I seem. I have allowed everyone, including you—out of necessity—to continue thinking, I mean, assuming ... that is, upon my arrival, everyone thought that I was a young man, when in fact ...," her words tumbled out in a rush and then stopped abruptly.

"I don't understand. What are you saying?"

She looked directly at Piero and spoke slowly and distinctly.

"I'm a woman."

Piero stared at her for a long moment, the mounting confusion playing across his face. He got to his feet slowly and walked to the bank of the stream where the horses were chomping on the young spring grass.

Liz sat perfectly still, waiting for the storm to break.

Piero knelt and scooped up great handfuls of water and drank noisily. He stood and rubbed his wet hands on his face and through his hair.

At last, he turned and faced her. She remained seated, immobile.

Great, fat tears slid silently down her cheeks. They landed unchecked on her hands resting in her lap.

The sight of her wet cheeks and the pathetic expression on her face moved him. He read pain there and something else—something elusive that defied definition. He turned and scanned the horizon to the north before walking slowly back to stand over her.

"Who else knows of this?" he asked.

Droplets of water clung to his hair.

"No one. I have confided in no one else."

"You admit you lied. How do I know you are now telling me the truth?"

Liz heard the disapproving tone in his voice. She gathered up her courage like a cloak and stood to confront him. All the words she had planned left her. She swiped carelessly at the telltale tears, unwilling to suffer his contempt, before she spoke.

"I am telling the truth, and I never lied. I never corrected the misunderstanding under which … but I never lied."

Her voice, even to her own ears, was thick with tears.

"I had my reasons and they were sound ones, and afterward—well, I was afraid to say anything. I didn't mean to deceive anyone. It couldn't be helped."

Drawing herself up to her full height, she still only reached to his shoulder. Nonetheless, in a quavering voice, she persisted in her defense.

"I must ask you to accept that I had no choice in this and to accept as well my apology for misleading you."

"This changes everything," he said, his expression grim.

"How? Nothing has changed except that you now know the truth. That I'm a woman. No one else knows, and no one else needs to know. We can continue as we began."

"How can we? It is impossible."

"I can still serve you as your apprentice and your servant. What has changed? Have I not served you well? What complaint can you have against me? That I am a woman? What would you have me do? Confess to everyone that they made a mistake? What good would that do?"

"What if you are found out? What then?"

"If you are afraid for yourself, you can claim that you were duped, as were they all … or you can tell the Duchess, if that is what you decide you must do. The decision is yours."

"No more arguing, and do not make suggestions for what I should do or should not do." He nearly shouted this last protest at her, and his green eyes flashed with anger. "I must think on this—on what must be done."

His upraised voice shattered the peaceful countryside. Liz had hoped for understanding, even acceptance, from him, but that was a futile hope.

Maybe he just needs time, she thought; besides, it'll do no good to push him, she told herself.

Piero tried but failed to mask his shock and disappointment. His initial reaction to his apprentice's disclosure was one of total shock and disbelief.

His temper had erupted because he realized that he had been completely taken in, made a fool of. What kind of an idiot am I? Had no one guessed? Am I surrounded by fools?

For both their sakes, he hoped that he was.

CHAPTER 13

▼

"I'm sorry this happened. What more can I say?" Liz put her palms together in a gesture of supplication. Then let her hands drop to her side.

She stalked to the stream and knelt to drink. She splashed a couple of handfuls of water in her face to mask the tears that she was powerless to stop.

"Let's start back," Piero said, coming to stand next to her. Then, almost as an afterthought, he added, "I'm sorry too."

She turned and looked at him. She turned away, unable to meet his gaze. His furrowed brow and the somber expression in his eyes wordlessly, but eloquently, mirrored her feelings.

Tense and mute, they mounted their horses.

Dark storm clouds rolled in bringing cooler Alpine air from the north. The sunny afternoon that held such promise had turned cool and cloudy, leaving behind a bleak landscape full of shadows.

"It was wise to rest the horses for it looks like we'll have to push them to out-run the storm," Piero said. From his tone, he might have been speaking to the horses instead of to her.

The horses lifted their heads high and smelled the air. *Zingaro* snorted and Piero gave him his head. *Argento* followed closely behind at a brisk canter.

Liz's heart sat heavily in her chest like a stone. His muttered apology, half-hearted and clumsy though it was, seemed genuine. She repeated to herself over and over that everything would work out for the best even as she felt her blood slow down as if ice crystals had formed in her veins.

Piero allowed *Zingaro* to set the pace. The sound of the horses' hooves beat the time of the mantra that ran silently through her brain—'everything will be fine.'

"Are you all right?" Piero called out to her.

"Of course. Don't worry about us. We can keep up," Liz answered.

The wind whipped her hair and stung her face, carrying her words off. She waved him on. She felt the air grow heavy with moisture.

No need to spur the horses, for their warm dry stable seemed to act as a lure.

Before long, she saw the city looming ahead.

At the gate of the city, Piero pulled *Zingaro* up and stopped. He turned the horse and walked his mount to stand beside *Argento*. The horses' lathered sides heaved with the strain of their labored breathing.

"We made it," Liz said, scanning the storm clouds to the north.

Piero nodded in reply. He looked at her directly for the first time since they had started back. His eyes resembled two chips of cold jade.

"We can take a moment to talk here before we go back inside where ears and eyes are everywhere."

He hesitated, and then continued in a quiet voice she strained to hear over the sounds of the wind and far off thunder.

"Do not judge me too harshly, Cosimo. I must have time to think about this."

"I understand." She waited, eyes cast down, but if she expected him to say more, she was disappointed.

"Are we still going to the seashore tomorrow?" she asked, knowing what the answer would be.

"I don't know."

"It will look strange if we don't. Questions will be asked since we've made plans and talked of nothing else all week. What would we say by way explanation?"

Piero didn't respond.

"Please," Liz persisted, adamant that they work it out, and pushed Piero for an answer, "it will give us a chance to talk … away from those ears and eyes you speak of."

Argento jerked on the reins, and Liz strained to hold him. She felt space close in on her. Will I disappear into a tiny point of light? She suddenly found the question she asked herself had a certain appeal. She wished she could just disappear—through that elusive portal.

"We will see," he replied at last.

She pressed him no further. Instead, she reached out and laid her hand on his arm in a gesture of entreaty.

Piero looked down at her hand and saw there for the first time what should have been obvious to him. Her hand, utterly feminine with its long, delicate fingers and soft contours of flesh, gripped his arm with a gentle pressure.

He raised his eyes to hers, and the expression in her gaze held him. With startling clarity, he recalled the look on her face as she sat by the stream—the look that had confused him. Now he recognized her expression for what it was—a look that held affection—no love! She loved him.

Everything that had happened since her arrival seemed to lead up to this moment. He marveled at how easily she had complicated and enriched his life, and in such a short time.

On an impulse, he lifted his arm and brought her hand to his lips.

"I see now what a fool I have been. I'm sorry for …"

Piero suddenly recalled the times she had attended to his bath and changed his bed linen. He was so overcome with acute embarrassment that his apology died on his lips.

*   *   *   *

They reached the stable and turned their mounts over to the care of the waiting grooms who would walk them and rub them down before giving them their feed and water.

Still smarting from his embarrassment, Piero walked toward the *Palazzo*. He glanced back and stopped to wait for Liz to catch up.

"Before I eat, I'll wash up. I suggest you do the same. We'll speak later."

Then, he turned on his heel and was gone.

Dismissed as summarily as if she were no more than the lowliest of servants, Liz was left wondering when she would be welcome back in their quarters.

The back of her hand was still warm from his kiss. From the coldness of his departure, it might never have happened. But it had happened.

She knew he needed time to think things through—away from "Cosimo"—calmly and without distraction, but his abrupt parting left her hurt, humiliated and, above all, angry.

Anger, so ferocious in intensity that it frightened her, flared up like flames about to engulf her. She stomped into the stable, muttering to herself under her breath in English. The horses continued to eat their feed and swish their tails contentedly, oblivious to her fury.

She went into *Argento's* stall and put her arms around the horse's neck, giving in to her tears. Not since she was a child and learned the incontrovertible truth that Santa Claus was Uncle Frank dressed up in a Santa suit had she shed such a deluge.

Her tears flowed for all the recent losses she had suffered. She wept for the loss of her family and, most of all, for the loss of her dream of a life with Piero.

"Just who does he think he is? How can he treat me this way?" she asked *Argento*, through bitter sobs.

Argento turned his soulful brown eyes on her, but Liz slumped to the floor of his stall, too distraught to notice or care. When her crying ceased at last and her mind cleared, she thought things through dispassionately—something she thought near to impossible in her state.

Powerlessness, she concluded, would only increase her feelings of vulnerability and leave her at everyone's mercy, especially Piero's. Instead of floundering about aimlessly, she had to take control of the situation.

Understandable though it was that her deception had disappointed him, and she had no choice but to bide her time until his anger ran its course, she could not forgive his boorish behavior. Hurtful. Humiliating.

Was this the way things would be from now on? His moods as mercurial as the spring weather? What if he turned on me in his anger? And what were the chances that one day I wouldn't slip on my own and be found out? What then? What would become of me?

She weighed her few options and decided to try again to get back to her own time. She told herself that she had nothing to lose. If she stayed, she had everything to lose.

Leaving the stable, she ran all the way through the rainstorm to the kitchen door. She raced up to the chapel to see if the portal had reappeared.

Lightning bolts cast the only light into the chapel, barely enough for Liz to make out her image on the wall. The likeness was almost complete. Piero had not finished the hands and feet, and many little details were missing. She touched the image in several places, but it was rock solid beneath her touch.

The idea struck her that when Piero completed the image, if she could stand in front of it with the amulet, maybe the energy emitted by the amulet would be powerful enough to force the portal to open.

There was a chance it would work. And since she had nothing else to go on, a plan formed in her mind to accomplish just that.

She returned to the kitchen, stood at the open doorway, and looked across at the artisans' building. A faint light shone in the upstairs room. Piero was still there.

The courtyard was deserted. Though the storm dumped quite a lot of rain, it had passed quickly. The world was washed clean, and the cobblestones gleamed in the faint moonlight.

Kitchen maids lit lamps. Soon everyone would be filing into the kitchen for their evening meal. The fare would be lighter than what was served at lunchtime, but the crowd would fill the kitchen.

Dirty and dejected, she decided to go back to the stable and wait for Piero to leave the artisans' building before going to her room to clean up. She passed several stable hands on their way to the kitchen pump. Mistress Isabella strictly forbade anyone from entering her kitchen until they had washed off the filth from the stable.

The stableyard was deserted as well. Everyone had gone to their homes. Rainwater sloshed ankle deep over the cobbles and filled the water troughs to overflowing.

Liz entered the stable again and went directly toward *Argento*'s stall.

The last thing she did, before being struck from behind, was reach out for the latch on his stall.

*   *   *   *

When she came to, it was pitch dark and eerily quiet, as if she had been thrown down a deep dark hole. When she tried to sit up, she found that her hands and feet had been tied. She almost cried out for help, but stopped herself in time. Suppose the person who struck is still nearby? It would be best to keep quiet rather than signal him to come to finish the job.

From the smells around her, she could tell she was still in the stable.

She attempted to free herself, but could get no purchase against the ropes. She ceased struggling and lay perfectly still, listening to her breathing and the rustling sounds of the horses.

Her head throbbed as if it was ready to explode and jagged flashes of light crossed her field of vision.

While keeping the rest of her body as motionless as she could, she concentrated on freeing her hands. Tears sprung to her eyes from the pain in her head.

At last, she managed to work her hands free. She sat up slowly and had to rest before she was able to work at the rope binding her ankles. Her head still pounded, but not as badly, and she hoped the tears she shed accounted for the dampness running down the side of her face.

Gingerly, she reached up her hand and felt a gash with a serious lump above her right ear. Her ankles were still bound, and a hollow dizziness crawled inside her, ready to swallow her up. She forced herself to take several deep breaths because she felt inches away from slipping into unconsciousness.

Her eyes had become accustomed to the dark, and she detected faint light coming from somewhere nearby. In the gloom, she traced the trail of blood from the gash on her head down her neck to her wet and sticky shirt.

As she wondered how long she had been unconscious, the unmistakable smell of smoke hit her.

A noise caused her to look around in time to see two dark shadows descending a ladder from the loft. She could make out that one wore skirts. She called out to them. "Please, help me!"

When they reached her, she recognized one of the young kitchen maids with fair-haired Emilio Romano.

"What happened to you?" the young apprentice asked, stooping to untie Liz's ankles.

"I don't know," she responded, struggling anew against another bout of dizziness that confused and disoriented her thinking.

"Well, we don't know either," the young man said, a trifle defensively.

"Thank you for untying me. I think I can stand if you help me."

"You're bleeding," the maid offered.

"I know. Did you see anyone?"

The maid blushed furiously and looked away. The young man wore a sheepish expression and merely shook his head. Liz understood, muddle-headed though she was, that they were in the loft for a reason and were probably too engaged in their sensual pursuits to take much notice of who clobbered her.

The smell of smoke grew stronger, and Liz hurt far too much to waste any more energy on them. She wobbled a bit, but her legs held her weight.

"Smell the smoke? See if you can find the source."

Liz leaned on one of the wooden pillars supporting the massive slate roof. The maid had gone to the main door of the stable.

"It's bolted on the outside! I can't open it!" she cried out.

"So is the back door to the tack room," the young man called out.

"We can't get out. We're trapped!" the maid screamed, her hands flying to her face.

"Listen to me," Liz said to the young man. "Go back up to the loft and get out the loft door. Jump if you have to, and then open up the front." The authoritative tone in her voice jolted him into action.

In a minute, the main stable door flew open. The maid rushed out into the smoky night.

"I think the fire is at the back corner of the stable," he called to Liz, while pointing toward where thick, black smoke billowed.

Once the large front doors were open, the stable rapidly filled with smoke.

Loud popping sounds propelled Liz to release her hold on the pillar. She staggered to the back of the stable where the stalls of both *Argento* and *Zingaro* were located.

"Go get help!" Liz shouted to the young man.

The horses didn't want to leave their warm stalls, but she pulled at *Zingaro's* bridle and murmured endearments, coaxing him and *Argento* out into the stable yard.

Circling the outside of the stable, she found where the fire had been set at the back wall. Debris and tree limbs mixed with dry hay had been piled up at the base of the stable wall under the shelter of the roof. The stable backed up into the hillside so the wooden braces of the stable roof met the stone foundation, practically at ground level, a perfect spot, relatively dry and well hidden, for a fire to take hold.

Liz pulled the tree limbs away from the wall and kicked the debris and hay to scatter it, but she saw that the wood had already caught. The fire traveled under the eaves along the roof line. She heard loud voices calling out and sighed with relief that help was on the way.

Stopping first to soak her handkerchief in the water trough, she covered her nose and mouth and re-entered the stable through the main door. Eyes burning, she opened the remaining stalls at the back of the stable and brought first one and then another horse out of the stalls through the dense, acrid smoke.

The voices and shouts outside grew louder, but she could see no one through the inky smoke.

Flames shot up into the night sky, and the smoke compelled her to waste precious time wetting her handkerchief twice more to keep her from choking.

At last, others joined her, and they succeeded in saving all the horses in the stable. As luck would have it, many more were still in the pasture.

She heard Captain San Martini before she saw him. He was directing the stable hands and others who were fighting the fire. Soldiers milled about or made ineffectual attempts to help, but merely contributed to the general chaos of the scene.

Even though the stable was made mostly of stone and slate, enough wood and the hay that was stored in the structure sent the flames higher and higher and generated intense heat.

Liz ran and grabbed a bucket and hauled it back from the water trough to the stable. With the horses safely out, a serious effort could be made to bring the fire under control.

"Have them get more buckets and fill them," Liz called to Captain San Martini.

"Do it!" he shouted, and the soldiers jumped to obey.

She formed them into a bucket brigade to fight the fire at the back of the stable where it had a strong foothold. She couldn't believe how quickly it raged, and she hoped the earlier rainstorm would keep the fire from taking the entire building down. The flames licked at the wooden roof supports, threatening the collapse of the heavy slate roof.

The soldiers wound their way up the hillside and soaked the roof with the rainwater from the water troughs.

The battle at last turned in their favor, but despite their efforts, the damage was extensive.

While Captain San Martini inspected the damage, Liz stumbled to the closest wall and succumbed at last to exhaustion and the effects of the blow to her head.

✳   ✳   ✳   ✳

Piero worked in his room, sorting through sketches for the next series of figures for the chapel wall and trying to put the problem of Cosimo out of his mind. The smell of smoke reached him. The primordial fear of fire that ruled their lives drove him from his room to investigate. He ran down the stairs of the artisans' building and into the courtyard.

A running surge of humanity greeted him in the courtyard—shouting figures, madly intent on charging down toward the barracks and stable. He joined the crowd which now mimicked a teeming school of fish migrating in the sea.

The blaze was visible against the night sky, and the fire was like a wave of heat that rushed at him and broke over and around him.

The stable!

His first thought was of his apprentice, for he knew without a doubt that she would be with the young horse.

In the stable yard, he was confronted by a mad scene out of "Dante's Inferno."

He reached Captain San Martini's side.

"Have you seen Cosimo?" He had to shout to be heard over the noise.

"He was here. I don't know where he is now."

Piero searched the courtyard frantically. No one could remember seeing his apprentice.

He almost tripped over a little pile of clothing against the stone wall, but saw a glint of golden hair that stopped him in his tracks.

When he picked her up, she was so light he feared the life had gone from her.

Refusing any offers of help, he carried the girl up to his room.

CHAPTER 14

▼

Piero placed Liz gently on his own bed and looked down at her with dismay. She groaned, and he instantly regretted his foolhardy decision to refuse all offers of help.

He bent over her and began to remove her muddy boots.

No, try to think. What would Mistress Isabella do first?

He had not a clue where to begin. His only thought down in the stable yard had been to prevent anyone from finding out that the young apprentice was in fact a female in disguise.

So much blood! True, he had experience with superficial injuries, but this was way beyond him.

But here he was with a seriously injured girl on his hands, one that could possibly die. She was depending on him. He gritted his teeth and set to work.

Inept he may be, but he had to try if she had any hope of recovery. And he acknowledged to himself that he wanted, more than anything, for her to survive and get well.

First, he fetched a basin of water and a clean cloth.

Next he removed her bloody shirt. For the sake of modesty, he left her in her breeches and bindings. They too were sodden with dirt and blood, but there was nothing to do for it.

While she remained unconscious, he checked her for broken bones, feeling the joints and limbs thoroughly. Good, he thought, no breaks that he could discern.

He washed off as much of the dirt and grime from her face as he could, looking for the source of all the blood that covered her head and soaked through to her undershirt. He found the deep gash on her head and congratulated himself as he cleaned it. He probed a little and removed small bits of wood clinging to the wound.

He was preparing a dressing to bind up the wound, which mercifully had stopped bleeding, when Liz's eyelids fluttered.

By sheer will, she forced herself into consciousness. When she tried to open her eyes, they seemed to be stuck shut, as if they were weighed down by invisible thumbs pressing them closed.

She felt something warm and wet washing over her eyes and a gentle cloth wiping them until she was able to open her eyes and see. Her mind was as clouded as her vision.

A face loomed over her, a face so blackened by soot and dirt that she failed at first to recognize him. Then she detected, under all the sweat and grime, the unmistakable green glint of his eyes glowing in the flickering candlelight.

Piero!

As he leaned over her and washed her face, he managed a weak smile. She choked as some of the soot drifted off his face and landed on her neck like a malignant snowfall.

Their eyes locked on each other, and the only sounds in the room were the audible sigh that escaped his lips and the sound of her ragged breathing.

"*Grazie, per Dio,* I did not think you would live," he said, wiping the soot from her neck.

She looked around and realized she was in his bedroom, on his bed, and he was bathing the blood and grime from her face and neck.

Aware now of how her body ached and the terrible dryness in her throat, she tried to sit up, but Piero pressed her back onto the pillow.

"None of that. Stay still, *Piccolino.*"

"Am I your *Piccolino* again?" Liz croaked, even as a fit of coughing shook her, and tears leaked from the corners of her eyes.

"Yes!"

The pain in her head reared up and threatened to push her into unconsciousness, and she retched violently.

And then, most wonderful of all, Piero lifted her to a sitting position and cradled her in his arms until her coughing and retching subsided. He wiped her face again with the damp cloth. Anyone seeing them would find them either pitiful or comical.

Liz could swear puffs of smoke escaped her mouth when she coughed.

The choking fit may have subsided, but it took so much of her energy that she fell back against the pillow exhausted by the effort.

Piero stood and removed the basin and came back with fresh water. He wet a clean cloth and washed her arms and hands.

Liz watched him and thought of the times she had washed him, or his brushes, or his clothes.

She reveled in his tender ministrations, too sore and too tired to object. Even if she had a mind to, which she didn't, she had no desire to stop his gentle touch.

He bent and brushed his lips shyly across hers in a sweet kiss.

"I thought I was going to lose you," he whispered.

His kiss—at once so gentle and unexpected—startled her and kept her from slipping into unconsciousness. Liz held on to reality even though the black void beckoned where Piero could not follow.

He recovered his composure first and stammered, "We must finish cleaning you up."

"Not yet," she whispered.

Liz pulled him to her and they kissed again. But this time, Liz would not settle for a gentle brush of his lips.

This kiss was the kind for which she had yearned—demanding and possessive. Never taking her mouth from his, she caressed the back of his neck and the edge of his jaw, now rough with stubble. As their kiss lengthened and deepened, she let her hands roam through his hair and linger at will, imparting all her longing into that kiss.

Piero took her hands in his, and she felt the rough fingertips and the smooth palms. Pressing his hands to her breasts, she used her tongue to draw him ever more into her, his sigh blending with hers into a purr of pure contentment.

Emboldened by her earthy, but natural, sensuality, he stretched out in the bed beside her and covered her face with kisses.

"That's much better," Liz said, smiling at him.

Before he could recover his power of speech, there was a knock at the door. Piero stood and tossed a blanket over Liz and went to open the door, looking back, his look telling her that they would resume their pastime at the first opportunity.

Mistress Isabella stood on the threshold holding a basin of water with towels draped over her shoulder. She brushed past Piero followed by a young boy carrying a tray.

"He's awake. That's a good sign," she said, immediately taking command of the situation.

"I tried to get our master painter here to let me tend you, Cosimo, but he would hear nothing of the kind. He rushed up here with you in spite of my protests."

"What have you there?" Piero asked, his tone wary.

"I have dressed the Duke's own wounds of battle, Master Piero. I assure you I know what I am doing."

"I was just getting ready to put a dressing on …"

"I'm sure you were, but I'm here now and he must have a proper dressing."

She dismissed Piero as next to worthless and went to work expertly examining Liz's head wound.

"Are you hurting anywhere else, Cosimo?"

"No, Mistress, just this gash on my head."

"There's a good size lump too, but you seem alert enough, and your color is good."

Liz glanced in Piero's direction and smiled. He thought her smile was silky, like a cat's, and he couldn't help but smile back at her.

"I will put some healing herbs and a compound of alum on your wound and bind it up," Mistress Isabella clucked like a mother hen. "And it looks as if our painter here did quite a good job of cleaning your wound," she added, nodding at him as if to let him know that he was not so worthless after all.

"I am sure you will feel better in the morning for you are young and strong. And I will have some supper sent up for you both. Eat, that is the best thing to get your strength back."

When she was satisfied with the dressing, she gathered up her things and made ready to leave.

"Try not to sleep for a while. That would not be a good thing yet. But, eat whatever you feel like eating from the tray I send up to you, but don't force yourself. And as for you, Master Piero, do not try my patience again. It is my place to tend the sick and wounded here, not you."

With a pointed parting look at Piero, she left.

"Thank you, Mistress Isabella," Liz called after her retreating figure before beckoning Piero back to the bed.

"I'd like a bath before I eat, Piero, please."

"All right, I'll go down and get the water myself. If Mistress Isabella asks me, I'll tell her it's for me for I don't think you should be moving around too much."

"I promise I'll be still until you return. You can help me for a change."

Liz chuckled to see Piero turn away in embarrassment, knowing full well that her jab had hit its mark. What he was recalling to himself, no doubt, were the times she had helped him bathe. His cheeks were probably red under all that dirt.

"I'll be right back."

Piero raced from the room to do her bidding, leaving Liz to muse on the turn of events that landed her in Piero's bed.

Her head ached a lot less. A bath and clean clothes would do wonders for her.

For a time, as she lay there, she indulged in a sweet reverie of the life she would have with Piero, the dream she had thought lost to her. They would live and work together and perhaps one day marry, if no sinister forces contrived to drive them apart. As it turned out, her unknown assailant had done her a great favor, she thought, smiling to herself.

Then, thoughts of that unknown assailant filled her mind. Who would so blithely end my life? What kind of person would do that? And more importantly, when he learned he had failed, would he try again?

Meanwhile, Piero went to the kitchen to fetch the water for her bath, grateful for the opportunity to put some distance between them. It seemed to him that she had aroused him easily and completely, and he was prepared to admit he had never been kissed as expertly or as thoroughly as his apprentice—in her wounded state—had kissed him.

The courtyard and kitchen were crowded with the comings and goings of weary, dirty and hungry men. The servants busily tended to all of them, so Piero went himself to the cauldron in the larger of the two fireplaces and poured hot water into two large kettles.

"Do you need help?"

Piero recognized the voice of his friend, Captain San Martini.

"No, Luca, thank you. I think I can manage."

"How is the lad?"

"Cosimo? I think he'll be all right. All that blood was from a gash on his head. A good night's sleep, and he'll be fine."

Captain San Martini noticed his friend appeared nervous and awkward in a way the good Captain had not seen before. Piero did not seem able to look directly at the Captain when they spoke, so very unlike Piero's usual behavior, which puzzled the Captain to the point of suspicion.

"Is everything all right?"

"Yes, everything is fine. He'll be fine."

"Good. I'd like to speak to him about the fire. When would be a good time?"

"In the morning … I think that would be best. He needs rest and food right now."

"Of course. You know, he did well in fighting the fire. He got most of the horses out of the stable by himself."

"I didn't know. Are the horses still in the paddock?"

"No, we moved them down to the pasture for the night. I'm afraid we lost all our store of hay and feed, but we were able to save most of the tack including two of the Duke's best saddles."

"And the stable?"

"It will need extensive repairs. What I want to know is how the fire started. Maybe Cosimo knows something since he was already there when the fire was first detected."

"Very well. We'll come down to meet with you in the garrison first thing in the morning."

"Good."

"I'd better get back."

Captain San Martini clapped Piero on the back as he strained to walk under the load of the heavy kettles of water.

"*Buona notte*, Luca."

"*Buona notte, amico.*"

Captain San Martini watched his friend leave the kitchen and could not rid himself of the notion that his friend was somehow not his usual self. Something's afoot. It was probably nothing more than his own overactive imagination or Piero's concern for his apprentice, but he resolved to get to the bottom of things in the morning. There was a riddle here to be solved, and he liked riddles very well indeed.

✳   ✳   ✳   ✳

When Piero reached his chamber, he put the kettles down and unlocked the door. The bed was empty. He continued through to the privy chamber and poured the water into the hip bath.

"Where are you, Cosimo? I've brought the bath water."

"I'm just getting some clean clothes in my room."

"You shouldn't be moving around. Let me get them."

"It's all right. I'm feeling much better. Really."

Piero readied the soap and towels.

"I'll hold up a towel for you to shield yourself while you step into the bath."

Liz reentered the privy and was testing the water with her hand.

"All right. Have it your own way. The water's just right."

Liz stripped out of her bloody clothes and stepped into the hip bath. She sank down to luxuriate in the feel of the warm water coursing over her skin. Piero placed the soap, cloth and towel within her reach and started toward the door to his room.

"Wait. Stay and talk to me."

"That might not be a good idea."

"And why not? Several times now I have assisted you at your bath while you chattered away and ordered me about."

"It's not the same, and you know it."

"You're right, of course, I don't expect you to shave me or cut my hair," Liz said with a laugh.

"Just tell me what news you've learned downstairs, and then I'll let you go. With this bandage on my head, I'll have to wait until tomorrow to wash my hair, but I promise you can help me then."

While Liz scrubbed herself clean of grime, soot and blood, Piero relented and sat on the floor with his back against the door.

"I saw Luca, and he told me of your bravery in getting the horses out. They're down in the pasture for the night. The stable was extensively damaged and the stores of hay and feed are gone. But thankfully, no one was killed or hurt. Except for you, of course. How did you get that gash on your head? Did something in the stable come crashing down on you?"

"You might say that. I didn't get hurt fighting the fire or getting the horses out. I was in the stable when someone hit me and knocked me out. I was tied up and left unconscious to die in a fire that this person most probably set to cover up the fact that I had been murdered."

Piero jumped to his feet.

"What??!! Why didn't you tell me this before? Luca expects us to come down to the garrison in the morning to tell him about the fire. But I think this is something I better tell him now. Will you be all right to get dressed after your bath? He may want to come up to speak with you," he called to her from his bedroom.

"Don't forget to bring me back some supper!" Liz called out to him.

Piero re-locked the door behind him and dashed down the steps and through the artisans' quarters into the courtyard. He saw Luca standing by the door to the kitchen talking to Mistress Isabella.

"Luca!" Piero shouted.

Mistress Isabella and Luca both started to walk toward Piero, but Luca quickened his pace when he noticed his friend's agitated demeanor.

"What is it?" Luca demanded.

"Is the boy all right?" Mistress Isabella asked.

"Yes, but listen. Cosimo did not get hurt fighting the fire. Someone hit him before the fire and tied him up and left him for dead and then started the fire to cover it up. He ... he just told me."

Mistress Isabella and Captain San Martini exchanged an anxious look.

"Maybe I should go up now and speak to him," Luca said, which came out sounding more like a question.

"I think that's a good idea." Piero nodded his assent as they started back to Piero's room. But Piero stopped short when he saw that Mistress Isabella was accompanying them.

"I think, Mistress, that it might be best if you give us a few minutes. Will you be kind enough to come up in a little while with our food?" Piero asked with a disarming smile.

"Yes, I will do as you ask."

But Piero caught the look she directed at Luca, as if to say, you better tell me everything later—or else.

Piero and Luca found Liz, now fully dressed, sitting on a chair next to the large round table in Piero's room waiting for her supper.

She related to them both how she had come to in the barn, the two young people who had helped her—the Romano cousin and the young kitchen maid— and how she had managed in spite of her head wound, to save the horses. She entirely omitted the conversation with Piero and her feelings about how they had parted.

"I will be sure to question your two young saviors in the morning," Luca commented. "And you are sure you have no idea who struck you?"

"I was hit from behind and saw no one."

"I suspect one or both of the Cevas," Piero said.

"Probably instigated by Raffaello," Luca added.

"I tend to agree with you," Piero said with a nod, "but what are we to do about it? Cosimo could be in danger still. And without proof ..."

"It's all right, Piero. It will be taken care of. You needn't worry so. You can always go away for a few days and take Cosimo with you, when he's better, certainly. But meanwhile, we will both keep an eye out for his safety. We can do nothing until morning, in any event."

Luca spoke in a soothing manner and succeeded in calming Piero, but only just.

"There is something else which you may want to consider," Liz said.

Both men turned to look at her.

"And what would that be, Cosimo?" Luca asked, a patronizing smile curling his lip.

"If I were you, I would post a guard or two in the pasture."

"In heaven's name, what for?"

"It may have been that the arsonist's real purpose was to eliminate the garrison's horses, and I was in the way, or he saw it as a lucky chance to kill me and get rid of the horses at the same time."

Captain San Martini instantly grasped the practical logic in what Liz said. And all that her words implied. Suppose she was right, and an attack was imminent? It would be his fault if he overlooked an obvious attempt to render the garrison immobile.

Liz watched the concerns roll across his face in wave after wave, triggering a ribbon of scarlet along the facial scar. She had a sudden and abiding admiration for him, for she sensed he was a man whose duty and loyalty came before everything else.

"And another thing," Liz went on, "there are cisterns beneath the *Palazzo*, are there not?"

"How do you know this? It is not common knowledge."

"For the sake of expedience, let's just say that I know. And is there a conduit that leads out from the cellars?"

Consternation written plainly on Captain San Martini's face, he glowered at Piero.

"Did you tell him this?"

"When I did not know of it myself?" Piero responded.

"Anyway," Liz continued, looking from one to the other, "if I were you, I would also post guards at the exits of the conduits, for they could also serve as a way into the *Palazzo*."

Captain San Martini glared at Liz a moment or two before stomping out of the room with Piero a step behind. When they reached the landing, Luca whirled on Piero.

"How would he know this?" he demanded.

"I don't know ... Is he right?" Piero asked, his tone somber.

"Yes, damn the little *spauracchio*. To think that a young insect like that would be reminding me of my duty. He's got a fine military mind, I'll say that for him, and I admire him for saving the horses. Tell him I will take care of it, and that I apologize for not saluting when I left."

With a rueful smile, he rushed down the stairs—his anger dissipated—to carry out his orders.

Piero remained on the landing, going over the conversation in his head. So, there was more to Cosimo than even she was willing to admit. He was determined to have all the truth from her.

He heard a noise on the stairs and turned to see Mistress Isabella and a serving maid as they reached the landing.

"Your supper, Master Piero."

"*Grazie*, Mistress. Let me take the tray."

They entered Piero's quarters, and Piero put the supper tray down on the table. He drew another chair up to the table. He averted his eyes, but missed not a word of what was said. Liz thanked Mistress Isabella for taking such good care of her.

"No, no need to thank me, Cosimo, I should thank you. Everyone is talking about your bravery in the face of the fire." The good lady waited in hopes of a tidbit of news, but Cosimo had started in on her food.

Piero busied himself with his food too with an occasional peek at Cosimo, her expression one of light and innocence.

"I'll leave you now to your supper and your rest. *Buona notte.*"

"*Buona notte*, Mistress Isabella," Liz said.

Piero stood and walked Mistress Isabella to the landing.

"He looks better already, Piero. Take care of him. *Buona notte.*"

Piero waited until Mistress Isabella was at the foot of the stairs. He took a deep breath, squared his shoulders and re-entered the room.

Liz looked up as he entered the room, and the smile on her face died. Piero's full lips were drawn in a tight line, and his expression caused her full stomach to lurch.

"What's the matter now?"

"I want to know how you knew about the cisterns—Luca will want to know too tomorrow—so you better tell me now and decide how you will explain it to him. He's no fool. And while we're at it, I dislike deceiving him. He's my friend, and I've a mind to tell him everything."

Liz tried to compose her features in the face of this frontal assault. Tread carefully, she cautioned herself. Torn between refusing to indulge him and the unpleasant memory of being on the receiving end of his temper once before, she knew no good would come from stoking his anger now.

She rose and lit more candles in an effort to steady her nerves and calm her voice.

"I think we better finish our food before it gets cold. Then we'll talk."

Piero had no choice but to comply. The silence was pervasive as they ate.

When they finished their meal, Liz faced him.

"The time has come to tell you how I came to be here. Come. Pull your chair next to mine, and I'll do my best to explain. As for Captain San Martini, you will have to decide what you can tell him, for you know him better than I."

Piero did as she asked and allowed her to take his hand. His desire for her was growing in equal measure to his distrust, and the combination roused fear and anxiety in him. Could she possibly be a spy sent by Malatesta to find their weak spot? If so, she had found his easily enough.

"Do you remember the conversation we had several days ago … when I asked you if you believe in fate?" Liz began. They were still seated at the table with the remnants of their supper in front of them. He looked down at her hand which was trembling in his.

Piero nodded, "I remember."

Liz released his hand and took another sip of wine. She rested her arms on the table and continued.

"Sometimes things happen for which there is no explanation. Remember I said that to you? I have no explanation to offer you. I don't understand it myself. I can only swear to you that what I am about to tell you is the truth."

Then Liz related how she had stepped through a time portal which transported her from the future back into his time. She watched as Piero's expression changed from amazement, to incredulity, and finally, to dismay.

"You tell me a preposterous tale like this and expect me to believe it. To take your word for it. Well, I don't believe it! What kind of fool do you take me for? That you can sit there and lie to my face tells me more than anything what kind of woman you are."

Piero had risen from his chair and was pacing the room.

Liz rose slowly and went to her room. She returned a moment later and came to stand facing him in the middle of the room. She clutched something in her hand.

Piero half suspected it might be a weapon.

But no, she held out her hand and opened it to show Piero a glimmering object that rested in the palm of her hand.

"What is that?" he asked.

"Good question. Have you ever seen anything like it before?"

"No."

"Have you any idea what it could be?"

Piero shook his head as he stared at the object she held.

"It's the one thing I had with me, other than the clothes I wore, which may prove to you I am no liar. Since you need proof, take it. Examine it!"

Piero took Liz's wristwatch and examined it. Liz seated herself back at the table to observe his reaction to the piece of hard evidence he held in his hand. Piero turned the watch over and over, inspecting it. He followed the movement of the second sweep hand—the intrinsic foreignness of the object obviously perplexing him, for puzzlement was written on his face.

"If you thought I was a liar before showing you this, now I suppose you will think me a witch," Liz said at last. "You, who claim to be an enlightened scholar, you know nothing but what you can see and touch."

Her tone was scathing.

"There it is then, your proof," she continued. "You can wonder all your life about what the future holds. Well, I know what the future holds. I am no witch. Only a traveler, who now must rely upon the likes of you for my safety. Imagine how consoling that must be for me."

Liz rose from her chair and took the watch from Piero.

"Look. It is worn on the wrist, like so." She strapped on her watch.

"It's a timepiece," she continued, explaining to Piero as if he were a child, "so that I always know what time it is merely by glancing at my wrist."

"What kind of metal is it? It resembles silver."

"It's what is called 'stainless steel'—an alloy. It's forged under heat like a sword. It was a gift to me from my parents."

Liz could feel tears welling up inside of her, but she refused to give in to her tears.

"Inside is a tiny power source that will last indefinitely. Tell me, then, have you seen anything like this before?"

"No."

"And in all your scholarly pursuits, have you ever heard of anything like this?"

"No."

"Where does it come from then? What is your conclusion?"

"I don't know."

"Well, I do. It has been said that when you have exhausted all possibilities, the logical conclusion—even if the only one left to you seems improbable—is the correct one."

"I have seen large clocks. The Duke possesses two fine examples in the *Palazzo*, but they are large and use weights to tell the time. There is nothing like this, so small, so very small. And you say there is a power source inside? Amazing!"

"In my time, the future, everyone I know possesses a watch like this. This one is shockproof and waterproof."

Piero smiled and shook his head, but Liz felt on the verge of tears.

"So you believe me?" Liz asked him, unshed tears glistening in her eyes.

"Yes, I suppose I must."

"Good."

Without another word, she put the watch inside her shirt and gathered up the dirty plates and cups and placed them on the tray.

"I'm taking the tray down to the kitchen. I need the air. And then I'm going to bed. I think you should too. You have a lot to think about. Like what you plan to tell Captain San Martini in the morning."

CHAPTER 15

▼

From his bed, Piero surveyed the encroaching dawn through bloodshot eyes, watching the night slip from pale gray to rosy yellow, while trying to make sense of Cosimo's revelation.

He had spent the sleepless night propped up in his bed against the pillows meant to ease his aching back. But nothing eased his soul as the night stretched on endlessly. He felt like he was in a deep pit deprived of air and light.

In between pacing, worrying, and furtive barefoot trips to the door of Cosimo's room, he prayed for guidance.

Doubt and uncertainty blanketed this dawn and the upcoming interview with Luca like the gray storm clouds that hung over the city.

Robbed of sleep, he was still no closer to a decision on what to do or what he was going to tell Luca. He knew Luca to be an honorable man, but one full of superstition. Luca would never be able to accept Cosimo's story despite her irrefutable proof. Piero was certain Luca would kill her first and ask questions later.

And so, he was torn between his loyalty to his old friend and fear for the life of his new friend. His overwhelming need to protect her compelled him to lie to his friend. Always a rotten liar—how to carry it off was driving him to desperation.

Sounds of Cosimo moving around in the privy saved him from further useless deliberation. He tapped gently on the door.

"Don't come in!" she called to him, startled at the sound of his knock. Her courage and temper had fled during the night. Facing Piero this morning held no allure because this could well be the last day of her life. Doubtless, the uncommonly bitter taste in her mouth was fear.

She had slept fitfully, and to top it off, she awoke with her period. She had no way of knowing if the slight headache she felt stemmed from that, or from the head wound which itched under Mistress Isabella's tight dressing.

After she pulled herself together and straightened up the privy, she opened the door to Piero's room.

The pathetic sight that greeted her moved her to pity and remorse for the way she had talked to him the night before. How could she have been so stupid and heartless to expect him to accept her story outright? She had lost her temper last night, but it had evaporated into the night air like mist.

He was dressed in the same clothes he was wearing the day before and badly in need of a shave.

"I've been awake all night trying to think what to do," he said with no preamble, dropping wearily into a chair.

"I know. I heard you pacing. Why don't you get cleaned up, and we'll go down and have some breakfast before we seek out Captain San Martini."

"What will we tell him?"

"We don't have to talk about it now. I want to apologize for the way I spoke to you last night."

"We must talk about it," Piero replied, waving off her apology.

Liz sighed and gave in. There was no preventing this conversation.

"There is nothing that I said to Captain San Martini that can't be explained. So what if I knew about the cisterns beneath the *Palazzo*. Lots of people could have learned about that. Workmen could have spread word of what's throughout the entire *Palazzo*. And if we don't bring it up and make it an issue …"

"I don't think he will let anything pass."

"Then I'll say I heard about it from some travelers before I got here. The wonders of Duke Federico's *Palazzo*. It'll be all right. I promise you he would never suspect the truth."

Liz stood beside him and absentmindedly stroked his hair as she would soothe a frightened child.

"Come on," she continued, "go get cleaned up. I'm hungry."

Piero rose and noiselessly closed the door to the privy chamber.

Liz busied herself getting some clothing ready for Piero, and then sat waiting for him to rejoin her.

Heavy steps sounded in the hallway and stopped outside the door. Liz felt the loud knock in the pit of her stomach before it sounded.

"Maestro Piero, it's Mistress Isabella. Quick, let me in. Please, open the door."

Liz ran to the door and stepped back as Mistress Isabella burst into the room nearly knocking Liz to the floor.

"*Buon giorno*, Cosimo. How are you? I must speak with Maestro Piero"

"I'm much better, thank you, Mistress."

"Where is he?" she asked clasping Cosimo's arm.

"He's in the privy."

The good lady's exertions climbing the stairs had raised two bright red spots on her cheeks, and she wrung her hands nervously.

"Sit down here, Mistress, he'll only be a minute more. What is it? What's happened?"

"I'll tell you both when he finishes," she replied.

"We were just coming down to have breakfast."

Mistress Isabella sat in a chair, and her gasping breaths eased.

The door to the privy chamber opened and Piero, washed and freshly shaven, stepped into the room to finish dressing.

The two women turned to look at him when he entered the room. He stopped short when he saw Mistress Isabella sitting near the window.

He was clad only in his breeches and attempted to cover himself by reaching for the shirt Liz had laid out on the bed. In that brief moment, Liz saw that Mistress Isabella, instead of modestly averting her gaze, appraised Piero shamelessly with an appreciative gleam in her eye.

Piero evidently noticed as well for he flushed to the roots of his hair before turning his back and slipping into the shirt which only succeeded in affording Mistress Isabella a charming view of his delicious backside.

"Mistress Isabella! I'm sorry to give offense. I didn't know you were here," Piero muttered, turning around to face her.

"Nonsense, Maestro Piero, I've seen many men in far less than you are wearing. I am the one who should apologize to you for entering your chamber unannounced, but it is urgent business that brings me here from my kitchen. But I must say, despite those stairs, it has turned out to be a most pleasant mission."

"Will you tell us now?" Liz asked, trying to hide her smile from Piero's watchful eye.

"Captain Luca sent me up to fetch you. He needs to speak with you both right away."

At precisely that moment, bells rang out, not the stately and melodic call to prayer Liz was accustomed to, but a strident, ominous clarion that sent a small frisson of fear inching down her spine.

As Piero pulled on his boots, Mistress Isabella raised her voice to be heard over the bells and told them what little she could.

"All I know is that Luca went to speak to the Ceva brothers last night about the fire. They were lodging at the home of Giovanni Sanzio. Lucky for Luca he just happened to have two men-at-arms with him. As soon as Ghirardino Ceva saw the men approach through the courtyard of the Sanzio house, he rushed out at them and tried to cut Luca with his dagger. What a foolish young man! They think he was preparing to leave the city, you see, because he had a horse and a bag at the ready."

"Was anyone hurt?" Piero wanted to know.

"No. Luca and the two guardsmen quickly subdued him, and he is even now, as we speak, licking his wounds in a cell in the garrison."

"So Luca is all right then?"

"Oh, yes, but he is worried because Ghirardino's brother, Febus, who has not been seen since yesterday, is already gone from the city."

"Then why are the alarm bells ringing?" Piero asked.

"I have no idea," Mistress Isabella replied.

Piero hastened to the door. Liz and Mistress Isabella followed him out.

"I think we should get down to the garrison right away," he called over his shoulder.

In the courtyard, they saw soldiers lined up to take weapons from the armorer. Saddled mounts, made skittish by the din from the bells ringing throughout the city, were being led up into the courtyard. No one, even those shouting at the top of their lungs, could be heard over the fearsome sound of the bells.

Piero saw Captain San Martini, flanked by his two lieutenants, standing in the doorway to the garrison headquarters and ran to him through the noisy maelstrom of men and mounts. Liz followed a step behind him with Mistress Isabella bringing up the rear.

The Captain didn't acknowledge them but stood with his hands on his hips, a tiny spot of calm in a roiling sea. He scanned the preparations his men were making for several moments before raising his right arm to signal to a guard up in the bell tower. One by one, the alarm bells fell silent. The church bells throughout the city soon followed suit, but Liz's ears continued to ring.

"Come inside," Captain San Martini said to Piero and Liz.

Mistress Isabella followed the three into Captain San Martini's office, but before she could enter, he stopped her and dispatched her to the Duchess.

"The Duchess will need your help. I suggest you go to her now."

Turning to Liz and Piero, he remarked, "The women and children will be pouring inside the walls of the city, and she won't turn them away from the *Palazzo*. It's begun. Two patrols came back early this morning and reported that Malatesta's force is on the move. I estimate they will be here by nightfall."

"How big?" Piero asked.

Captain San Martini smiled slyly, puckering the skin near his scar.

"Not as big as he should have. We'll have no trouble defending ourselves against his forces."

"Are you sure your patrol has seen the entire army?"

"Yes, I'm sure, both patrols, separately reported roughly the same numbers. By the way, Cosimo, you were right. We examined the conduits where they emptied outside the city, and one had been tampered with, the westernmost. The gate had been loosened and would be easily felled with a modest sneeze. Febus is probably with Malatesta at the head of the army eager to lead a small force into the city through that conduit. Ghirardino admitted—with some persuasion from me— that he, along with his brother, were here to gather information on our defenses for Malatesta. I'd give my right arm to know what it was that kept him here yesterday after his brother left."

"How did he expect to elude the guard and get out after the gates had been closed?" Piero asked.

Captain San Martini shook his head.

Liz did not voice the possibility that Ceva might have had help, instead deciding to keep her speculation to herself.

"What of the Sanzios?" Piero asked.

"They were upset, especially old Giovanni. The son may have suspected something was going on, but I don't think he was a party to it. They used him too. But that young popinjay's involvement is enough to prevent the Duke from appointing him as his father's successor."

"What did you do about the conduit?" Liz asked.

"We repaired it, of course."

"May I make a suggestion?"

Captain San Martini glanced at Piero.

"Now what?"

"Well, I was just thinking that if you left the gate exactly as you found it...."

"Why would I do that?!!" Luca roared.

"Hear me out, please," Liz replied calmly.

"It would be a perfect spot for an ambush, don't you see?" she continued. "You could position several men in the conduit and more hidden on the outside.

When Malatesta's men, with Febus in the lead, enter the conduit, you would have them."

"It would give me great satisfaction to have both of them in my hands," Captain Luca said, rubbing his hands together in anticipation. "I will give your suggestion some thought."

Observing the expression on his face, Liz did not envy the Ceva brothers their fate.

"The Duke will have the pleasure of dealing with them, and that brings me to what I want you to do, Piero. I have sent two men out to attempt to reach the Duke and his army. I want you to try as well; I cannot spare any more of my men. I have them busy checking all the fortifications to make sure Ghirardino wasn't remaining here to dismantle any more of our defenses. In any event, the Duke may have already started for home; for all we know, he may have reached *Firenze* in which case he and his army will be the guest of Cosimo de Medici. I want you to go east toward Pèsaro."

"Why east?" Piero asked in astonishment.

"You will first take a message to the Duchess's father in Pèsaro and then continue south. Your route will be safest going east and then south along the Montefeltro's border with Sforza lands. Then head west over the mountains to *Firenze*. God willing, you will find the Duke there."

"And if not?" Piero asked.

"Seek an audience with the Medici, explain our situation and get word to the Duke from there, even if it means getting a fresh horse and continuing on to find the Duke yourself. Will you do it?"

"Yes," Piero answered without hesitation.

Captain San Martini clamped a massive hand on his friend's shoulder.

"I knew I could count on you. I want you to leave as soon as possible. Get some food to carry with you and leave within the hour."

Liz waited awkwardly by the door while the friends took their leave of each other.

"*Buona fortuna*, Luca."

"*Buon viaggio, mio amico, vai con Dio!*"

*   *   *   *

In addition to the soldiers and horses trying to leave the courtyard, a crowd of people with their children and possessions in tow poured into the courtyard, slowing down Piero and Liz's progress toward the kitchen. The result was a swirling mass of men-at-arms, horses, carts, families with screaming children, and their animals creating a traffic jam of monstrous proportions.

Buffeted by a donkey cart, Liz lost her footing and nearly collided with a hay-wagon. Piero pulled her to safety, and they squeezed past servants carrying baskets and crates of stores into the kitchen.

Catching their breath against a wall inside the kitchen, they watched a sea of noisy humanity pass by the open doorway seeking a safe haven within the thick fortress-like walls of the *Palazzo* whose graceful design belied its original purpose.

"Why are all these people entering the *Palazzo* courtyard? Aren't the city walls enough to protect them?" Liz asked.

"They are mostly the country people, who would have no protection outside the walls of the city. Some are residents of the city who feel safer inside the *Palazzo*. Up here on the hill, the *Palazzo* provides a clear vantage point from which to survey the surrounding countryside. And it's too high for the big cannon to reach us up here. Our enemy knows that as well and may have developed new weapons to reach us. But, first they'll try to breach the walls."

Liz had information from her old life that the original buildings in the *Palazzo* had been expanded to form an architectural gem, but the thick stone walls could still withstand repeated assault from engines of war.

The early, more primitive armaments—such as catapults, battering rams, and the fearsome trebuchet—had given way to cannon and artillery. The Duke, first and foremost a master of the military arts, had made it his business to storm and successfully capture enough fortresses to learn what mistakes the defenders had made that had supplied him with his victory. These lessons had served him well, and he had fortified Urbino so that the entire city was an impregnable fortress.

"The Duke will help the country people rebuild their homes and reclaim their land. The people know this. They are here to fight with us, to defend their city. Do you see Mistress Isabella?" Piero asked Liz.

Liz shook her head as her eyes roamed over the crowded kitchen. Piles of stores were heaped in every corner, and Liz jumped up on a barrel to get a better view. She spotted Mistress Isabella and pointed and yelled to Piero.

"She's over there, to the left of the hearthplace."

She jumped down, and taking Piero's hand, they threaded their way through the mass of people and materiel to reach Mistress Isabella's side.

She was directing the transport of the stores down the steps to the vast labyrinth in the lower reaches of the *Palazzo*.

"I gave instructions that the crates and barrels be labeled and placed so you can read the labels, but I know what will happen. Be careful there!!" she shouted at one poor soul who caught her eye.

"Mistress Isabella," Piero bent to whisper in her ear. "Captain Luca wants me to try to reach the Duke, and he has ordered me to leave right away. Can you have some food prepared for me to take?"

"For me too, Mistress Isabella," Liz piped up, "I'm to accompany him."

"Oh, no, you're not!" Piero rounded on Liz.

"Yes, I am!"

"Impossible."

Piero took Liz's arm and pulled her a little ways off until he found a quiet corner.

"I'm not staying here while you go off. How do I know you can get back in here once the siege begins? And besides, you may need me," Liz argued.

"Ssh! Lower your voice," Piero sputtered. "You'll slow me down."

"No I won't. *Argento* and I can keep up. I won't stay here!"

"You'll be safe."

"Don't make me laugh. I'd be safer with you riding to find the Duke than I would be in here when the fighting starts. And what if *Zingaro* goes lame? What would you do without me and *Argento* to help you?"

Piero clenched and unclenched his fists and glared at her.

"Please, Piero, I would rather take my chances with you out there than stay here and worry about you. Please!"

*   *   *   *

Moments later they were in their quarters stuffing a change of clothing into saddle bags. Liz took soap, towels, her comb, and the unmentionable clean cloths for sanitary use.

"Why do you need all that?" Piero asked.

"I think you would call it my 'course'."

"Oh! I'll take an extra oilskin for you."

"I can take the food and water on *Argento* because we'll each have a blanket, oilskin, and clothes, and you'll have the weapons and ammunition to carry."

"Good. We'll deal better with the supplies when we get to the horses. *Andiamo!*"

After one last meeting with Luca to pick up the message from the Duchess and to let him know Cosimo was going along, they departed on their mission to find the Duke and his army.

CHAPTER 16

▼

Horses laden with their provisions, they left the eastern gate of the city—the same one they had used on their last ride together. Only this time, they were on serious business, not in search of fun. The weather was holding, and they set off at an easy canter. They would need to pace their horses if they wanted them to be strong enough to carry them as far as *Firenze*.

"At the stream, we'll make our first stop to rest the horses and let them drink," he said.

There was no need to identify the stream, for she knew what stream he meant.

After a short silence, she asked, "How long should it take us to reach Pèsaro?"

"Not long, about an hour or more past the stream. The plain is flat, and the weather is fair; I would say not later than mid-afternoon. I'll deliver the message from the Duchess to her father, and then we'll be off."

"Maybe the Lord of Pèsaro will give us something to eat so we can save our provisions for tonight on the road."

"*Buon' idea!*"

Liz's main worry was the completion of her image on the wall of the chapel, which would now have to wait until their return to the city. And nagging at the back of her mind was the greater worry that her escape route back to her own time would be lost forever if the Duke's forces were not able to withstand the onslaught from Malatesta's army. She hoped and prayed the chapel would still be standing with her image intact when they returned.

"Tell me why this Malatesta fellow is attacking the city. What's that all about? I don't understand how he can just do that."

"Doesn't that happen where you come from? Or should I say when you come from?"

"In some places, it still does. There are wars, mostly prompted by age-old rivalries and blood feuds. You know, your people killed my people hundreds of years ago, so now it's my turn."

"So it still goes on. People still live in fear. I had hoped all wars would have ended."

"No, I'm afraid war still happens. Only the consequences are far more deadly. There was a world war fought to end all wars, but it didn't work."

Piero was silent trying to digest her words.

"Strange, I have never asked you when you ..."

"2007 A.D."

"Five hundred years."

"Closer to 550 years, I think."

"And you don't have any idea how this happened?"

"Well, I do, but it's just a guess on my part. Did you secure the amulet in your room before we left?"

"Yes, why?"

"Because I think somehow it is the cause. It may emit some kind of kinetic energy. I think it was responsible for opening the time portal, and I fell through it. Maybe it was meant to be me, and I am here for some purpose, or just anyone would have come through. I don't know."

In what seemed like a very short while, they reached the stream and dismounted to rest the horses. Liz walked *Argento* and *Zingaro* around to cool them off before letting them drink.

Piero rested under a tree and gazed at her thoughtfully. Then he joined her at the edge of stream. They stood together and watched the horses drink. Silence coiled like a snake between them. Lost in their own thoughts, they never expected the snake would strike.

"So you intend to return then?" he asked.

His question took Liz by surprise, and the tone of his voice made her heart leap.

"When you finish the image of me on the chapel wall, the thought occurred to me that if you brought the amulet near the wall, it might re-open the portal. I might get back through. Don't you want to be rid of me?"

"I don't know. I've come to depend on you."

"A lot of people in my own time depend on me."

Piero turned away before he blurted out something stupid as his thoughts warred with each other in his brain. He knew he should say something—anything—to convince her to stay. But mightn't it be better for Cosimo if she did return to her own time. After all, what could he offer her, certainly not security, the life of a painter living on commissions that could dry up at the whim of a patron? Or where danger lurked everywhere? He would miss her, it was true, for he had come to have feelings for her. Was that enough to make a life together? He wanted to say so much, but he said nothing.

Liz cleared her throat and reached for the horses' reins.

"I think we should get going."

"You're right." He took *Zingaro*'s reins.

"And try not to cause me any more delays, all right?" Liz teased.

This elicited a smile from Piero, lightening the mood, which was exactly what she intended.

When they were mounted and following a northeasterly track, they picked up the thread of their earlier conversation.

"You were going to tell me about this Malatesta and the feud with Duke Federico."

"Not just with the Duke, although their rivalry goes back about twenty years."

"How old is the Duke now?"

"About forty years of age."

"The Duchess is so young," Liz commented, shaking her head.

"The families of the Malatestas and the Montefeltros originated in the same area. From the time of the Duke's grandfather, the families have vied with each other for territory, power and influence. The Duke's father, Guidantonio, managed to outdistance the Malatesta clan with his prowess as a military leader, a *condottiero* of immense skill. Even so, the Montefeltro found their territories slipping away, and with no access to the sea, their trade was limited."

"Then what happened?"

"The balance of power shifted. When the Duke took over the reins of power, he captured the Malatesta stronghold in San Leo. The Malatesta family ruled in Pèsaro, and the people of Pèsaro sent a secret mission to Duke Federico begging him to free them from Malatesta's tyranny. They claimed that Sigismondo Malatesta was cruel and arrogant and cited instances of outright murder and destruction by him and his henchmen. So Duke Federico mounted a campaign and ousted Sigismondo Malatesta and replaced him with a branch of the Sforza family."

"The Duchess's father."

"Yes, her uncle is the Duke of Milan."

"So the marriage sealed the relationship with the Sforza family and secured Pèsaro, on the seacoast, for the Duke."

"Exactly," he said with a nod before continuing.

"The Duke has struck an alliance with the Florentines, and brokered a peace between them and Venezia. He's a stabilizing influence in the whole region, and because of that, and his skill as a negotiator, he was called upon to head the Italian League which has managed only barely to keep the peace. The Pope and foreign kings have heaped honors on the Duke, and he deserved every one for he's a moral man and liberal leader. And the people of Urbino have prospered under his rule, while Malatesta has holed up in Mantua, just waiting for an opportunity to make his move. We fear that this present Pope may be helping Malatesta, which is why we must call upon the Duke's allies."

"He should have killed him when he had the chance."

"You're probably right. Luca would have been happy to do it."

"Did you ever meet this Malatesta?"

"Oh, yes, I worked for him right after my apprenticeship in *Arezzo* ended. I did several portraits for him."

"What's he like?"

"Let's just say, I left as soon as I could and came into the Duke's service. It happened because of Luca. I first met him in *Arezzo*."

He paused a moment while he negotiated *Zingaro* through a tricky patch of ground. Liz had not noticed, but they had left behind them the fertile lands with large tracts of forested area for the more exposed and windswept seacoast. They had traveled on remnants of an ancient Roman road for part of their journey and skirted small farms and settlements, but the view now was bleak and deserted.

"You must understand what happened in Urbino to inspire such love for the Duke among his people."

Liz was absorbed in the tale and waited for him to continue the story. When he didn't resume, Liz asked, "What was it that happened?"

"Am I boring you with this talk?"

"No, you monster, continue and be quick about it. What happened?"

Piero chuckled and picked up the story.

"When the Duke's father died, control passed to his legitimate son, Oddantonio, who was by all accounts just as bad a character as Malatesta."

"You're joking."

"No, he was a fiend, a rapist, and a murderer. There was no depravity in which he would not indulge. And he had his friends too, like Malatesta, who were just as bad."

"So what happened?"

"The people rose up, stormed the *Palazzo* one night, dragged him out and killed him."

The idea that the people of Urbino, whom she found to be kind and gentle, could rise up and murder anyone shocked her beyond belief.

"Look," Piero said, "there's Pèsaro. We'll be there in a few minutes."

Liz was not to be distracted so easily, besides Pèsaro, after a quick glance in the direction Piero pointed, was not as impressive as Urbino. It looked like a backwater.

"So then the Duke took over? And the people accepted him?"

"Not as easily as that. When his brother was ruling in Urbino, the Duke was living in Mantua where he'd been raised while being held hostage ever since he was a boy."

"Wow!"

"So the people of Urbino begged him to come to Urbino and take over their government. When he agreed and returned to the city, he got a surprise. The elders and merchants of the city met him outside the gates of the city, greeted him very cordially, and presented him with a Code of Conduct—rules they expected him to follow. They respectfully requested that he sign the document and agree to its terms."

"And he did."

"Yes."

"Or they would give him the same treatment they gave his brother, right?"

"Right. But, he surpassed all their expectations. He's much loved by his people."

"And you said Oddantonio was the legitimate son of Guidantonio. Does that mean that Duke Federico is illegitimate?"

"Yes."

"That's quite a story. And it just goes to show you that you can never assume anything about anybody."

"That's right."

"We're here. There's the Costanza Fortress up ahead.

"The rest of the town doesn't look like much, but the fortress is pretty impressive."

"We'll present ourselves, and I'll request an audience with the Duchess's father. Meanwhile, you see to the horses and getting us something to eat if you can. I hope this won't take too long, but you never know with the nobility."

"Can't you just leave the message for …"

"No, Luca wants me to present it to him personally and stress with him that attack is imminent. In case the Duchess has to flee with young Lord Guidobaldo, her father's got to be prepared to receive her here."

"You think it could come to that?"

"I hope not."

Piero and Liz entered the fortress under the watchful eyes of the guards. They pulled up their horses in the courtyard and were led to the Captain of the Guard. Then Piero followed the Captain and two other soldiers into the fortress. Liz was left to tend the horses. No one approached her to offer her any assistance.

She led the horses over to a water trough and stood with them while they drank. She surveyed her surroundings and could see that there was little prosperity here, unlike Urbino, for the courtyard was ill kept with piles of foul smelling rubbish everywhere and cracked and dirty windows in the buildings.

Eventually, one of the guards strolled over to talk to her. He was as dirty and ill kept as the courtyard, with a torn, badly patched uniform. Greasy-haired and unshaven, he reeked of body odor as if he hadn't bathed in weeks. Liz sensed that beneath his filthy uniform, his heart skipped in anticipation of a juicy bit of gossip from this outsider. In Pèsaro, as in Urbino, the rumor mill—a very dubious source of information—was all there was to make sense of their world. Information added to one's status, and this fellow looked like he could use a step up in status.

"*Buon giorno*," he said to Liz. "I'm Marco." His grin revealed a mouth full of rotten teeth.

Liz smiled and sidestepped around him to put some space between her and the vile smells wafting in her direction from his entire person.

"Good day to you, *signore*. I must tend to the horses for my master. Clean hay would be most welcome."

He led her toward the stable and left her without another word. He appeared to be pissed off about something, but she had no intention of spending more time around him, not when she had the care of the horses.

After making sure that the horses were getting clean hay with no trace of mildew, she asked a ragged stable boy for the way to the kitchen. She found it easily enough, but was dismayed to see that it was as filthy as the rest of the place and decided against getting anything to eat or drink.

Liz returned to the horses and checked their saddles and the bundles to make sure everything was secure and then sat down to wait. She wanted desperately to relieve herself, but decided it was too dangerous until they were clear of the city.

After an hour or so, she spied Piero returning with the Captain of the Guard. She stood between the horses with her head cast respectfully down. Piero took his leave of the Captain, and they mounted their horses and made for the fortress gate. As they picked up their pace and cantered away, Liz saw the soldier called Marco looking at them from the corner of the courtyard. Liz thought nothing of it, but was content to leave dirty Pèsaro behind them.

When they cleared the city, Liz could contain her curiosity no longer.

"How did it go?"

"Well enough. It's hard to tell with the nobility. At first the old man said nothing, just took the letter and read it, but I think he will receive his daughter and grandson should it come to that. At the end, he nodded and said "very well." Did you get any food?"

"No. The kitchen was dirty beyond belief so I decided against it. We'll eat what we have."

"Fine."

They continued east, and in minutes, the landscape changed again. The ground became uneven and rocky with limestone outcroppings causing them to slow their pace. Soon, Liz heard the unmistakable roar of the ocean. After riding to the top of a slight rise, the Adriatic stretched to the horizon.

They slowly descended to the narrow, rocky beach. The air was fresh and clean with that wonderful sea scent that Liz loved. As they neared the soft sand by water's edge, *Argento* shied and backed away from the sight and sound of the water. He snorted as if he didn't care for the smell either.

"What's wrong with you?" she asked *Argento*, wrestling for control of the powerful young horse.

"I don't think he has ever seen the sea before so it must frighten him," Piero said.

He sat regally on *Zingaro* who was calmly ignoring the water.

Liz gave *Argento* his way and stopped fighting him. The horse returned to the edge of the rise they had clambered down.

"I'm going to relieve myself," she called to Piero.

Piero waved in acknowledgment as Liz dismounted and walked to a nearby cluster of boulders. She still held the horse's reins.

Still mounted on *Zingaro*, Piero rode down the beach to give Liz the privacy she needed and to take care of his own business. He calculated how much longer it would take to reach *Firenze*. He knew they would be able to travel south along the seacoast for miles before they turned inland at Monte Conero. They might pass a few fishing villages, but if they met no obstacles, they would reach the Frasassi Caves where they could rest and eat before continuing.

They would cross through Umbria and reach Medici lands early in the morning and should arrive in *Firenze* by late afternoon tomorrow. By his reckoning, with luck, they would find the Duke camped with his army on the outskirts of *Firenze*.

Liz had gone behind one of the boulders with a clean cloth from her bag and left *Argento* munching on salt hay that poked up from the rocky dunes. She squatted to relieve herself, replaced her sanitary cloth with a clean one and covered up her urine and dirty cloth, like a cat in a litter box. She was in the process of pulling up her breeches when she was shoved from behind down into the sand by a powerful blow that forced the air from her lungs and left her gasping.

In an instant, a pair of hands grabbed at her and threw her onto her back. Other hands grasped her breeches and pulled them down further. Two soldiers from Pèsaro—the dirty one named Marco—and another one who she had never seen before pinned her to the ground.

Liz forced air back into her lungs before Marco straddled her. She screamed before he clamped a dirty hand over her mouth. Her scream startled *Argento* who took off up the beach at a gallop.

"We had orders to follow you. Imagine my surprise to see you squat to piss. You never told me, and I thought we became such good friends," Marco muttered contemptuously.

He was so close as he leered at her that she could smell his breath which stank of onions and garlic. The other soldier had her hands and arms pinned down over her head in a vise-like grip. She was completely at their mercy, vulnerable to assault.

"Enough talk, Marco. Do it before the man comes back. I want a turn too," the other soldier said.

Liz ceased struggling against her attackers. Marco mistook her attempt to quell her fear for acquiescence and removed his hand from her mouth to fumble with his breeches. Liz screamed and renewed her efforts to unseat him.

At that moment, she heard the sound of hoofbeats. Both men heard it too, and the soldier holding her arms released her to stand to look. That was all Liz needed. She made a fist and struck Marco in the softest part of his throat. Next, Liz grabbed the booted foot of the other soldier and gave a mighty yank. He sprawled on the sand, but scrambled to his feet in time to greet an angry Piero coming at him with his knife drawn.

It was Marco's turn to gasp for air as he tried vainly to recover. In one swift movement, Liz had gotten to her knees and pulled her breeches up. Covering her nakedness seemed important, but it cost her two precious seconds, enough time for Marco to grab at her.

The other soldier was no match for Piero, who was almost twice his size.

Marco drew his knife, and Liz readied herself for a fight for her life.

She surprised him with a well-placed kick straight to his mid-section. She closed in and jabbed her thumb in Marco's eye, and he bellowed in rage. She brought her knee up in a violent thrust to his groin, and he crumpled to the ground. Liz knelt on his neck, grabbed the knife, and turned her attention to Piero. She saw Piero slit the throat of the other soldier. She heard a gurgling sound and stared in utter horror as blood gushed from the soldier. Then, as he lay still, the sand around him turned crimson.

Piero pulled Liz off Marco, and calmly and methodically slit his throat too. Despite her hatred for the man who only moments before had attempted to rape her, she crawled away unable to control her revulsion. She was seized by paroxysms of vomiting caused by the smells emanating from the two dead men.

Several minutes passed before she recovered sufficiently to return to the scene. Piero glanced at her momentarily while he dragged Marco down to the water and threw his body into the surf. Shaking so uncontrollably that she was of no use, she sank to the ground and watched helplessly as he repeated the process with the other soldier.

Piero walked over to Liz where she knelt on the sand and opened his arms to her. She ran to him, wrapped her arms around him, and wept into his chest. It had happened so quickly, only minutes, and yet it seemed as if time had stood still.

"Are you all right, *cara*, did they hurt you?" he asked into her hair.

"I'm all right."

She stepped back and looked up at him with tear stained eyes. "What can I do to help?"

"There must be no trace. The sea will take them," he said looking over his shoulder at the bodies bobbing in the surf. "We'll leave no sign on the beach. No one will come looking for them until tomorrow morning. By then, the sea will have removed all trace of what happened here."

"Why did you have to kill them?"

"Because they would have killed us both. Or if they managed to get away and got back to Pèsaro, they would have told everyone you were a woman, and we can't have that getting back to Urbino. It would complicate things for us. I can't believe you would waste any pity on those two after what they tried to do. They would have raped you and murdered both of us. Do you require more reasons?"

"You're right," she agreed, but she was far from sure.

"What's done is done. Let's clean up quickly and get away from here."

CHAPTER 17

▼

Zingaro's nostrils flared as the powerful horse breathed in great gulps of air. Lathered, sides heaving, he whinnied loudly causing *Argento* to shy and prance away. *Argento* too was covered in lather, and his withers twitched from the strain of their journey. Piero had pushed the horses hard—harder than he should have. Anxious to put as many miles as he could between them and that morning's scene of bloody horror on the beach, he charged hell-bent down the coast and inland into the hills.

Not a word passed between Liz and Piero about the attempted rape or the two soldiers who had lost their lives. Not even when they stopped briefly to rest the horses.

Liz was as spent as the horses and moved slowly and painfully as she dismounted. Piero helped her and winced at the sight of the wicked bruises that stood out starkly against the pallor of her skin.

✳   ✳   ✳   ✳

Night had fallen by the time they reached the remote sanctuary of the Frasassi caves. Piero put down the oilskins on the cold ground, and Liz wrapped herself in blankets before lying down inside the entrance to one of the caves.

"I'm going to walk the horses to cool them down and see if I can find a source of fresh water. Don't be afraid. I'll be close by." He was unsure if she heard him, but then, like one drugged, she nodded in response.

As he unsaddled the horses, he gazed up at the star-studded sky and agonized over whether to bring up the deadly encounter with the soldiers. Maybe, he decided at last, it would be best to let her broach the subject first, if she wanted to.

Liz needed a hot meal and sleep. He knew the bruises would heal, but she had been brutalized, and her spirit would take time to recover. And as for the horses, before he put more demands on them, they needed at least several hours rest. He knew that their survival and the success of their mission depended on the horses. Otherwise, they might never make it to the Duke's encampment. The burden of his mission and his care of Liz and the horses weighed heavily on him.

The Frasassi caves were the perfect shelter where they could have a meal and rest the horses and themselves in safety before continuing on their journey.

Piero found a spring-fed pool of fresh water. While he filled their water bags, the horses drank their fill. The air was fresh and cool. Abundant pine and hickory forests grew over a thick carpet of ferns and mosses. While the horses grazed, he returned with the water bags. Liz was no longer on the blankets.

He saw firewood piled near the entrance and heard sounds from inside the cave. He started a fire and soon had a blaze going to brew tea and cook some of their food.

Liz came out of the cave and again wrapped herself in a blanket. Sitting by the fire, she looked so small and fragile that she reminded him of a child waiting to be told a story.

"I found a fresh spring. If you want, I can heat up some water for you to wash," Piero suggested.

She stared into the fire and ignored his remark.

"What are these caves?" she asked, her voice listless with exhaustion.

"They extend for miles from the seacoast until they disappear into the Appennino Mountains. They reach all the way from here—the Marche—into Umbria."

Liz picked up a piece of firewood and poked it in the fire. She got to her feet and walked back into the cave with the lit torch.

Piero continued to prepare their food and called to her when it was ready.

She came out of the cave and sat near the fire. "There are drawings and carvings on the walls of the cave," she remarked. "I'd like to look at them again in the daylight, if we have time."

"We'll see," Piero answered. "It's not surprising. Who knows what you would find in there? Ancient people called Piceni once made their home in the caves. Long before the Romans and the Etruscans, they lived here. The Umbri lived further inland. They gave the region of Umbria its name. It's sad in a way. Those drawings are likely the only thing to mark their passing."

"Yes, it is," Liz nodded. "This world is fleeting, for all of us. We have our time, and then we are gone."

With that final truth said, they sat quietly eating their meal while the horses continued to graze nearby.

The night was brilliantly clear, and the full moon bobbed like a float on a dark sea. They listened as the cricket song swelled as if it had been ordered especially to accompany their meal.

When they finished eating, he replenished their tea and sat next to her on the blanket.

"I've never seen anyone killed before," Liz said, breaking the silence. "Once, my friend's father was killed in an accident, and I went to his funeral. That was the only time I came close to death."

"You are fortunate. I have seen too much death. There was a time, when I was young, when illness spread very quickly, and the dead were piled in the streets. My father died in one such plague shortly before I was born. The first time I saw the dead stacked in the street like cords of wood, I became sick. But then strangely, I became accustomed to it."

"I don't think I could ever become accustomed to it."

"No, maybe you would not. But now, you must rest. I will be standing guard so you have nothing to fear."

"What about you?"

"I'll rest tomorrow when we reach *Firenze*."

Liz lay back on the makeshift bed of oilskin-covered blankets. Piero covered her with another blanket and sat down near the fire. The familiar night sounds kept him company as he watched her sleep.

She had removed the bandage from her head, and the firelight played on her hair, turning it first to silver and then to gold like an alchemist's trick. Free to indulge himself, he studied every detail with his artist's eye. The fire cast shadows over her features, and he knew one day, very soon, he would paint her portrait.

What was it about her that provoked such feelings? he wondered. He confronted his feelings—a heady mixture of respect, tenderness, admiration, and lust. He accepted that he was willing to do anything to keep her with him. He would fight to protect her. He had killed to protect her, and he would kill again, if necessary.

In this solemn place, among the wandering souls of the ancients, he admitted to himself for the first time that he considered tying himself down to one woman. Up until this moment, the mere idea of marriage meant nothing but a loss of his freedom. And so, he had always made it his business to avoid the trap. But with

Cosimo, it was different, maybe because she was different. She was not a silly woman full of vanity or venom, who made unreasonable demands on him or expected him to dance attendance upon her. Instead, she was bright and resourceful, and her presence never failed to soothe him.

She was a paradox, modest and beautiful at the same time. He could see himself making a life with her. What more, he asked himself, could a man wish for?

Besides, he was tired of running from women. Maybe, he thought with a shake of his head, it was time he let himself be caught.

As he watched her sleep, thoughts tumbling pell-mell through his brain, he remembered the kiss they had shared. He had never been kissed like that before. He had lain with a woman only three times in his life, and each time had been a hasty, clumsy fumbling in the dark. He thought at the time that he liked the young women well enough. But there had been no heat. There hadn't been time. It was a hurried business that left him disappointed.

Certainly nothing worth sacrificing one's freedom for.

Piero now found himself wishing for a closeness with Cosimo that could only come with sharing the same bed—forever.

He got up and added more wood to the fire. Squatting near the fire, he dropped his head in his hands. However do I speak of love to this young woman? Do I just blurt it out? Do I tell her how I feel? How do I put it into words? He despaired of finding any answers to these questions. He was an artist, not a poet.

His thoughts stopped as a nasty thought popped into his head. What if she doesn't want me? How can I be certain she feels the same? What if …? There must be a way to convince her to stay. To marry.

Marry! He who for so long had adroitly avoided marriage. The irony of the situation in which he found himself made him laugh, but he checked his laughter before he woke her.

Liz stirred in her sleep and made little whimpering sounds. When she thrashed around, Piero was there in an instant to hold her as she awoke from her nightmare. He shook her gently and whispered her name. She sat upright suddenly, her eyes wide with fear, panting as if she had been running.

"Cosimo, wake up!"

She looked at him with unseeing eyes. Piero shook her again, and this time she focused on his face, fully awake.

"Piero!" Liz cried between sobs. She clung to him. After a few moments, her crying subsided, and he felt her relax in his arms. He stroked her hair and murmured soothing endearments.

"I wanted to go to the beach with you, for us to be together," she said at last through her tears. "Instead, it has turned into this awful memory. I see their faces … I can't get them out of my mind."

"You must! It is done. You cannot dwell on it. No harm will come to you ever again. I promise!"

Unprepared for the intensity of his words, she freed herself from his embrace and turned to look at him. Her breath caught in her throat. Fire glowed in his green eyes. Liz recoiled at the depth of his passion—so long buried only inside his art—but visible now and dangerously close to flaring up and consuming them.

Fearful of being burned like a moth is burned by the flame, Liz hesitated, but then she recalled the promise she made to herself and knew that she could not turn away from the love he was offering her.

Her hand drifted slowly to his face and touched his lips. Never taking his eyes from her face, he grasped her hand with both of his and kissed it fervently.

He pulled her down with him on the blankets, and they lay together for long moments just looking at each other. Tentatively, gently, they kissed.

Liz clung to him. She wrapped her arms around him and pressed herself against the length of his body.

Her response intoxicated him, and he kissed her cheeks, her eyes, and the tender hollow at the base of her throat. Caught up in the night, the warmth of the fire, and the mingled scent of their bodies, they explored each other with their hands and their mouths.

In the unknowing dark, they existed only for each other. They laughed as they frantically shrugged themselves out of their clothing and surrendered to their desires.

Piero caressed her breasts. He filled her with delight when he ran lazy circles with his tongue on her breasts, avoiding her nipples until she thought she would scream her need out into the night. He gripped her hips as he coaxed and licked at first one breast and then the other until fire traveled to her innermost core. His kisses trailed down from her breasts to her taut midriff and slightly rounded belly.

"Ah, I've waited too long to feel like this. It's you. You make me feel like it's the first time," he whispered.

He looked down at her from what seemed like a very great height, and the warmth emanating from him set her ablaze.

"My thoughts exactly, *caro mio*, let's not wait another moment."

His eyes widened in wonder. Before she had a chance to change her mind, he positioned himself between her legs. She reached for him and guided him into her. In one swift stroke, he encased himself fully. Resolving to prolong their first coupling as long as he could, he made slow, measured thrusts to bring them to the edge of bliss. Then he stopped and kissed her passionately.

In this way, he was able to maintain their lovemaking for long minutes of delirium before she wrested control from him. Her desire for release overwhelmed him, and he gave in to the captivating tremors deep within her that shook his resolve and took them to the brink one final time. Their bodies covered in a fine sheen like a silken cocoon, they hurtled over the edge into paradise.

*   *   *   *

Later, hours before dawn, they stirred and broke camp. The horses—with full bellies and restored energy—strained at the reins and flew at a gallop as if the devil himself was on their tail. *Argento* tried to keep up and match the larger horse's stride.

Liz barely had time for one last wistful look back at the campsite where she had known such happiness. Piero caught her look and smiled. He sensed what she was thinking. He knew that recapturing that moment in time was nigh impossible, but he was ready and willing to give it a try.

Even though the night sky was lit with a full moon, the terrain was rugged, so Piero subdued *Zingaro's* headstrong plunge. He slowed the pace down lest a spill bring down both horse and rider.

They rode side by side, letting the steady tattoo of the hoofbeats lull them into a state of post-coital tranquility. They spoke to each other in whispers even though they had not seen a soul since they left the seacoast.

Liz's thoughts turned again and again to their lovemaking. It had been lush and juicy, and she continued to savor the taste of it as she would a particularly pleasant meal. Piero had murmured sweet words of love in her ear afterward as they were gathering up their clothes. She never understood the meaning of a "sweet nothing." And now she understood what the expression meant. How lucky I am! she thought, nearly pinching herself to convince herself she wasn't dreaming.

After they had finished making love, they bathed in the spring and dressed hurriedly, the pangs of guilt reminding them that this trip had a greater purpose than giving them the opportunity to be alone and indulge themselves in carnal delights.

Piero was optimistic that they would reach *Firenze* by late morning and find the tents of Duke Federico's army encamped on the outskirts of the city. He led the way west, sticking to the main route through the mountains. And he was right, for they made good time, and other than the occasional small herd of cattle or night-hunting birds of prey, they saw nothing.

When they stopped at daybreak to rest the horses and let them drink at an inviting stream, Liz and Piero dismounted and drank from their water skins.

"We'll be through the mountains soon. We'll bypass *Arezzo*," he said between gulps from his water skin. "As soon as we see the Arno, we'll follow it through the *Val di Chiana* to *Firenze*."

Liz nodded as she stooped to fill her water skin from the stream.

"This water is sweet," Liz said, as she cupped her hands and drank from the stream.

"Not as sweet as you, Cosimo," he said, beckoning her.

Their eyes locked, and Liz rose and walked toward him.

"Cosimo," Piero pulled her to him for a kiss.

"Wait, Piero. Now that we are lovers, I must tell you...."

"What more could there be to tell me, *cara*?"

The question made Liz smile.

"Well, for one thing, my name. It's not Cosimo."

"Of course, it isn't. It can't be," he said with a rueful laugh. "Tell me, *cara*. What are you called?"

"Elizabeth, I mean, Elisabetta."

"A sweet name. And is there nothing else you must tell me? No other secret?"

"A lot more, but we have a lifetime, no?"

"*Spero di sì, cara*."

"I hope so too."

After this heartfelt exchange, they kissed again and mounted the horses, bound for *Firenze*.

CHAPTER 18

▼

After riding the rest of the morning, they cleared the mountains, as Piero called them, but to Liz they were more aptly called foothills, or "Piedmont."

Now, with the sun climbing high in the sky, they peered down from the crest of the last hill above *Firenze*. The city lay below them, spread like a silken carpet of ochre walls and red tile roofs.

Piero pulled his spyglass from his blanket roll and surveyed the city. He moved the glass from north to south. Firenze nestled in a curve of the Arno River, as a beautiful woman lolls in the arms of a hopeful lover, and sunlight glistened off the river in the morning sun, turning it into a shiny satin ribbon.

"There!" he cried.

He passed the glass to Liz. With a little practice, she focused the glass and picked out the *Ponte Vecchio* proudly straddling the river like a splay-footed queen. She followed the river south and spied a massive camp on the outskirts of the city.

"Can you see the camp? Look down and to the right—by the river."

"I see it!" she called out.

The camp looked like a movie set with pennants floating in the breeze atop the tents, tether lines with horses, men walking about and bathing in the river, and sunlight glinting off spears and shields.

"Come, Elisabetta, let's get to them quickly."

"That's the first time you've said my name," she said. Her heart hammered in her chest at the sound of his voice speaking her name.

"Only out loud. In my heart, your name sings."

"If you don't stop saying things like that, you'll have me wanting to make love constantly."

"And is this a bad thing, *cara?*" he asked, a playful grin lighting his face.

"When we rejoin people, and I mean now, when we go down there to the Duke's camp, I'm your apprentice again, remember?"

"Yes, you're right" he replied soberly. "But I don't have to like it."

"I don't like it either, but we can't look at each other like moon-faced fools and speak to each other in any way differently than we did before, or we'll give ourselves away."

"I agree. But we must resolve this situation soon."

"When we get back to Urbino and this conflict is settled, we'll find a way to be together."

"Always."

"Let's go down there now like actors going out onto the stage and make our audience believe only what we want them to believe."

$$* \qquad * \qquad * \qquad *$$

They rode into the camp to the shouted welcome of the soldiers who immediately recognized the dusty horses and their riders as *paesani* from home.

Piero waved in greeting and threaded his way, Liz trailing behind, through the maze of campfires and clusters of soldiers. On a rise in the middle of the camp stood a large tent flying the eagle pennant of Duke Federico.

They dismounted in front of the tent, and Piero greeted one of the sentries by name. He tossed *Zingaro's* reins to Liz and strode into the tent with another sentry.

Liz drew the horses to an open space on the far side of the tent where a makeshift water trough had been set up. She let the horses drink while the activity of the camp swirled around her.

A short time later, Piero returned, and they led the horses a short distance away from the main camp into a small copse to an area where they could graze the horses and set up their own satellite camp.

"Did you see the Duke?" Liz asked when they were out of earshot.

"No, he's in the city. But they know about the siege. One of Luca's couriers reached the Duke during the night. He was wounded but managed to get the message through. We must assume the second courier was killed or captured. *Che Peccato!* What a pity! He was a good man. The Duke is conferring now with Piero de Medici, trying to get a contingent of Florentine militia to return with him to help defend Urbino."

"Piero de Medici? What about Cosimo?"

"The old man is not well. They don't expect him to live much longer, so the Duke is conferring with the son, Piero, and Cosimo's grandsons, Lorenzo and Giuliano."

"Lorenzo?"

"*Sì.*" He detected the mixture of surprise and wonder in her voice. "What is it?"

"Nothing. It's another one of those things I have to tell you."

Changing the subject, she asked, "When is the Duke expected back?"

"At any moment. They will send for me to give him my report. He plans to leave tonight once the men have rested for they only arrived yesterday morning. Whether we have any Florentines with us or not, he already informed his officers that he's going to march on Urbino come nightfall. The men will have had little more than twenty-four hours of rest."

"That doesn't seem like enough."

"It will be enough for them once word spreads through camp that their families are in peril. They'll be eager to return to defend their city. Besides, if the Duke says 'March!' they'll march."

"Will I get to meet him?"

"I'll see what I can do, *cara*, but if you do meet him, try not to stare."

"His eye?"

"Yes, he lost his right eye in a jousting tournament. And also, he has a hawk-like nose that was battered in the same tournament. He bears the signs and scars of many battles."

"If I could get used to Luca's appearance, I won't flinch when I set eyes on the Duke."

He laughed, and they went about unsaddling the horses and setting up their camp. Liz gathered wood while Piero went to scrounge some provisions from the Duke's soldiers.

They had a quick meal and were just finishing when they heard the jingle of harness and the shouts of the men heralding the return of Duke Federico and his party.

"Wait here, *cara*," Piero whispered.

He hurried to the Duke's tent and joined the sentries.

Liz's heart swelled with pride at the sight of him standing head and shoulders above the other men, the breeze ruffling his hair.

He was hers. She said it *sotto voce*, and it sounded strange to her ears, but there it is, she thought—undeniable—not just her mind—but her heart, body and soul reverberated with love for this man.

As the Duke neared, Piero looked back several times to reassure himself that she was still where he had left her. Even amid all the commotion, the Duke spotted Piero at once.

The Duke signaled to Piero, and he grasped the reins of the Duke's horse—an enormous white stallion with flaring nostrils and proud bearing.

Duke Federico dismounted and hugged Piero to him, giving both cheeks a kiss, and Piero went down on one knee in obeisance to this ugly little man who had endeared himself not only to his people, but to the man she loved!

The cheers from the men at the return of their commander prevented Liz from hearing any of the exchange between Piero and the Duke. She left the little copse and advanced a little so she could get a better look.

Undeniably, Duke Federico was the ugliest man Liz had ever seen. The years of battle and sovereignty had weighed heavily on him. In addition to a scar that pulled his right eyelid down and askew, he had a misshapen nose that looked like it had been broken several times. His skin was light olive in color, and he stood only about five foot, seven inches tall. His hair was black and worn very short, almost like a monk's tonsure.

His authoritative bearing commanded Liz's attention as he led Piero toward his tent, and she noticed that in addition to his scarred face, he had a wound to his leg or foot that caused him to limp.

It was nothing short of a miracle that he had survived so many grievous wounds and still commanded an army of loyal followers.

Piero beckoned to her, and she hurried to enter the Duke's tent three steps behind Piero, who immediately presented her to the Duke. She fell to one knee as she had seen Piero do.

"This is my young apprentice, Cosimo, Your Grace, who has served me well and insisted on accompanying me on this important mission. Our Luca, believe it or not, has come to value his brave heart and shrewdness. He has aided us in the defense of your city."

"Rise, young Cosimo, and let me look at you. I rely on Piero's sound judgment when he tells me you are worthy of my trust and favor."

Liz stood and gazed into his eyes which were nearly level with hers. This warrior prince who struck fear into the hearts of his enemies smiled warmly. She found that she could look at his deformed face without qualm. His remaining eye was dark brown, but it was his reassuring demeanor which conveyed not only his strength but his innate goodness. She could understand why the young Duchess had come to love this man.

The Duke turned his attention back to Piero, and Liz retreated to stand by the tent flap. A servant scurried in with a decanter of wine and cups on a tray followed by more servants bearing platters of food.

"Come, Piero, take a cup of wine with me and tell me of the situation in Urbino when you left. Have you eaten?"

"Yes, I have, Your Grace, thank you."

The Duke took the decanter from the servant and poured each of them a cup of wine, and they sipped companionably—the Duke stretched out on a divan—as Piero related to the Duke what had transpired and what measures Luca had taken to defend the city.

"He is concerned, Your Grace, that the Duchess and young Lord Guidobaldo could fall into Malatesta's hands, so he had me go first to Pèsaro to deliver a letter from the Duchess relating to her father the gravity of the situation. Luca was hopeful that Sforza would receive the Duchess and the young Lord should it come to that."

"She won't leave. She is headstrong and loyal. She would spit in Malatesta's eye at the first opportunity."

"I think Luca will not give her that opportunity. He realizes how vulnerable you would be should Malatesta take them hostage."

"He's a good man and will do what is necessary. And I will tell you this—I would rather be here dealing with the Medici than there in Luca's shoes telling the Duchess what to do."

The two men chuckled over that remark, while Liz, like a fly on the wall of the tent, marveled as these men traded jokes on the very eve of battle. After his refreshment, the Duke's lieutenants filed in, and the Duke relayed the results of his visit with the Medici.

"We leave at nightfall as planned. *Firenze* will provide several hundred armed *contadini* to accompany us to Urbino."

"Farmers with pitchforks," one of the lieutenants scoffed contemptuously. If he had not been standing in the Duke's tent, he would probably have spit for added measure.

Curses flew from the mouths of the other officers. One, in particular, his color rising ominously, added, "Is that all they can spare us after what we did for them in Siena?"

The Duke nodded. "And we owe even these to the good offices of Piero's sons, Lorenzo and Giuliano, for Piero is afraid to do anything at all. They convinced their father that he must honor Cosimo's agreement with me, so they are at least sending these. Lorenzo will come with us to command his forces, and they are not farmers with pitchforks—well, they are farmers, it is true—but they are strong and well armed for I have seen them, and they will swell our numbers. That fool Malatesta will fall back when he sees the size of the army marching against him which is all that is necessary. Giuliano will remain here to raise volunteers from the city militia should we need them. All in all, I am pleased with the result of my visit. Your orders are to break camp and be ready to march east before the sun sets. I want to see the walls of my city by sunrise. Now go!"

*   *   *   *

Piero and Liz took their leave of the Duke and sauntered through the encampment to their little patch of ground. The horses stopped grazing to watch them approach, and *Argento* whinnied and tossed his head in greeting. Liz borrowed a curry comb from one the soldiers and cleaned *Argento* while Piero made them tea.

"He's only going to need it again when we get back to Urbino," Piero said.

"I know, but he wants attention."

"You spoil him."

"That's because I've grown to love him. Are you jealous?" she teased.

"Now that you ask, I think I am."

Liz finished with the young horse and sat down next to Piero at the fire so they could drink their tea and watch the soldiers readying their weapons.

"We might as well get some rest while we can because it won't take us long to break camp," Piero commented, as he finished his tea and settled down for a nap.

*   *   *   *

"*Cara*, Elisabetta," Liz awoke to Piero's voice whispering in her ear. "Time to get up. The army is starting to move out. I have everything packed and the horses saddled."

"You should have awakened me so I could help."

"It is no matter. You were sleeping so peacefully, I didn't want to wake you. If you want to relieve yourself, go back into the trees there, and I will stand guard with the horses to screen you from view. We can have a quick wash at the river while the horses drink."

"Is it all right? We won't hold anyone up?"

"No. The Duke's *cavalleria* (cavalry) is leading the column, then the foot, and finally the wagons and artillery. Lorenzo's *contadini* will bring up the rear. And that's where we will ride, so we have plenty of time."

While Piero was explaining all this, Liz had risen and shaken and rolled her blanket so that it was ready to be tied to the back of her saddle. It was close to sunset so she hurried deep into the dark little copse of trees to relieve herself where none could see her.

In no time, the horses had drunk their fill and were ready to ride east behind the Duke's army.

Piero pointed and Liz looked to see a large contingent of men standing about in a rather haphazard manner—the *Fiorentini* who were waiting to fall in. They milled around as at a country fair, talking and gesticulating wildly in response to mounted men who were moving among them, trying to form them into some sort of cohesive unit.

From where Piero and Liz sat astride their horses, it was difficult to discern who was in charge. Unlike the Duke's men who wore uniforms with insignia, these men were dressed in country clothes with their weapons tied at their waists with cord or slung over their shoulders in leather scabbards. But, as a group, they appeared tall, strong, and robust with ruddy color on their cheeks.

"Do you see Lorenzo?" Liz asked.

"No. I don't see him among those on horseback."

"Would you know him if you saw him?"

"No. I've never met him, but I could guess. I have heard that he has a magnificent *castano* (chestnut) horse and almost never wears anything but brown. It's his trademark."

Armed with this information, Liz craned her neck and carefully scanned the horsemen again but saw no one to fit that description.

"It doesn't look like he's arrived yet," she said, relaxing in her saddle and abandoning her search.

"He's probably outfitting himself as befits a princeling. It is said he is a proud fellow who keenly appreciates his exalted position and is sensitive to any sign of disrespect. I'm certain he will be traveling in extravagant style."

"That takes time and planning."

"Exactly, and he's had little of either."

The *contadini* moved out behind the Duke's artillery and wagons. Piero and Liz fell in with them. The men shuffled along slowly, keeping pace with the wagons. After several minutes of trying to control the natural instincts of their horses to pass these slow moving creatures, Piero looked at Liz and shook his head.

"This will never do. Their mouths will be ripped from pulling on them all night. Let's ride up ahead of the wagons and let them set a faster pace."

They maneuvered the horses away and to the left of the *contadini* just as they spotted three riders on the road leading from the city. A light wagon trailed behind them at a short distance. The group veered in their direction.

In the growing darkness, Liz was barely able to make out the young man in the lead. He was dressed from head to foot in brown and mounted on the most beautiful horse she had ever seen. The horse was dark chestnut with a white blaze and was decked out with outrageously opulent trappings on saddle and bridle. As they got closer, still several hundred yards away, Liz got her first clear look at Lorenzo the Magnificent.

Brown suede fairly dripped from the top of his head to the tips of his toes. His cap was intricately worked with bands of gold and encircled his head like a fat *bandeau*. It held a cone shaped cloth in place which draped down one side of his head to end in a gold tassel. The cuffs of his riding gloves and knee-high suede boots matched his cap. A cape fell from his shoulders in soft folds. Gold spurs glittered on his feet, and a large topaz dangled from his right ear. He wore his hair long. It was dark brown, almost black, in color, and of a coarse texture. His complexion was swarthy, and his face bore the look not of a Tuscan youth, but more closely, that of an eastern prince. The overall effect was almost piratical, but it was not enough to disguise the fact that he was still a boy. Liz judged him to be no more than fifteen years old.

"Lorenzo de Medici," she murmured, a reverential tone in her voice, almost like a prayer, as they passed.

Piero and Liz had stopped to watch the new arrivals catch up to their cohort. Lorenzo and his companions moved to the front of the *contadini* to join the other mounted men in the lead, and they now rode six abreast.

She turned to Piero and felt her eyes well up.

"You can't possibly know what it means to me to see him, Piero. His name will go down in history as synonymous with the Age in which we are living."

"This boy?"

"Yes, this boy."

"You must tell me more, *cara*."

"I will tonight, *tesoro mio*, when we reach Urbino."

CHAPTER 19

▼

Urbino, Present Day

Passengers crowded into the aisle of the train, desperate to get ahead of their fellow travelers, as the train pulled into the Urbino rail station. Lou Cummings waited patiently to remove his bag from the overhead rack before joining the queue snaking its way up the aisle to the exit.

As he waited for the people in front of him to move, he peered out the rain-streaked windows, wondering if the train's twenty-minute late arrival meant he would have to find a taxi. He silently prayed that someone would still be waiting on the platform to meet him.

He stepped down off the train and searched the faces of people milling around on the platform. The crowd thinned as passengers hurried off, and his eye settled on two individuals by the outer gate—a man and a woman—who appeared to be looking his way. They exchanged a few words before slowly approaching him.

"Mr. Cummings?" the gentleman said, extending his hand.

Lou returned the gesture. "Mr. Nelson?"

"Yes. That's right. You resemble your sister quite a lot," Steve Nelson remarked, smiling awkwardly before turning to the woman next to him. "This is Dr. Grasso, the University liaison. We're sorry to welcome you to Urbino under such circumstances."

"If you mean the disappearance of my sister, I accept your apology. What I'm anxious to learn is what you've done about finding her."

Steve Nelson flinched as though he had been struck in the face, but Lou Cummings pulled no punches. Lou sized Nelson up as possibly inept or worse, maybe somehow complicit in Liz's disappearance.

His parents had received a call from this man, and then had immediately called him in California. Distraught, almost hysterical, they had exacted a promise from him. He would go to Italy in their place and bring Liz home, and he had every intention of fulfilling that promise.

"I'm here to find out what has been done and what has not been done to find my sister, and, if necessary, to pick up the search for her myself," he pressed. "I'm aware that for you and the University, this is an embarrassment or a situation, but please remember, it's much more for me. And for my parents. They're counting on me to find Liz. Accomplishing that is my only concern, and I expect full cooperation."

"I understand completely." Steve answered, swallowing hard and shifting nervously from foot to foot.

Lou could tell that Nelson was shaken by their exchange. He also noticed that the color of Dr. Grasso's face had gone considerably paler. Good, Lou reflected to himself, studying their faces, that's exactly why I've come, to shake them up.

They exited the gate three abreast into the rainy parking lot.

"We have a car waiting," Steve said leading the way to a tiny red car. "You must be tired from your long flight. Your room is waiting for you. Maybe you'd like to take a little rest."

Dr. Grasso put the key in the lock and opened the car door for him. He turned to ask her how she expected him to fit his six foot, three inch frame into the tiny car, only to see her holding the front seat forward for him to climb into the back seat.

"No thank you," he said in reply to Steve Nelson's suggestion. "I want to see my sister's room first." He wedged himself into the tiny back seat and curled his knees up to his chest.

"As you wish. Liz's room is exactly as she left it the day she disappeared. On the way, I'll try to answer your questions."

✳   ✳   ✳   ✳

Dr. Grasso inched the tiny car expertly along narrow angled streets clogged with traffic, the windshield wipers clicking noisily, but ineffectually at the rain.

"I'm afraid it is the time everyone is going home for *il pranzo*. That would be the mid-day meal," Dr. Grasso added, seeing the bewildered look on Lou's face. "It will be quiet later."

Steve Nelson sat up front in the passenger seat with Lou's bag wedged on the floor between his feet. Lou—squashed in the back like a huge bug in a tiny ant-sized shell—grunted in reply and turned his attention to the view from the little car window.

Something sinister about the glistening ancient stone streets prickled his skin and made him shiver. He decided he didn't like it.

"Everything appears very ... old," he remarked to no one in particular.

Steve slued around in his seat, as much as he was able in the cramped space, to face Lou.

"Coming from the States, that's the first thing everyone usually notices. You'll get used to it."

"I don't think I want to be here long enough to get used to it, if it's all the same to you," he responded sullenly.

"I'm sorry the car is so small," Dr. Grasso interjected. "It was the only one available to us. Not many people own a car in Urbino. But it is not far."

*   *   *   *

Lou expected to feel something when he crossed the threshold of Liz's room, but he was disappointed. Nothing of his sister lingered here to trigger a connection to her. She might never have been here at all. She was someplace else, he felt certain. An aura of cold impersonal sterility hung in the air, and Lou fervently hoped his sister had found a safe haven wherever she was.

Because the others were with him, and he had insisted on coming here first, he felt obligated to look around the room. Her personal items were piled on the left side of the dresser, her clothes folded neatly at the foot of the bed, her bags lined up in front of the closet door.

"It's not quite as she left it. The police wanted her roommate moved into another room, and they have been through Liz's possessions, looking for clues, I suppose," Dr. Grasso said.

"Tell me what happened ... from the beginning. Please."

He saw the look that passed between Dr. Grasso and Nelson. Dr. Grasso took a step toward Lou, her hands spread in supplication.

"Signor Cummings, why don't we go to the dining hall for coffee, and we'll tell you everything we know."

"We'll drop your bag off in the room we've assigned to you," Steve Nelson added. "It's on our way."

Lou thought this sounded too pat—as though they had rehearsed it beforehand. Like they were covering themselves against a lawsuit, but sued for what, he wondered.

*   *   *   *

Only a few diners lingered in the dining hall when they entered. Dr. Grasso directed him to a table and sat down with him while Nelson went to get the coffee.

"Turnabout is fair play, even in Italy, I see," Lou said.

"*Mi scusi?*"

"Never mind. That was just my lame attempt at humor."

Now it was Lou's turn to feel nervous. He looked around hoping Nelson hurried with the coffee.

Maybe, he thought, he should try switching the cups around in case they planned to poison him.

This silly idea made him chuckle, and Dr. Grasso looked at him like a bug had just crawled out from under his shirt collar.

Oh, great, he thought, here I am sitting with the most beautiful woman I've ever seen, and I make a total idiot of myself.

Steve Nelson approached the table with three cups of coffee on a tray. Dr. Grasso jumped up to help him, giving Lou the distinct impression that she wanted to scream and run out of the dining hall.

*   *   *   *

"So what you're telling me, Dr. Nelson, is that my sister left her room and vanished off the planet," Lou said, after hearing a recap of the events that brought him to Italy.

He gripped his coffee cup, his knuckles growing white, and stared at Steve Nelson.

"She went to her room. At some point, we don't know when, we think she left her room. We don't know where she went," Steve Nelson explained. "It wasn't until later that we realized she wasn't in her quarters. We phoned around the campus that evening. The next day, her things were found in the chapel."

"Then what?"

"We called the police immediately." Reacting to the hardened expression that appeared on Lou's face, Steve quickly explained. "You have to understand. At first, there was no reason for worry. We thought she possibly had met someone she knew and spent the night. After all, she was an adult …"

Lou winced. "You mean she is an adult, don't you?"

"Of course. I'm sorry. What I mean is, until we found her rather expensive camera and sketchbook, we thought she just forgot to tell anyone she wasn't coming back to her room. Just an innocent oversight. But we knew then that something was terribly wrong."

"We made copies of her picture and plastered the campus and the center of the city with them. The police said it was all right to do that," Dr. Grasso added.

"The police began to expand the search ..."

"It was awful. Every time they suggested a line of investigation, it was worse than the one before."

"They notified police departments in other cities. Train stations, bus stations, and airports were alerted."

Dr. Grasso lowered her head and looked as if she was about to cry.

"Very well," Lou conceded at last. "I'll grant you that everything was done that could be done. But what about her camera? That turned up nothing?"

"The police said it could have been left there by Liz or by someone involved in her disappearance or by some innocent bystander who simply found it. Lots of people go in and out of that chapel. Tourists, staff, workmen. But only her fingerprints were found on it. Every lead they explored went nowhere," Steve said, shaking his head.

"Two reports came in that Liz was seen traveling from Urbino to Venice," Dr. Grasso said, "but when they investigated, it turned out to be a student backpacker who looked like her, but, of course, it wasn't."

Lou sat back in his chair.

"What I'd like to do is look around myself for a bit. I'd appreciate it if you could set up an appointment for me with the police officer in charge of the investigation for tomorrow morning." He looked from one to the other.

"I have the card of the investigator in my office. I'll be happy to call him and make the appointment. And I'll get you a map of the campus," Dr. Grasso volunteered.

"Thank you." Lou stood and slid his chair under the table in a gesture of finality. The interview was over. But he got the feeling there was more they weren't telling him. He decided to play a waiting game, gain their confidence, and worm it out of them later.

If he made enough of a nuisance of himself, they would tell him everything or anything just to get rid of him.

*   *   *   *

Lou studied the map in between unpacking his bag. He numbered the sites on the map he wanted to explore in the order of their importance and stuffed the map in his knapsack with his camera and a bottle of water. He left the room, carefully locking the door behind him and pocketing the key.

His first stop would be the *Palazzo*. He had no trouble finding it in the narrow streets because it was a landmark clearly visible from every corner of the town.

On his way, he passed posters with Liz's picture on them. They were plastered on the walls of buildings and pasted in shop windows. The Italian written on the poster was unintelligible, but he had no trouble figuring out what the boldly printed word spread above Liz's picture meant—**Scomparsa**. She was missing, all right. He ripped down one of the posters, folded it, and stuffed it in the pocket with his room key.

When he reached the *Palazzo*, he stopped. He gazed up appreciatively at the building.

He decided to make a complete circuit of the building before entering so he had a notion of where the exits and entrances were. He noted that the doors and windows on the ground floor were alarmed.

Finally, he entered the building and got a pamphlet with the floorplan from the counter, paid his entry fee and went through the turnstile.

His destination was the chapel. He followed the diagram and barely noticed the art lining the walls of the corridor leading to the chapel. He was told there were workmen in the crypt beneath the chapel, but it was quiet and seemed deserted. He made a mental note to ask the detective in charge if these men had been checked out.

He stopped just inside the door of the chapel and let out a low whistle. Pretty impressive, he thought, and knew this place would draw Liz like a magnet.

Something happened here, he just knew it. But what?

He walked slowly around the chapel, his footsteps echoing on the marble floor.

A noise from across the chapel made him turn. The left wall shimmered like heat on the highway. Twelve to fifteen feet away from him, he saw it glow and pulsate.

He took a step toward the wall when a loud sound like an explosion filled the vast expanse. The blast sent him reeling backward, almost knocking him off his feet.

The sound of loud voices and running feet made him whirl around, looking for the source of the sound. At any moment, he thought a band of warriors would break through the wall and into the chapel to kill him.

If this happened when Liz was in the chapel, he wondered, if it was in fact what happened, if they came through and took her. Too fantastic, he decided.

Still, he covered the distance to the wall in four steps, took a deep breath and walked through the wall.

*   *   *   *

His legs buckled beneath him, as he landed on the floor. He clambered quickly to his feet, none the worse for wear except for slight dizziness. The building shook beneath him from another loud blast. Motes of plaster dust floated in the air.

He walked toward the exit of the chapel and saw it was blocked.

There had to be an exit somewhere so he searched for it and found an opening behind a large canvas.

When he pushed aside the canvas and stepped out of the chapel, a scene straight from hell greeted him. Screams of men and animals, foul smells and the sting of gunpowder that hung in the air made it difficult to breathe, forcing him to his knees.

He slid down the outer steps to the ground next to a barrel of water. Large chunks of rock landed around him as more shelling took out parts of the buildings and surrounding wall.

He plunged his head in the water barrel and came up spluttering. He struggled out of his shirt and dunked it in the water. The ground beneath his feet shuddered. He tied the shirt around his nose and mouth and took a few unsteady steps.

Where? Which way? People streamed past him toward a building to his right so he went along with them, sticking close to the wall and hoping a rock didn't land on his head.

Loaded carts and wagons blocked his way but he skirted around them, always staying as near to the wall as he could. A courtyard opened up near the building, and armed men dressed in a uniform he didn't recognize swarmed around a pile of what looked like bowling balls.

They were playing a deadly game with them. They passed them down a long line of men up to the top of the wall along the battlement where three big guns were surrounded by more of the oddly-dressed soldiers. They fired the guns in rapid succession, shaking the ground under Lou's feet. The sound and recoil caused a hollow ringing in his ears.

He was pulled roughly by the arm, and a gruff voice screamed in his ear.

"*Chi sta? Chi sta?*"

"I'm sorry," Lou said. "I don't understand you."

The soldier glared at him, then motioned to two of the soldiers who gripped him unceremoniously by each arm and marched him between them into a squat building in the corner of the courtyard.

Lou protested the rough treatment, but all he got for his pains was a cuff to the ear before being pitched head first into a dingy room. The door was shut and the bolt thrown.

CHAPTER 20

▼

Urbino, 1470

Far from being the journey of discovery Liz thought it would be, she soon learned that riding behind an army on a forced march where time is of the essence had to be one of the most uncomfortable experiences she'd ever had. The heat and dust raised by the tramping feet of men on the move and the smells from the horses made her miserable, and it wasn't long before the journey took its toll on her flagging energies.

She bumped along on *Argento*, growing more morose as the trek grew more tedious. *Argento* snorted constantly to rid himself of the dust flying up his nose causing Liz to lurch in the saddle as if she was riding a camel. She covered her nose and mouth with a dampened piece of cloth as she saw some of the other riders doing, and that helped.

But as the hours passed, her shoulders, back and arms grew weary with tension from the concentration needed not only to keep her seat but to keep *Argento* on track and away from holes or bumping into another horse in the growing darkness. Twice Piero had to grip *Argento*'s reins to keep the pair from stumbling over the rocky outcroppings of tufa.

"Are you all right?" Piero asked the second time this happened.

"*Sì*, Master." Bone tired, she put up a good front, but Piero knew how much she needed to rest because he was as tired as she. Dirty, hungry, and spent, he looked at the men and horses around him and saw mirror images of himself.

"The tufa is a good sign," he said, desperately wanting to reassure Liz that it wouldn't be much longer. "It means we are nearing the sea and Urbino—the more limestone we see, the closer we are to home." He couldn't see if she smiled or not because of the bandana tied across her face, but the blue smudges around her eyes spoke volumes.

With relative ease, they had resumed their former roles of master and apprentice. Still, Piero could not resist sending her the occasional knowing smile or wink to remind her that he was acting a part. A vehement shake of her head did nothing to dissuade him. She soon gave up trying. Besides, she was just too tired to care.

Five hours into their journey, with Liz half asleep in the saddle, one of the Florentine horsemen rode up alongside them.

"*Signore*, are you the painter, Piero della Francesca?" he inquired after the customary formal greeting.

"I am," Piero responded politely.

"I am Ignazio Carola. My master, Lorenzo de Medici, asks that you join him."

"*Certamente, al suo servizio.*"

Like a dose of a magic potion, Liz perked up at the mention of Lorenzo's name. As they fell back to the Florentine contingent, Liz was struck anew by the beauty and elegance of the horseflesh the *cavalieri* were riding. Any one of the horses was a match for *Zingaro* and *Argento*, both of which Liz considered incomparable.

Lorenzo rode in the middle of his group of young men, his *cavalieri*. He sat astride his magnificent horse with the poise and regal bearing of one mature beyond his years.

Liz saw him just at the moment when he reacted to some jest, as he held the reins with one elegant hand while with the other, he jabbed the ribs of the jokester to his right. Leaning in his saddle toward his neighbor, he straightened when he spied Piero, as if he suddenly remembered his exalted position. His color deepened like a child who'd been caught with his hand in the cookie jar.

"Ah, he comes to join us. Please, Maestro, ride with us, for the night is long, and these fellows are boring me with their jokes and pranks. How much can any man stand, *vero?*"

His uninhibited courtiers—all young men not much older than himself—laughed and made room for Piero who fell in beside Lorenzo. Liz maneuvered *Argento* behind them so she could eavesdrop on their conversation.

Liz had a view of the back of Lorenzo's head and a little of his profile. Though marred with irregular features that would never mark him as an Adonis, from a trick of the light or the force of his personality, he was transformed into an attractive young man. Or, maybe it was simply that Liz knew what his future held, and that knowledge colored her perception.

Piero smiled graciously at Lorenzo and bowed his head in salute. Lorenzo returned the smile, his quick mind evident behind the animated face. They seemed to Liz like kindred spirits.

"I must confess, Maestro Piero, that I am more eager to see your great *frescoes*, of which I have heard much from His Grace, Duke Federico, than I am to vanquish Malatesta, but since it seems I cannot do one without the other, so be it. I find myself, *in seguito* (as a result), with these fine *cavalieri* on this dusty path to the sea. *Che irritante*! Rest assured, I will make this Malatesta pay."

"*Mille grazie, è molto gentile da parte sua. Gentilissimo Signor de Medici, lieto di conoscerla, piacere!*"

With this very pretty speech, Piero instantly ingratiated himself, thanking Lorenzo and expressing his delight at knowing him. From Lorenzo's expression, it was apparent to Liz that even though Lorenzo was still a boy, he had been well schooled in the courtier's art. He could bestow compliments graciously and receive them equally well.

As the company rode ever closer to Urbino, the conversation was pleasant, making the time pass quickly. Liz fought her fatigue as she listened to Lorenzo and Piero discuss art. Lorenzo sounded well disposed toward what Piero had to say and displayed an extraordinarily broad knowledge of all art, from *fresco* to bronze sculpture to portraiture.

*   *   *   *

Late in the night, a soft rain fell, prompting Piero and Liz to dig out their oilskins. About the same time, the column came to a stop, and Lorenzo sent one of his *cavalieri* up ahead to find out why.

The moon rode low on the horizon as rain clouds scudded across the sky. The fields were washed by the rain and smelled of fragrant earth and wild flowers.

Piero and Liz climbed down from their mounts and waited under their oilskins, rain pelting them and the horses. Liz held *Argento*'s halter and consoled the young horse who looked as forlorn and miserable as Liz felt.

The *cavaliere* returned and reported that the column would halt for the remainder of the night. Within striking distance of Urbino, the Duke ordered that camp be set up where they stood.

"The Duke orders: no fires and no noise. Rest and ready weapons for the morning. Sunrise is no more than two hours hence."

The young *cavaliere* fairly bounced in his saddle with excitement as he continued his report to Lorenzo.

"The Duke hopes to take Malatesta and his forces by surprise, and is sending scouts forward to sound out the strength of the enemy. The Duke says, 'Without a doubt, Malatesta has his own outguard, so we are to post sentries.'"

Lorenzo's *cavalieri* fanned out swiftly among the men under his command to carry out the Duke's instructions.

"Tell them their orders come directly from me," Lorenzo added.

*   *   *   *

Piero and Liz were left alone with Lorenzo under the overhanging branch of a large umbrella pine.

"*Sua Eccellenza,*" Liz offered, "may I help you unsaddle your horse?"

"You may, but do not address me as 'Lord' for I am only a simple citizen of the Commune of Florence and bear no title."

"How shall we address you then?" Piero asked, looking askance at Lorenzo.

"I am Lorenzo di Piero de Medici, but Signor Lorenzo will do," he answered, flashing them a toothy grin.

With a wave of his hand, the simple citizen beckoned one of his men and instructed him to have his wagon brought to him. Meanwhile, he unsaddled his own horse while Piero and Liz tended to their mounts. Liz was glad Lorenzo took care of his horse because—despite her offer—Liz was not sure she could have handled such a spirited stallion.

Once the horses were tended to, Lorenzo sat on a camp stool to wait while his meal was prepared—by other simple citizens of the Commune of Florence.

"You are quiet, Maestro Piero, what troubles you?" Lorenzo asked.

"*Niente di grave.* It is but … I had heard you were a proud young man, and yet now that I have met you, I am amazed to find that you are *un uomo giovane coi piedi per terra* (a down to earth young man)."

"I have learned not to believe everything one hears," Lorenzo replied with a laugh.

"*È vero,*" Piero said, "I will remember this lesson in the future."

Lorenzo's servant brought out a cleverly designed folding table and additional stools from the wagon and laid out a light meal of cold fowl, cheese, bread, fruit and the ever present wine.

Lorenzo beckoned Piero to the table.

"*Per piacere*, share this meal with me," Lorenzo urged graciously. "I hate to eat alone, and it affords us the opportunity to continue our conversation."

Liz stretched out beneath the tree to rest. Piero glanced over his shoulder at her several times. One of Lorenzo's servants brought some food to her. She accepted it gratefully and tried not to appear too eager—though she was ravenous—even as she devoured every scrap.

When the meal ended, Liz jumped up to help clear away the plates and cups. As she trailed after the servants with an armload of cups and plate, *Argento* followed her.

"Look at how that horse follows your servant. He is a faithful fellow, indeed."

"*Sì*, he is that and sometimes a big nuisance. Like a baby, he constantly craves attention."

Liz returned to sit near Piero after helping with the clean up. The two men were in deep conversation. She sat with her back against the pine tree to listen, but *Argento* nuzzled her head. When he nibbled on her hair, she got up and walked him to the wagon to give him one of the dried apples from Lorenzo's stores. She returned with two more pieces.

"Signor Lorenzo, may I give a piece of dried apple to your horse?" she asked.

"*Certo*."

"What is his name, *Signore*?"

"*Morello*. I named him for the dark cherries my father gets from France. My brother, Giulio, and I have a fondness for sweets, and those cherries are our favorite."

Liz approached the big horse and stroked his neck. She spoke softly and held out the piece of apple. He snuffled it before nibbling the fruit gently and taking it from her. She called to *Zingaro* and he too sauntered over to get his piece of apple.

"Look at that," Lorenzo commented to Piero in disbelief. "*Morello* likes your servant. He does not usually allow anyone but myself and a few well-liked grooms near him."

Liz wiped her hands on her breeches and sat under the tree again near Piero's feet.

"Our Cosimo is full of hidden talents and surprises, *Signore*," he said, standing and gathering up his oilskin. "We have two hours to rest. We should while we can."

Piero tossed down his oilskin and wrapped his blanket around himself before lying down on the damp ground. Liz followed suit. She shivered. Was it from the damp or from the surreal scene in which she found herself. She couldn't tell.

She rolled herself up in her blanket and found a comfortable position on her side. If not for the fact that a battle for the city would take place in the morning, this night could be a pleasant camp out with friends. With worry creasing her brow, she soon fell asleep.

The rest of the night passed with nothing but the sound of the occasional owl hooting in the distance and the flutter of bats' wings as they returned to their haunts.

*   *   *   *

Faint morning sunlight in her eyes woke Liz. Her brain registered the sound of the camp coming alive. The clink of tack as horses were being saddled. Men moving silently about the camp. The only other noise being carried on the morning air was the song of birds announcing the arrival of another sunrise.

"Are you going to sleep all day?"

Piero stood over her and gave her foot a playful kick. "Up servant!"

"Ssh! We're supposed to keep noise to a minimum," she responded.

"Oh, all right, I'll get up," Liz said in a mock grumble as she got stiffly to her feet, sore from sleeping on the ground again.

Piero led *Zingaro* and *Argento* to her and whispered in her ear.

"While it's quiet, let's go to a little stream I found where we can wash. There's tall brush for you to use and it's deserted."

"Is Lorenzo up?" she asked as she followed him toward the stream.

"I don't know. He slept in his wagon. He'll be up and about soon."

"What's the plan for today?"

"We will stay as far from the fighting as we can. With my spyglass, we'll be able to see what's happening."

"Good. I'm glad to hear you're not going to engage in anything for which you are totally unprepared. Remember, Piero, you are a painter, not a soldier."

"*Tante grazie, mamma!*"

"I'm serious!"

"I will stay out of this battle because of you, not because I am afraid to fight."

They reached the stream. Liz squatted behind some shrubs while Piero stood nearby with the horses as they drank. The animals effectively blocked anyone's view; and when she finished, they went upstream to fill their waterskins and wash.

Liz splashed her face with the icy cold water and rinsed her mouth. She bent to get a clean shirt from her kit when a hand—warm and gentle—touched the back of her neck. Piero turned her to face him and kissed her with such ferocity, it took her breath away.

Minutes passed—minutes filled with desperate, furtive kisses, words of love and tender caresses. Then they separated to walk back to the camp to take up the pretense again that they were nothing more than master and apprentice, and not knowing when they would be together.

✳   ✳   ✳   ✳

When they returned to the camp, one of Lorenzo's servants gave them a chunk of bread. They washed it down with a long swig of fresh water from their skins. They were saddling their horses when Lorenzo descended from his wagon.

Lorenzo waved to them as he mounted *Morello* which had been saddled by one of the *cavalieri*. Liz thought at first that Lorenzo was wearing the same brown suede he wore the day before, but when he rode up to them, she realized it was different, with tan suede cut work trimming this outfit.

"Do you think it wise to don my armor now?" he asked no one in particular.

No one wore armor, so they shrugged collectively and followed the column moving out.

The wind had turned and an easterly breeze blew in their faces.

"Does it seem foggy to you?" Piero asked.

"Maybe it's the wind coming off the sea," Liz answered.

"I don't think so," Piero replied, his expression grim. "It doesn't smell like the sea. It smells like smoke."

CHAPTER 21

▼

The column marched north and east through an ominous haze. The artillery and extra field cannon made slow progress as they crawled laboriously over the rocky terrain—hauled by straining men and horses.

From a vantage point on a low rise, Liz and Piero peered through the smoke at the Duke's infantry and cavalry scurrying into position, reminding Liz of swarming ants. Her eyes stung from the dense smoke, and her stomach clenched with fear as the men inched ever closer to the moment of engagement.

She longed for the vision before her to fade into the mist like a magical Brigadoon. For Urbino—the city she had come to love—was under merciless bombardment by Malatesta's big guns. What of the inhabitants? She longed to know that they had survived unscathed. She longed to curl up in the safety of Piero's arms and to be in the refuge of her little room in the artisans' building.

The ground shook beneath them, and the air was heavy with the smell of gunpowder. Duke Malatesta's army was arrayed between them and the city. Puffs of smoke spewed forth from the muzzles of Malatesta's cannon to thicken the murky sky. Parts of the city were ablaze and holes had been punched in the outer wall. She knew the Duke's army had arrived just in the nick of time.

Liz looked to Piero for his reaction just as a roar of protest from the mouths of Duke Federico's men roiled back over them like a wave. Their clamor voiced their desire to charge the besieging force who continued to blast away at the walls of the city.

"We'll stay here for now," Piero said to Liz as he pulled on *Argento*'s rein.

"What do you mean, for now?" Liz asked.

"I don't know if I can stand and watch and not do something."

From the set of his jaw and the twitching muscle in his cheek, Liz decided not to press him.

Duke Federico's lieutenants rode among their forces exhorting them to remain in formation until the order to attack was given. The men were working themselves up into a frenzy. Their city, their families, were under attack, and Liz could understand their desire to inflict damage and pain, to exact their revenge upon the invaders.

The lieutenants converged at the front of the line, and Liz was transfixed, waiting to see where the lieutenants were headed and what would happen next.

Lorenzo and his men moved into positions in front of their force of *contadini* and awaited orders from the Duke's commanders. They were much calmer, stolidly bovine in their patience.

"Why don't they attack? What are they waiting for?" Liz asked, as Malatesta's guns poured on volley after volley. The city's defenders were outgunned, and were attempting to repair breaches in the wall even as the cannons blasted new ones.

"They're waiting to get their orders from the Duke."

"The city may not hold if he waits much longer."

Piero dismounted and took out his spyglass, intent on monitoring the Duke's strategy. Lorenzo joined them on the crest of the little hill.

"What do you think, Signor Lorenzo?"

Lorenzo wagged his head sadly and shrugged.

"My *cavalieri* and I are ready for battle. God willing, we will survive this day and be victorious."

Lorenzo's *cavalieri* dashed toward the wagon where the breast plates and helmets were being laid on the ground by the servants. Lorenzo left them to don his armor.

Liz held her breath at the sight of the deadly instruments of war—the swords, halberds, and pikes—being unloaded and stacked against the wagon. She dismounted and sidled up close to Piero for reassurance and the comfort nearness to him invariably brought. Piero glanced momentarily at her and resumed peering through his eyeglass.

"The Duke's soldiers are moving into position. And his light artillery is being readied to fire."

"Surely he's not going to fire on his own city?" Liz asked.

"No, it looks like he's going to try to take out Malatesta's guns, and a good number of his men as well. If he succeeds, this may be over soon."

Liz saw one of Duke Federico's officers ride up to the wagon and speak with Lorenzo. Almost immediately, the *contadini*, with the *cavalieri* and Lorenzo in the lead, moved into the middle of the field directly behind the Duke's cavalry. The remainder of the Duke's forces—his infantry—fanned out in flanking positions.

A blast from Duke Federico's artillery made Liz jump as three of his field pieces fired simultaneously. The noise was so loud, her hearing was gone momentarily. Dense smoke carried on the wind wafted back and obscured her vision.

Liz dropped to the ground, clutching at *Argento's* reins as the young horse skittered nervously. Tremblors rolled in waves beneath her, and smoke blew into her face, making her choke and her eyes water.

Piero stood his ground, his eye glued to his glass, trying to follow the progress of the battle.

Another loud explosion from the front of the field ripped the air. One of Duke Malatesta's field guns, with its store of ammunition, had been hit. An exultant cheer resounded across the field from the Duke's forces. They advanced—a hurtling, swarming mass—on Malatesta's line of defense.

"The Duke is closing in, and any of Malatesta's soldiers, who manage to break through the cavalry, will find themselves face to face with Lorenzo's force," Piero informed Liz, who had covered her mouth with a piece of her shirt.

Piero pulled on *Zingaro's* reins and mounted the big horse.

Liz jumped to her feet.

"Where are you going?" she shouted over the din.

"I'm going down on the field to be with Lorenzo. You stay here. Don't move from this spot. I'll come back for you soon."

Before she could respond, he rode onto the field of battle leaving Liz dismayed and fearful for his safety.

She pulled *Argento* toward her to calm him for she could see he was trembling with fright. She held him close and found herself instead being comforted by the gentle, young horse.

Suddenly, there was another loud explosion—this one much closer to her position—and she lost her grip on *Argento*. She saw the whites of his eyes roll for only a moment before the young horse bolted. Liz called after him, and knew it was hopeless. She watched his headlong flight and started off after him, even as she conceded to herself that it would be impossible to catch him.

Liz followed after the horse at a slow jog, but it didn't take long to lose sight of him, and she sat down, heavy hearted, to catch her breath and consider her options. She looked back and could hear the battle raging on.

She recalled *Argento*'s fright when he encountered the sea so she guessed if he headed further east, he would most likely turn back when he reached the very same terrifying wall of water. The similarity to the sounds of battle would force him west and south, so she decided that her best bet of finding him would be to head in that direction.

Any of Malatesta's soldiers who made it off the battlefield to find a young horse like *Argento* would consider himself lucky indeed. He wouldn't hesitate to steal the horse to make his escape. She realized how vulnerable she would be on foot instead of on horseback. All of these things ran through her mind, but above all, it was the thought of losing *Argento* that propelled her off her rocky seat to search for the young horse.

$$*\qquad *\qquad *\qquad *$$

On the battlefield, Piero could see that Duke Federico's men had pressed home their advantage. He weaved his way through the men, horses, wagons and caissons until he found Lorenzo's position. The farmers under his command had dug themselves in. They made a formidable wall, and Piero shuddered to think what would happen to any poor *bastardo* who strayed into their line. Reassuring himself that Lorenzo was holding fast and well attended, he swung *Zingaro* around and headed back to the rise where he had left Liz.

When he didn't spot them through the smoke, at first he didn't panic, but stood in his stirrups to get a better look. He couldn't wait to tell her that the tide of battle was firmly in Duke Federico's favor.

Gone. Nowhere in sight. Now panic gripped him, and he spurred *Zingaro* along a zigzag course through the hilly area, hoping to spot them in a small depression or better still, returning to where he left them.

Why can't she do as she is told? he muttered to himself. Always getting in trouble. If she would just listen and do what she is told, she wouldn't …

He almost missed it. A splotch of pale color, a movement in the distance, and he rode full tilt. *Argento*, riderless. He caught up to the young horse and saw that he was in a sorry state. Sides heaving, foam-covered. Piero grabbed his reins and slowed the horse down. The horse shuddered convulsively until he saw it was *Zingaro* riding next to him, and then he stopped dead in his tracks. Piero could have laughed out loud at the young horse's reaction except for the fact that Liz was nowhere to be found.

Piero retraced his route—again zigzagging—hunting for Liz.

"Elisabetta!" he called out over and over.

She knew he was the only one privy to her real name. But suppose she was hurt or unconscious and couldn't answer. Suppose the young horse had thrown her or fell on her and broke her leg. The longer he searched, the more desperate his call became.

"Over here!" her voice, faint but clear, reached him at last. Relief flooded over him as he rushed to her side.

"You found him! Oh, Piero, I'm so glad."

He jumped down from *Zingaro* to embrace her.

"*Cara*! Are you all right?"

Before she had a chance to respond, his joy at finding her safe and sound was overshadowed by a flash of temper.

"Why did you leave? Didn't I say to stay there."

"I'm sorry, but I had to find *Argento*. A wicked cannon blast scared him, and he ran off."

"That damn horse! You disobeyed me. You should have …"

"Now wait just a minute! You seem to be under the impression I take orders from you. I take orders from no one. I'm my own person, Signore, and you would do well to remember that."

Liz turned her back and stomped off to busy herself checking the cinch on *Argento*'s saddle and the rest of his tack.

"Listen."

"What?" Liz asked, still peeved at him.

"It's quiet, the battle must be over."

They looked at each other, and their mutual anger melted away like a summer hailstorm.

"Elisabetta," Piero said, reaching for her hand, "let's go home."

*   *   *   *

It took only minutes to return to the rise that gave them the best view of the battlefield. The big guns were silent—replaced by the moans and screams of the wounded and dying. Bodies were strewn across the field like colorful flowers that had been leveled by a summer squall. Duke Federico's men could be seen crisscrossing the area, putting the wounded to the sword and rounding up prisoners.

Piero and Liz rode down onto the battlefield—still a very dangerous place—and picked their way through the smoke and detritus of battle. Small fires threatened to detonate ordnance littering the field near the guns, and Liz noticed several men were removing and stacking small barrels of precious gunpowder so they wouldn't blow everything and everyone to kingdom come.

The wind had not slackened, and the smoke that stung their eyes made it difficult to avoid the craters and the cannon shot—some of the cannonballs as big as bowling balls—and to keep from stepping on the bodies of the dead.

Piero spotted the flag of the *Commune* of *Firenze* and turned the horses in that direction. Liz gripped *Argento*'s reins so tightly her knuckles were white.

She gaped in horror at the destruction all around her. The scene unfolded, it seemed to her, in slow motion, as if any movement would summon the Angel of Death ever closer.

Bloody hands lifted slowly in a silent plea for water, for help, for God!

Bile rose in her throat from the sights, sounds, and smells all around her. She covered her mouth with her hand and tried to take some deep breaths. She closed her eyes to control her trembling and prayed she would be able to control the violent feelings of revulsion that threatened to make her sick.

"Shouldn't we stop to help?" Liz asked.

Piero turned in his saddle to eye her. Unbeknownst to Liz, he had been watching her and had seen her tremble and turn pale. He had known all along that the life he contemplated asking her to share would be too strange and harsh for her to endure.

"No," he answered. "We'll find Lorenzo first. They will come with litters soon to tend Duke Federico's wounded."

Almost as soon as he uttered the words, she observed the approach of men with litters to carry the Duke's wounded into the city.

"Surely, they won't kill all of Malatesta's wounded. Piero, say they won't."

"They will. They will take the able-bodied as prisoners and make an exchange for them—gold for prisoners. Maybe Malatesta will pay, maybe he won't," he said sternly, the statement so matter-of-fact.

"It is the way it is, Elisabetta. I cannot change it. I wish, for your sake, that I could."

"What happens if Malatesta refuses to pay? Would the Duke have the men killed … in cold blood."

"No, he will take them into his army, and for what he pays, they will fight for him. He will make them into soldiers. It's not a bad life for them."

"I think it's a terrible life."

Piero only shrugged, unwilling to argue the point further.

CHAPTER 22

▼

Lorenzo was safe. They found him with his men, swaying slightly, but still on his feet, bloody sword in hand, directing the removal of his wounded to the city.

When he spied Piero and Liz, he pointed his sword toward the city. Piles of rubble and a large jagged hole in the city wall could be seen to the left of the western gate—where the gate tower once stood. The gate was pockmarked, blackened with soot and hung at an odd angle, but just barely. The right tower remained—a lonely bastion—battered, to be sure—but intact. The city had held. Thankfully, they were spared the need to flush the enemy from the streets and homes of Urbino.

Liz passed by more bloody bodies with terrible wounds and eyes open and fixed on the heavens that set her to trembling anew. She tore her gaze away and looked straight ahead as she trailed behind Piero and Lorenzo. She couldn't be sure that the stinging tears running down her cheeks were caused by the acrid smoke. Maybe they were the result of the relief she felt that the battle was over at last or the fearful prospect of what lay ahead when they entered the city.

The defenders flung wide the gate and a multitude of voices thundered their approval at the return of their noble Lord and the liberation of their city.

Lorenzo, Piero, and Liz joined the Duke's army on the road leading to the gate of the city. To the resounding cheers of the jubilant victors and citizens, the Duke on his beautiful charger rode triumphantly into his city at the head of his army.

Duke Malatesta had fled with a small remnant of his men, but a contingent of the Duke's army was in hot pursuit.

Piero and Liz followed behind the Duke and his commanders with Lorenzo's force and his *cavalieri*.

The people streamed from their homes into the broad avenue, and the expressions of relief on their dirty, tear-stained faces moved Liz to tears.

So much death and destruction, and for what? Liz thought.

Those people without flags or pennants waved white cloths of welcome. The victors' procession brought out the shopkeepers, artisans, and mothers with their babes-in-arms. As they approached the front courtyard of the *Palazzo* with its grand rotunda—the Court of Honor—it grew quiet.

"This is not good," Piero mouthed to Liz. He was dry-eyed, but lines of exhaustion and fear were etched on his face.

The entire household had assembled in the courtyard, but they were oddly silent, their heads bowed. On the top step of the landing, the Duchess waited to greet her Lord.

Liz scanned the crowd searching for Mistress Isabella, but she was nowhere to be seen. Luca was not there either. Several officers of the garrison that had defended the city left their posts and ran into the courtyard. They waited while the Duke dismounted.

The Duke showed himself briefly to the assembly. Then he limped wearily up the staircase to the door of the *Palazzo*. The Duchess made a formal greeting—something between a bow and a curtsey—and then tenderly touched his cheek. The Duke took her hand and kissed it. The poignancy of this gesture touched Liz deeply. A lump caught in her throat, and she noticed how pale and tired the Duchess appeared.

The Duke and the Duchess of Urbino bowed to the crowd and entered the *Palazzo*.

"What has happened?" Liz inquired of Piero. "The Duchess looks as if she's aged ten years. Piero, we must find out."

"We will. Let's see to Lorenzo first. Everyone seems to have forgotten him."

*   *   *   *

Liz trudged wearily up the steps to their quarters in the artisans' building. She had gone with Piero to the stables to see to their horses and familiarize Lorenzo's *cavalieri* with the available accommodations for their mounts. It would be a tight squeeze, especially in view of the loss of a large portion of the stable. The stable hands and soldiers would have to manage to get enough feed and hay somehow.

Lorenzo was another matter. He merited different treatment than a visiting horse; his accommodations would have to reflect his status. Only the best apartments in the *Palazzo* would do.

By his aloof expression and manner, Liz assumed that Piero still smarted from their heated exchange for her failure to obey his order to remain on the rise while he rode onto the battlefield, but she was too tired to care.

Everyone was tired. With a good meal, a bath and a good night's sleep, Liz was confident the chasm that yawned between them would close.

$$* \qquad * \qquad * \qquad *$$

Liz expected the artisans' building to be abuzz with activity, but it was practically deserted. Their rooms on the second floor were exactly as they had left them. Nothing had been disturbed, and there had been no damage to the building, at least none she could discern—just a fine layer of dust covering the windows, floor and furniture.

She crossed immediately to the large window in Piero's room and found the view toward the sea altered hardly at all. She scanned the city walls on this side of the *Palazzo* and found them to be unmarred and intact.

She went to her room and looked longingly at her bed, but she thought that if she so much as sat down, that would be the end of bathing, eating, and checking on the chapel. So, turning reluctantly away from her bed, she pushed herself to stick with her plan.

It was a warm afternoon, and the rooms were a little stuffy, but that was quickly remedied. The stench of death was still in her nostrils, but a fresh breeze with the tang of the sea would soon dispel that and make a cool bath so much better.

She took her time lugging up buckets of water from the kitchen-yard pump to fill the bath, and her reward after three trips, was a wonderful bath, her first in days.

Relaxing in the bath gave her time to think. Time—so much depended on time. Too much time. Too little time. Am I in the wrong time? And how am I to know what is the right time for me?

Her heart told her to stay. Her head told her to try to return to her own time—when it was more civilized.

But who's to say which time is more civilized. Her own time possessed merely a veneer of civilization that hid the violence in men's hearts. There were killings in her own time. There was war. There was sickness and death. No time escapes these truths.

Could I get used to the things I saw today? Would I want to? All these thoughts ran through her head as she sat in the bath until she shivered in the cool water.

She scrubbed her hair clean and noticed the wound on her head was almost completely healed. Her hair dried while she dressed in clean clothes, and then she gave it a good brushing to bring out the shine. It had grown quite a lot, so much so that she was able to tie it up with a piece of cord. She realized she felt almost human again.

Then she reversed the process, emptying the bath and cleaning it for Piero.

On her last trip down to the kitchen, she peered in to see if Mistress Isabella was there. No one was about except for two kitchen maids who said they would prepare a tray with cold fowl, some soup and bread and send it up.

In hushed tones, the two girls reassured Liz that it would be no time at all before things were back to normal. They blessed themselves when they said this, as if offering their words up as a prayer of sorts.

God willing, Liz hoped, things could return to normal.

She told the maids she was going to the chapel to say a prayer of thanks and asked them to cover the tray and leave it for her to pick up.

When she reached the chapel, she was greeted by the lone figure of Leonardo who knelt near the main altar. She had met no one on the way through the *Palazzo* to the chapel. The halls were quiet and as desolate as a tomb—the usual hubbub, strangely absent.

Leonardo saw her enter and ran to her full of questions about the Duke's campaign. She tried to answer as best she could, but he wanted far too many details.

"You will have to ask Maestro Piero, Leonardo, for he saw much more of the battle than I did. But, tell me, what of here in the city?"

Leonardo wagged his big head from side to side, and filled her in with what had transpired there during the siege.

"And then the cannon took out a big section of the wall near the gate. Captain Luca was thrown from the battlement and a very large piece of stone fell on him. It would have killed a lesser man outright, but he still lives. Everyone is saddened for it is certain that he will die very soon."

Leonardo's news shattered her fragile equilibrium. She needed to be alone, to cry in private.

She excused herself and, hiding her tears, left Leonardo, nearly forgetting to inspect her likeness on the wall of the chapel. But Leonardo would not be put off so easily. He followed her and babbled on.

"Tell Maestro Piero that I myself have stood guard over the chapel. They said I was too old to fight, so they left me here. All the young ones went to the walls, but not me."

Then he began to cry. She regretted putting him off and patted the old man's arm to comfort him.

"Were there many casualties besides Captain Luca?"

"Not too many, only about twenty-five dead and wounded, mostly among the soldiers, a few of our young men who were on the walls when the artillery fire took it down and a few on the ground. *Bastardi sfortunati!*"

"Ssh! In church, Leonardo." She thought she heard something and wanted to shush the old man.

They were standing in front of Liz's likeness … but something about it was different.

"I am here now, Leonardo, why don't you get something to eat or get some rest. You have done well." She tried to tune him out, wanting to inspect the area of the portal more closely.

"Then they sent me to the garrison to help guard the prisoners."

"What prisoners?" Liz asked.

"Ceva and the possessed man," he answered, crossing himself.

Liz stared at him. Then slowly a trickle of fear inched up the back of her neck and took hold.

"Leonardo, please … tell me about this man," she pleaded.

"There is not much to tell. No one can talk to him. He yells and speaks gibberish. He is possessed, and no doubt he will meet his end and go right to his master, the devil," Leonardo said the last word in a hushed whisper, as if saying the word could conjure up Satan himself. "He must be watched in case his master comes to free him."

"Thank you, Leonardo, for telling me about Captain Luca and the rest. I'll tell Master Piero right away." She repeated her offer. "Get something to eat and rest since I'm here now."

Leonardo did as he was bid and left her.

She turned her attention to the wall where earlier she could have sworn she had heard muffled voices. The portrait of her as the young page and the surrounding wall shimmered. She reached out her hand and touched it, but it was solid.

Something nagged at her. Leonardo told her that the man was possessed, which would be what these people would immediately conclude about someone who ranted and yelled unintelligibly. But she was convinced there was more to it—something that bore further investigation. First things, first.

*   *   *   *

She raced up the stairs of the artisans' building—her breath coming in ragged gasps—forgetting the tray of food.

She took the key from Piero's *armadio*. She fumbled with the lock on the chest under his bed, and pulled out the amulet.

Hurrying back to the chapel, she approached the wall. The wall still shimmered, and she heard distant, muffled voices. She placed the amulet on the floor in front of her likeness and waited a moment or two and then stepped up to the wall and touched it once more.

Damn! Still solid.

"What are you doing?" came a voice from behind her.

Liz jumped with fright and whirled around to see Piero standing there, ashen-faced, eyes red-rimmed.

"Look, Piero, at my picture that you painted," she said, recovering a little. "And listen, can you hear the voices?"

He stepped closer to the wall and listened carefully. He made out a distant hum, like voices talking in another room. The wall glimmered as if lit from behind. He turned to Liz.

"What does it mean?"

"I don't know … exactly. It seems that the portal wants to open, but doesn't yet. What's missing? I brought the amulet down here, thinking it might help. I came through before. I should be able to go back through it. Oh, Piero, something may have distorted the portal. I don't have a clue."

"You want to leave then?"

"Don't you want me to leave? I thought you did. Maybe I was mistaken?"

"You are mistaken. You are also outspoken and pigheaded, but I want you to stay."

"I see. You make me sound like quite a catch."

"What do you mean by that?"

"It means I'm irresistible," she retorted, beginning to lose her temper.

"To me, you are."

"I'm sorry. I shouldn't have answered you like that. You don't deserve it. I seem to lash out one moment, and the next, I'm crying like a spoiled child. Come, I'll prepare a bath for you. Let me help you as I did that first day. We'll talk of this later."

Liz scooped up the amulet, and they went together to the kitchen. Liz scrounged around for fruit and cheese and added them to the tray. The bowls were next to the tray so she ladled some soup into them, and Piero carried the tray while Liz carried two cups and a decanter of wine she got from the larder.

She draped his amulet around her neck, and they toted their evening meal up to their rooms, the tantalizing aroma of the soup whetting her appetite.

He put the tray on the table and waited until they were inside with the doors locked before he took her in his arms.

"First the bath, then we eat, then we love," Liz told him.

"Bossy, too. I left out bossy."

New lines of weariness and worry creased his face. He sat down as she stowed his amulet back under lock and key.

"Are you all right?" she asked.

When she got no answer, she looked up from beside his bed. He was still seated at the table with his head down on his arms.

Liz came around the bed and bent over him, putting her arms around him.

"You saw Luca." It was a statement, not a question, her voice thick with concern.

He let her hold him, and she felt the silent sobs wrack his body. He turned and gripped her waist, burying his face and crying onto her breast as if his heart would break. She held him until he recovered, and then she busied herself with the tray of food.

"I didn't want to be the one to tell you. I'm glad someone else broke the news. Let's get you washed up. We can talk in the bath."

He told her everything he had learned. Mistress Isabella and the Duchess had been nursing the wounded. When Luca was injured, Mistress Isabella commandeered the women of the city to help the Duchess so that she could attend Captain Luca herself. She was near collapse from exhaustion, but she would not let anyone but the Duchess near him.

The Duchess had begged Luca to allow a priest in to hear his confession and give him Extreme Unction, but he would have none of it.

She went to the church of *San Bernardino* and begged one of the Franciscan Friars to attend him, but when the Friar approached Luca's bed, Luca cursed him. The Friar said he would not come again.

The Duchess was running out of priests willing to come in to see him. She had two more come in, but both left in ill temper after Luca fired off insults at them, calling them every vile name in the book.

"Does he know he is dying?"

"Of course he knows. The Duchess is appealing now to Duke Federico. He was going in to see him, and she thinks he will obey the Duke if he orders him to confess."

"That's absurd."

"Yes, it is. He has a grievance, no doubt, that he has harbored since he was a boy, and I'm afraid he'll take it with him to his grave. I would hate to be St. Peter when he arrives in heaven."

"Do you think he will—arrive in heaven, I mean?"

"I love him as a son loves a father, as a brother, as a dear friend. I think he will go to heaven, in spite of himself."

"Why does he hate priests so much?"

By this time, he was seated in the bath, scrubbing his arms and chest. Liz laid out his breeches and his robe, got the towel, and his shaving things ready.

"When he was a boy, a woman and two men—neighbors of theirs from the same village—went to the priest claiming that Luca's mother was a witch. In those days, it didn't take much to denounce someone for witchcraft for the people were extremely superstitious." Liz peeked through her lashes at him, smiling to herself as she recalled her conversation with Leonardo of a few minutes ago. "People suspected demons roamed everywhere. But these people were greedy for her land, and because his mother was a widow with three young children and very vulnerable, they devised a way to get it. She had no family to protect her. Luca was her middle child."

"Oh, yes, the middle child syndrome."

"What?"

"Nothing. Go on with the story."

"They took his mother out and burned her as a witch. Luca and his older brother saw her die. She had been a good woman and attended church faithfully, but it did her no good. The priest, of course, would not bury her in consecrated ground. Her little family was thrown out and the accusers took the land."

"I'd say he has a very good reason to hate priests."

"When he grew up, he became a soldier. One night, the priest, by now an old man, left his church and rode out from his village to visit another church in another district where he was needed. He met with foul play. It was said that it was robbers who slit his throat, but some thought otherwise. Of course, there was never any proof to lay the murder at Luca's door, but ..."

"He never told you he did it, did he?"

"No."

"Well, then it very well could have been robbers."

"Except the priest had two gold coins still in his robes when he was found."

"But I'm sure there were others the priest had harmed."

"Doubtless there were many more. Luca would only say that he got what he deserved, and no one should waste their prayers on that wicked old priest."

Piero shaved and donned his breeches and robe and joined Liz at the table for their meal—the first decent meal in days. The soup was still warm—like the bread, and the wine was cool from being in a stone decanter in the larder.

Liz ate ravenously, which surprised her for she thought for certain after witnessing the awful events of the day, that she would not be able to swallow a morsel. But her young body responded to the need for nourishment, as it should.

The same could be said for lovemaking. She asked herself how could she put the pictures of the dying from her mind long enough to cross the great gulf separating her and her lover's arms. But cross it she did, their quarrel forgotten, for without the warmth and closeness, the security and strength of their love, life could prove to be a burden too heavy to bear, for both of them.

CHAPTER 23

▼

This time, their lovemaking, unlike their first time, had a leisurely intensity. Locked away in Piero's room, they abandoned all caution to revel in each other.

Eager to explore and perhaps discover secrets and hidden treasures, they fell into each other's arms and indulged in the tender kisses and foreplay of new lovers.

"I don't miss the stony damp earth of our first time together, do you?" Liz asked.

"No, *cara*, this is much better. Now I know that every light touch is yours, not some bug that has crept into the blanket."

"Excuse me! I'm sorry I mentioned it."

They whispered and laughed like playful children while resting in between bouts of lovemaking. With dusk, the night grew cool, and they watched the moon rise in the sky above their bed.

"What were you like as a little boy?" she teased.

"My mother says I was a bad little boy. You will meet her soon, and she will fill your head with such terrible stories. I am her only child so there was no other who could have made me appear better."

"But now she is proud of you?"

"Yes, I think she is. But enough of this idle chatter."

Piero tossed her carelessly onto her back, and for a mere three seconds, she lay open to his gaze before he lowered his body over hers. She never took her eyes from his as their lips met.

They traded places as Piero rolled and took her with him. She straddled him and leaned her body into his. She shimmied toward his feet and took his shaft in her hands, toying with him shamelessly, until he stopped her.

"*Basta*! Enough. You'll unman me, you little witch."

"I wouldn't want to do that," she answered with a sly smile.

She positioned herself to guide him into her and watched as his shaft disappeared into her moist core. She stroked his chest and leaned forward again to gain more control as she rode him. He kissed her when her warm mouth came in range. Their hearts beat in unison—slowly at first—and then rapidly as they reached the height of their passion.

The sight of the gentle smile that hovered about her lips and the tears that trickled from the corners of her eyes elicited a sigh from Piero.

"Why do you cry, *cara*?"

"Because I've never been happier. I never want to leave you."

"I pray to God you never will. I love you, *Piccolina*."

"You haven't called me that in quite a while. I love you too. You know that I do—I think from the moment I first saw you. You looked to me like every romantic dream I ever had."

"And now?"

"My dream has come true."

"*Cara*, morning will be here soon. We must get some sleep."

"Is all the wine gone?"

"We drank the last of it hours ago. Shall I get more?"

"No. Tell me you love me once more and then we'll sleep."

"Do you promise?"

Liz nodded.

"*Ti voglio bene*. There. Have I said it enough?"

She kissed him and then with a satisfied smile rolled onto her side to cuddle next to him.

"Your mother is wrong. I don't think you're such a bad boy," she pronounced sleepily.

*   *   *   *

Liz stirred and opened her eyes to see the faint light of dawn creeping into the room. Covered only in a sheet, she reached for Piero and sat up when she found the bed empty. She called his name softly.

She noticed that the door to the privy was ajar. Piero came out clad only in his breeches at the sound of her voice. He scooped up a shirt from the chair.

"It's still early, *cara*, go back to sleep," he whispered, kissing her.

"Where are you going?"

Putting on his shirt, he sat on the bed to button it and pull on his boots.

"I'm going to see how Luca is. I'll bring breakfast for you in a little while. Sleep until I come back. It will be time enough for you to get up then. Come, lock the door."

He stifled her protest with another kiss. A moment later, he had unlocked the door and was gone. She locked the door behind him and went back to bed, for once in total agreement.

Luca's death would be hard on Piero and Mistress Isabella. Everyone admired and respected Luca, but these two and the Duchess loved him dearly and would be profoundly saddened by the loss.

In dawn's half-light, she made a quick visit to the privy and tried to go back to sleep, but thoughts of the gravely injured man filled her mind.

She deliberately refocused on what needed to happen in order for her and Piero to be together. Damn, she mused, what use is there in daydreaming about something over which I have absolutely no control. Our future lies in Piero's hands.

She threw off the sheet and got up.

After she washed and dressed, she straightened the rooms. She was in the process of lugging the dirty chamber water to the door when there was a knock.

"Who is it?"

"Piero."

Piero stood on the threshold with a tray.

"We must eat quickly. Luca wants to see you. And Lorenzo is waiting for me to take him to the chapel."

"How is Luca?"

"I don't think he will live to see another sunrise," he said. "He refuses food and drink. The doctor forces strong draughts of opium on him for pain. He wakes from sleep in pain and they give him more."

When they hurried through their breakfast of honeyed *polenta*, fruit and tea, Piero helped Liz take the water down to the kitchen yard. He accompanied her down the hill to Luca's room in the garrison where they parted ways.

"I'm going to meet Lorenzo in the chapel. Come there when you're through."

"I'll check on the horses first and then come up. All right?"

"*Bene*," he answered, leaving quickly to find Lorenzo.

When Liz went to the dying man's room, it was to find him with Mistress Isabella and the doctor in attendance. Two of Luca's men stood guard just inside the door.

Mistress Isabella spotted Liz hesitating in the doorway—not sure if she should enter. Mistress Isabella beckoned to Liz, then leaned over Luca, and Liz heard her whisper, "It's Cosimo come to see you."

"Come here, boy, before the opium takes effect."

Liz was shocked at Captain Luca's appearance. Once a giant of a man, he had shriveled to a dry husk. His face was gray and his breathing labored. A fine sheen of sweat stood out on his forehead. Mistress Isabella picked up a cloth and a small, blood spattered basin from the bedside table.

Liz knelt by the side of his bed and took his once-powerful hand—now only skin and bone.

"I'm so sorry, Captain Luca."

"Death comes to us all, boy, but I have had the honor of serving one of the greatest men ever to draw breath. I did my duty. His commendation is my reward."

"Luca, don't talk. Conserve your strength," Mistress Isabella interrupted, the basin trembling in her hands, as he struggled to utter each word.

"This silly woman," Luca said indicating Mistress Isabella. "She thinks … I don't know I'm dying. Come closer, boy."

Liz scooted closer to Luca. The smell of death hovered in the air, and Liz shuddered but did not release her grip on his hand.

"Listen to me…. Take care of Piero. He needs you…. He is too sensitive by far, and you … you are a smart lad…. There are those who would take advantage of him … He's been a true friend to me…. Watch out for his welfare."

"I will, Captain Luca, I promise."

Liz bent her head and kissed his hand. She rose before her tears could fall on him, but he held onto her hand. His life may have been draining away, but his grip was still strong, like a vise.

"You were right, you know."

"About what?"

"We waited for them at the…."

He coughed then, rising up nearly to a sitting position, and Mistress Isabella held the basin to his lips. When she took it away, Liz saw it was filled with blood.

Mistress Isabella wiped his mouth and eased him back onto his pillow. She took the draught of opium from the doctor and helped Luca drink from the cup. He quieted almost immediately.

"We waited for them at the grate ... where they thought to enter the city. We took ten men by surprise ... and killed them all, including Ceva.... The other one is still locked up, and I was happy to tell him that I had taken his brother's life.... The Duke will deal with him when I'm gone."

Mistress Isabella motioned to Liz with a jerk of her head that she should leave.

Liz bid a final goodbye to that great soldier who had been the first human being in her life to truly frighten her. But as the opium took hold, she didn't think he heard her.

Liz stumbled from the room, her tears blurring her vision, certain that she would never see him alive again. She waited outside for a chance to speak to Mistress Isabella, but she never stirred from his side.

Surely, another time would present itself, Liz thought.

She took great gulps of air as she ran to the stables, desperate to outrun the Angel of Death lurking in the corner of Luca's room.

*   *   *   *

She looked for *Argento* or *Zingaro* among all the horses crowded into the stable and the makeshift corral. At last, she saw them jammed in at the far end of the corral. She sought out the head groom and suggested he take some of the horses down to the pasture in shifts so they could graze.

"They're going to begin fighting in there pretty soon," she told him. "You've got too many crowded in there, and they don't know each other. The big males ..."

"Don't tell me how to do my job," the groom said, rudely turning his back on her and stalking off.

Realizing she would have to go over his head, she marched back to the garrison and talked to one of the officers. She explained the situation, and he said he would take care of it. Even so, despite his assurances, she returned to the corral and found one of the grooms.

"I want those two cut out so I can take them to the pasture," she demanded.

He looked at her askance, but opened the gate nearest to *Argento* who immediately came to her when she called.

She grabbed hold of *Zingaro*'s halter and led them out and down to the pasture at a slow, leisurely walk, talking to them, and reassuring them. She sat down on a rock in the pasture and watched the horses run around, drink from a stream and graze.

Zingaro whinnied loudly, and Liz looked around to see a couple of the grooms leading horses to the pasture under the direction of the officer to whom she had spoken. He left a groom and two armed men to guard the horses.

She glumly watched *Argento* grazing awhile, perched on the rock, her head in her hands. Nothing made any sense to her anymore, and she gave up trying to explain to herself the evil that had transpired.

Argento snuffled at her hair, blades of grass falling onto her shoulders.

"What's the big idea?" she stroked his soft muzzle.

She rose from the rock, rubbed her cheek against his, brushed off the seat of her britches, and left to find Piero in the *Palazzo*.

✳   ✳   ✳   ✳

On her headlong rush past the garrison, Liz suddenly remembered what Leonardo had told her about the possessed prisoner. She spun around and retraced her steps to see this prisoner for herself.

The two guards at the door to the jail recognized her and let her enter.

"I want to see the prisoner you're holding—Ceva," she said.

"If you want to see Ceva alive, it's good you came now for he won't be for much longer," one of the guards informed her.

"Why is that?"

"Duke Federico is going to hang him from the battlement. Word will get back to Malatesta, and he'll think twice about...."

The other guard laughed. "After tomorrow, you'll be able to see a dead Ceva hanging anytime you want...."

"Please, let me see him," Liz said, feeling the hair rise on the back of her neck.

They led her down a dark corridor of stone cells, each with a heavy wooden door and a small barred opening in the center. They pointed to the end cell on the right. She lost her nerve for a few seconds. But then, she gathered her courage and looked through the opening.

Sprawled on his back on a cot under a tiny window placed high in the wall, she could see, even in the shadows, that his face was swollen and purple. He had been severely beaten. She could even feel pity for him, for the Duke's justice would be swift and merciless.

She turned her back on him and addressed the guard.

"I heard you have another prisoner, a man that may be possessed. Is this true?"

"Him, yes," the guard answered, a note of pride in his voice. "Would you like to see him too?"

"Yes. I've never seen a man possessed by a demon."

"Over here," he said, pointing at the opposite cell.

Liz had no clue what to expect, but the sturdy door reassured her that whatever danger lurked behind it, she would be safe.

She peeked through the opening. It was so dark that at first she didn't see anything. Her eyes swept from left to right and back again. Then, a slight movement. Her eyes, adjusting enough to the dim light so she could focus, found him.

He moved his foot into a small pool of light, and incomprehension seized her. She looked at a white athletic shoe and then a leg clad in dirty jeans.

She looked over her shoulder and saw that the guards were observing Ceva in his cell and exchanging jokes.

She whispered through the bars in the opening. "Who are you?"

He stood and approached the door, his manner wary, his step shaky.

"Lou!"

He rushed at the door. "Liz! Is it really you?"

"Oh, my God, Lou." She couldn't believe her eyes. His voice sounded husky, but unmistakable.

"Get me out of here."

Liz looked around and saw that the guards had forgotten all about her.

"Shush! I'll get you out."

"Now!"

"I'll get you out as soon as I can. Let me think." She could see that he was in pretty bad shape, but she couldn't just go get the key and let him out.

"What are you waiting for?"

"This is going to take a little planning. I'll be back with reinforcements. Sit tight and don't make any waves."

"Don't make any waves?!! You get me out of here right now."

Liz turned to leave, but he reached through the bars and grabbed her sleeve.

"Please, Liz. I followed you here. I don't know how, and I don't know why, but we've got to go back."

"Don't you think I haven't been trying? Somehow you came through the portal, while I've been unable to go the other way. For all I know, it's a one way trip."

She hesitated, reluctant at this point to tell him about Piero. And, more importantly, she asked herself, how will I explain Lou to Piero?

"There's been a complication," she explained lamely.

"What do you mean, a complication?"

"I'm going to need some help getting you out. I'll be back. Trust me."

He released her, and she walked over to the guards.

"Thanks. I'll be going now, but I may be back with Maestro Piero. He expressed an interest in seeing the prisoners too. Will it be all right?"

"Any time. We've nothing better to do."

Liz beat a hasty retreat out of the garrison and ran as fast as her legs could go to the *Palazzo* to find Piero.

✳   ✳   ✳   ✳

She found him with Lorenzo viewing the frescoes in the chapel. She stopped just inside the door to catch her breath. They were talking in low tones so she was unable to hear anything of their conversation. Every now and then Piero glanced in her direction and smiled, and she sensed something momentous in that smile. Whatever Lorenzo was saying, Piero seemed pleased.

Telling him about Lou would take the smile off his face pretty quickly, but she had to have his help if she was to succeed in getting her brother home.

Finally, Piero's conversation with Lorenzo ended. The workmen filed in to resume their duties which Lorenzo's visit had interrupted.

Lorenzo strolled out of the chapel and along the gallery admiring the sculptures placed in niches along the walls.

Liz hurried over to Piero, who waited for her near the altar, far out of earshot of the workmen.

"Well, how did it go?" she asked, stalling for time while she figured out a way to tell him about her brother.

"It could not be any better for us. He wants me in *Firenze*." Piero bubbled with enthusiasm, barely containing his excitement, as he related his news.

He held up a hand to stop Liz from interrupting.

"Now listen to me and hear me out before you say a word. This is our chance, what we've been hoping for. We can make a life there together. He wants to start a school for young painters and sculptors. He wants me to teach and take on commissions too, both for him and for others he will recommend to me. He says I can live next to the school in a building the Medici own, and I can bring anyone I want with me to help me start the school. He has others who will participate, but he wants me to direct it. These are men I have admired, and we can take on joint commissions for the Commune. He wants to make *Firenze* into a city of artists and craftsmen."

He spoke so rapidly she was having a hard time following what he was saying. "What about your commission here?" she asked.

"That's the best part. Only the chapel is left to finish, and it can be finished in a few weeks. Lorenzo has asked the Duke if he would like him to stay with his men to help with the repairs to the city wall and the stable, and the Duke has agreed. Lorenzo will return to Tuscany with the *contadini* in time for the harvest, and we will go with him."

"How do you think the Duke will feel about your leaving?"

"He will be glad for me. There is nothing wrong with my accepting Lorenzo's offer. And it will resolve the trouble between the Sanzios and me. I never really wanted to be court painter, and the Duke knew this. It's too limiting. Well, *cara*, say something; aren't you pleased? We can stop in *Borgo San Sepolcro* to be married and arrive in *Firenze* as *Signor e Signora della Francesca*."

"I'm stunned. Of course, it seems too good to be true. It certainly sounds like it's everything we've dreamed of. Let's walk outside where we can discuss it."

He ran his hands through his hair in a gesture of frustration at her lackluster reaction. He expected her to be more excited.

"I thought you would be happy."

"I am," Liz said, thinking she wouldn't get a better chance than now. "Listen, Piero. Something's happened, and I'm sorry, but I'm a bit preoccupied because of it."

"What?"

Liz related finding her brother in the garrison lock up. She waited while he digested this information before asking for his help. He took her arm and led her out of the chapel and into the courtyard.

"We have to get him out and help him go back to the future," Liz demanded. "I owe him that. It's my fault he's here."

"But we've had no success with the door through time so how are we going to get it to open for him?"

"I don't know. But we must get him out of the cell. We'll worry about the portal later. The guards told me Ceva's going to hang tomorrow. Suppose they decide to make it a double hanging?"

The rising panic in Liz's voice stirred Piero to action, and he started toward the garrison, pulling her along.

"Let's go then."

"Wait. First, we have to have a plan as to how we're going to do this. We can't just walk in there and tell them to open up the cell."

They walked a few yards, thinking about the alternatives.

"I told the guards I'd be back with you. What I think we should do is come up with a plausible story, one they'll be certain to believe, and go to the garrison just before these two guards are finishing their shift."

"Ah, yes, I see. They'll be hungry and eager to leave," Piero said, nodding in agreement.

"Exactly. And you should wear the amulet to remind the guards of how you are favored by the Duke. We'll take along a change of clothing for my brother so he won't draw any attention when we take him to the chapel. But what reasonable story can we come up with?" Liz wrung her hands in desperation. She couldn't come up with anything. Seconds ticked by. Her mouth went dry—with fear.

"We can say he is a traveler from another land, and that I met him once before ..." Liz began.

"That's good," Piero interrupted. "But we'll say that I met him. You've already seen him, and the guards may grow suspicious that you didn't recognize him before. I'll say he's a student from the northern countries, and we'll apologize for the treatment he received—in front of the guards, of course—but in the confusion of the siege, it was understandable. And then we will offer him a bed in the artisans' building before he moves on."

"Right. That way no one will question it when he leaves," Liz nodded. "Are you good at lying?"

"*Pessimo*, terrible." Piero hung his head and wouldn't meet her gaze. Liz grabbed his arm, and he looked at her. Their eyes locked.

"We've got to do this, Piero, and do it right or my brother could end up dead."

"*Io lo farò, cara*. I will do it. I promise. It will be all right."

✳   ✳   ✳   ✳

As soon as they reached their rooms in the artisans' building, Liz gathered up clothing from Piero's wardrobe for Lou to wear while Piero donned his amulet.

Liz tried not to dwell on everything that could go wrong with this operation. She only wanted it to be over and Lou out of harm's way.

They rehearsed what they would say to the guards, placed the clothes in a bundle, and left the building.

"You have to project an air of casual calm and pretend that you recognize him. You can talk to the guards and distract them while I clue Lou in as to what our plan is," Liz said, noticing a muscle twitch under Piero's left eye.

"*Va bene,*" he answered, but Liz could tell he was nervous.

"The tough part will be getting him out of the cell."

"We'll find a way, and you will have to make your brother understand that his behavior is the key."

"Literally and figuratively."

CHAPTER 24

▼

The guards were lighting lamps inside the jail when they entered.

"Your apprentice said you might come," the older of the two guards said to Piero. He appeared to be the one in charge and immediately led Piero into the corridor of cells. The other guard followed them.

Liz had told Piero which cell was Ceva's so he headed in that direction, making small talk all the while with the two guards. Liz brought up the rear, dropping her bundle inside the door, and casually walked up to the door of Lou's cell.

"Lou, just listen to me," she whispered to him through the tiny barred window. "We're going to get you out of here. But I want you to stay quiet, not a peep. No talking, yelling or carrying on. It just won't do. You're a student from the Low Countries or somewhere to the north. A traveler who doesn't speak Italian. Do you understand? Stay calm and pleasant, but no smiling or showing any teeth. These guys are soldiers, and they'd just as soon kill you as look at you."

Lou paled visibly and nodded his head.

"Good."

Piero's exchange of "hail fellow, well met" pleasantries with the guards soon gained their confidence. They suggested raising a drink in honor of the Duke and returned to the anteroom where one had a bottle.

Liz watched Piero trail behind them and slip the key off the hook by the door. He handed off the key to Liz who picked up the bundle and went back to Lou's cell.

Her hands shaking, she placed the key in the well-oiled lock and turned. The door opened on silent hinges, and Liz passed the small bundle of clothing to Lou.

"Change quickly into those clothes and come out when you're done. Make it fast."

Liz's heart pounded in her chest. Their plan, while it had sounded good back in the *Palazzo*, had been sidestepped by the guards.

She went back to the door of the anteroom to keep watch and saw the replacement guards arrive.

Piero greeted them and more wine was passed around from the bottle. She heard the first two guards' report that all was well before leaving the replacements in charge.

Piero took a chair and put his feet up on a table, settling in for a chin wag and more wine with the replacements. He never once looked in her direction. If they carried this off, it would be because of Piero's utter lack of nervousness.

Liz returned to Lou's cell just as he emerged.

"I stuffed my clothes under the cot."

"Good."

"Now what?"

"Now we wait."

Liz adjusted Lou's garments and pulled a slouch hat from inside her shirt. She yanked it down low over his eyes and led him to the door, putting her finger to her lips.

She watched Piero for any sign that they were ready to make a move.

In less than an hour, the first bottle was gone. Liz was afraid that their luck wouldn't hold much longer.

One of the guards offered to fetch another bottle from his quarters, the chance they were waiting for.

Liz watched him leave. The remaining guard sat on a chair, totally relaxed, his back to the cells, reliving the battle for the city in minute detail for Piero.

She knew she had to make a move before the other guard returned.

As she crept up behind the guard, Piero never took his eyes from the guard's face and even managed to laugh at one of his remarks.

One savage blow with her closed fist to the soft part of his neck, and he dropped forward.

Piero caught him and sat him back in the chair, positioning him so that his neck, with the bruise already purpling, faced away from the door. He looked like he had fallen asleep.

"Is he all right?" Liz whispered.

"He's breathing, but he'll have a headache when he wakes," Piero reassured her.

Liz motioned to Lou who came out of the inner room and walked with them toward the door. Piero stepped through the door first and looked around. He casually stretched his arms over his head and signaled to Liz that the coast was clear.

He walked at a moderate pace so as not to arouse suspicion. Liz and Lou followed close behind.

They cut through the courtyard and cleared the garrison before breaking into a run. They mounted the outer steps of the chapel two at a time.

"No lights," Liz cautioned.

They huddled in the dark chapel.

Lou had been too concerned with making his escape to say a word, but now he looked expectantly from Piero to Liz.

"Lou, this is Piero. He's the complication I mentioned to you."

Lou glanced at Piero before turning back to her.

Liz took a deep breath and continued.

"I'm not going back with you. I'm staying here with him."

"You've got to be kidding me," Lou snarled through gritted teeth.

"I'm not. My life is here now. There's nothing for me back in my old life."

"I'm not leaving you here." He stood and faced her, growing more belligerent. "You're coming with me."

"No! I'm not. Please understand. I love him, and he loves me. Besides it's not up to you. You're going to go back and never breathe a word to anyone."

Fiery sparks shot through Lou's blue eyes as he looked from her to Piero.

Liz could tell that Piero understood what she said to Lou, even if he couldn't understand the language. She saw fear in Piero's green eyes and anger in her brother's blue ones. She knew one of them would be disappointed with her decision. And she knew it would be her brother who would have to bear the bitter disappointment, for the thought of never gazing into Piero's green eyes again was unthinkable.

"I've made my decision, Lou. You're going back, and I'm staying." Lou's shoulders sagged in resignation. "And once you go, we're going to find a way to close the portal … forever."

Piero walked toward the wall where Liz's image glowed palely in the somber light. "We must hurry, Elisabetta!"

Liz took Lou's hand and led him up to the wall. She smiled up at him, every vestige of fight gone out of him. She hugged him close before releasing him.

"*Guarda*! Look!"

They turned to look where Piero pointed. The wall shimmered, and the glow spread outward, more intense than Liz had ever seen it.

"Piero, we've never been together with the amulet close to the wall. Maybe that's all it takes," Liz said. "It's worth a try."

Piero nodded, and they stepped closer to the wall, the amulet between them.

The glow increased and the wall pulsated—flashes of light shooting in every direction.

Lou kissed his sister on the cheek.

"I love you. I'll always love you," Liz rasped, her voice raw with emotion.

He kissed her hand one last time and stepped through the portal.

Liz stared in disbelief for a long moment at the wall.

Piero put his arms around her.

She cried into his chest. "Do you think he made it home?"

"We must believe that he did, that he's safe," Piero answered, a relieved sigh escaping his lips.

✳   ✳   ✳   ✳

The long evening stretched before them. Now that the danger was past, Liz seemed to be enveloped in fog.

Piero watched her stumble through the rooms in a kind of shocked stupor. She lit the lamps in their rooms and sat down on the edge of the bed.

"Are you hungry?" Piero asked.

Liz mumbled something in reply that Piero couldn't make out.

"What?"

"What is he going to pay you?"

"Who?"

"Lorenzo. What is he going to pay you for teaching at this school of his?"

"I don't know."

"Surely you discussed it. The duties may prove to be very demanding, cutting into the time you would need to devote to seeking commissions and carrying them out. So you need to know what your teaching salary will be."

"We did not discuss such a thing."

"When I last saw Luca, he spoke to me about you."

The abrupt change of subject had thrown him off-guard. He had been thinking of her brother. "What did he say?"

"That I should watch out for you. And that's exactly what I intend to do. Lorenzo is very young. It may not have occurred to him. So, you must bring up the subject to him about payment for this teaching. In addition to your lodging and food, of course. You are a great master who should pass on your knowledge, but you must be suitably rewarded. At the same time, you must be able to retain and even enhance your own creativity."

Piero stood open-mouthed at Liz's speech. She smiled at him, a smile that totally disarmed him; and, at that moment, the notion crystallized in his mind that behind her girlish smile lurked a very remarkable woman with a formidable intellect and the heart of a lion.

"I will speak to him immediately. Let's take a walk."

"To the horses?"

"*Bene.*"

They sat on a rock and watched the horses cavort. It was here sitting in the pasture in the evening that one of Luca's lieutenants sought out Piero to tell him that the Captain was dead.

Liz was unable to console Piero even though she wanted nothing more than to put her arms around him when she saw the sadness in his eyes. But she was forced to continue the masquerade and fall in step behind him as he returned to the Captain's room in the garrison.

*   *   *   *

Almost a week passed before arrangements for Captain San Martini's funeral were finalized, a week in which Liz spent long hours caring for the wounded. She was glad she was so busy, too busy to worry about whether or not her brother made it back to his time.

No mention was made of the possessed man who had escaped from the jail. Liz doubted that the guards even remembered that Piero had been there when he disappeared from his cell.

Piero was extremely busy too—carrying messages for the Duchess and running errands for the Duke.

Liz finally had a chance to express her condolences to Mistress Isabella. On a particularly hectic morning, Mistress Isabella paid a visit to the "hospital" ward. One look at her haggard appearance and the deep mourning clothes she wore were evidence of just how close the relationship between Mistress Isabella and Captain Luca had been. The care of the Captain and the other wounded had taken a physical toll on Mistress Isabella that only rest would remedy.

That's why Liz had volunteered for the work in the ward, so that Mistress Isabella could take to her bed and return, with limitations, to her duties managing the household.

"Thank you, Cosimo. The Duchess needs my help," Mistress Isabella had said after the Captain's death when Liz offered to step in.

"Oh, no you don't. I'm volunteering because I want you to rest and get well, and I'm sure you'll be of greater service to the Duchess when you are completely recovered," Liz said, a stern look adding weight to her response, which had the desired effect. Mistress Isabella agreed to take the time she needed to recuperate.

Piero and Liz were up every day at the crack of dawn and barely had time to see or talk to each other until they collapsed, totally exhausted, into bed at night. Because the care of the wounded kept her almost completely isolated from everyone, Liz learned what was going on from Piero.

He shuttled back and forth with the Duchess's message to the priests at *San Bernardino* in her futile attempt to get them to accept Captain Luca's body for burial. One by one, a priest from every church in Urbino was summoned to the *Palazzo* by the Duchess, and each one refused to accept the unshriven body of Captain San Martini for burial.

The priests of *San Bernardino* who had jurisdiction over the Montefeltro family crypt also denied permission for the body to be interred there. There would be no anointing with holy oils, no Mass of Requiem for him, and finally, no burial in the consecrated Montefeltro family crypt as she wished.

Climbing into bed late at night, Piero held Liz and recounted the latest news in hushed whispers.

One night, he was silent, and she thought him preoccupied with his work or just too tired to talk.

"Is something wrong?" she asked.

"There are rumors about your brother. People were bound to say something."

"What are they saying?"

"That the devil came and snatched him away. Some even reported seeing him whisked into the sky and away over the hills on dragon's wings."

"Oh, for heaven's sake."

"No, it is good for us that they think such a thing. Soon they will forget about him altogether."

Liz turned her head away. She had mentioned her brother less and less, and Piero was unsure about telling her the rumor about her brother, but he decided in the end that it was best she heard it from him.

"And what more of Captain Luca's burial?"

"The Duke gave his permission to the Duchess to try with the Franciscans, but he knew that the priests would never permit it. They know full well how Luca felt when he was alive. As much as she wants it, I think they will never acquiesce to her wishes. She's hammering her head against a wall if she thinks she will move them. Each priest praised her for her faithfulness and goodness and then refused absolutely to give Mother Church's blessing to the mortal remains of our dear friend. You can't help but admire her though."

"I'm so sorry, *caro*. What will happen now?"

"The Duke has a plan, and I think in the end, she will accept it. What other choice is there?"

Piero explained the Duke's plan, which was to construct a small burial chamber next to the family crypt where the body could be laid to rest. There could be no objection by the church officials since he would not be in the crypt.

Deeply hurt and distraught, in the end the Duchess agreed.

When Liz learned that Captain San Martini's body was being placed in the chamber, a big piece of the puzzle fell into place.

Piero was safe, and the Fates had been placated—at least for now. She would be allowed to keep her love.

Only the mystery of the amulet remained. Could the source of its power ever be known?

$$* \qquad * \qquad * \qquad *$$

The stonemasons worked around the clock to construct the chamber, inside the crypt all night by torchlight, and during the day, the work proceeded on the outside. So ingeniously was it designed that, when they were finished, it appeared from the outside to be part of the original crypt.

The Duke took advantage of the extra manpower on hand and made daily inspections of the repairs to the city walls and buildings that had been damaged by Malatesta's artillery. The stable too was being repaired. Piero often accompanied the Duke on his inspections and helped work out the details with the engineers.

The Duchess worried about Mistress Isabella, the Duke worried about the Duchess, and everyone worried about the possibility that Malatesta would return with reinforcements to retake the city before the fortifications were repaired.

Daily and nightly patrols were sent out to supplement the day guards posted on the walls and at strategic outposts in the countryside.

In addition to helping with the repairs to the walls, buildings and stable, Piero strove to finish the chapel by the time Lorenzo was ready to leave for *Firenze*.

"We have to be ready to go with him," Piero whispered to Liz late at night and repeated it like a mantra whenever she bumped into him, usually on the stairs. Liz was afraid he would get sick from so much hard work, but he refused to slow down.

She consoled herself by making certain he didn't miss meals so that he would keep up his strength.

CHAPTER 25

▼

Heavy rain clouds obscured the sun on the day of Captain San Martini's funeral. The Duchess arranged for his body to lie in state in the grand courtyard of the *Palazzo* where those of the town who wished could come to pay their respects.

The body was placed on a granite *catafalco* or bier at the bottom of the grand stairs and flanked by masses of flower offerings. A covering was hastily installed over the *catafalco* to ward off the impending rain from the threatening clouds that grew ever more ominous. Large candles were placed at the head and foot of the bier and Luca's officers stationed themselves as an honor guard. The skies opened and drenched the townsfolk who braved the showers to file silently past the body.

At sunset, the Duke and Duchess, family members, members of the court, and the entire household gathered in the courtyard for the service devised by the Duchess as a substitute for a Mass. The service included scripture readings and was intended more to be a consolation for the mourners than any religious ritual.

Fresh candles did little to dispel the gloom, but at least the rain had stopped. Liz stood alongside the workmen and artisans and listened as five of Luca's friends selected by the Duchess read the short passages from scripture—passages that the Duchess had translated from the Latin and Greek bibles in the Duke's extensive library into the Italian vernacular so that the people could understand them.

The last to read was Piero.

Dressed in the dark blue tunic he had worn the day of the birthday *festa*, he touched the bier as he passed to stand directly next to the body of his friend. Out of respect, he had taken extra pains with his appearance. The Duke's amulet rested on his chest, and it glowed with an unearthly transcendence.

Head held high, he recited from memory in a clear strong voice.

His voice quavered once, but he recovered his composure and finished flaw-lessly. She mourned the passing of the Captain too, but Piero's melancholy expression tore at her heart. She wished she could go to him and put her arms around him.

When the readings ended, each mourner lit a taper from the candles next to the body. With her lit candle, Liz fell in step behind Piero. The body was borne aloft by the honor guard up the grand stairs and into the *Palazzo*. Everyone from the household solemnly accompanied the body into the chapel.

Liz held her taper and waited with everyone else. While she waited, the final passage of Piero's reading from Acts, 11:34 echoed in her mind: "Now I really understand that God is not a respecter of persons, but in every nation he who fears him and does what is right is acceptable to him … that he it is who has been appointed by God to be judge of the living and of the dead. To him all the prophets bear witness, that through his name all who believe in him may receive forgiveness of sins."

How appropriate, she thought, when Piero nudged her and whispered in her ear, his voice raw with urgency.

"Look behind us at the wall!"

Liz turned and gasped.

The entire section of the wall with her likeness at the center glowed and pulsated.

She whispered anxiously to Piero, "I know what we must do."

She motioned to him to follow her.

"When you go down to the crypt," she directed him when they were out of earshot, "leave the amulet with Luca where it will do no more harm. I want to stay with you, Piero, and I'm afraid of what it might do.…"

"Are you certain, *cara*? If you're right, and the amulet is behind it all, it means you can never go back."

"I'm certain, Piero. I made my choice when Lou went back. Get rid of the cursed thing, please!"

Piero crossed the chapel. The Duke, Cesare Gonzaga and Morella da Ortona prepared to escort the body below. Piero walked beside them.

Before descending the stair, he turned and smiled at Liz, and his smile reached her core. His wistful smile told her wordlessly that he was sure of her love for him.

The womenfolk and the rest of the household were spared the final descent. They waited in the chapel for the Duke and Captain Luca's friends to complete their grim task. Liz never took her eyes from the wall. She prayed. Her prayers were rewarded as the pulsation diminished and the glow receded.

At last, the men filed back into the chapel. Liz craned her neck and gulped back tears when she saw that Piero no longer wore the amulet.

For the first time in weeks, she felt unafraid and free of the power the amulet exerted over her fate. She had cast her lot with Piero; for the rest of her life, she would live with this man in this time.

The mourners dispersed slowly and silently from the chapel, Liz fighting back tears as she shuffled beside Piero.

The affection in which Luca was held had turned the makeshift service from a pathetic parody into a moving outpouring of love. There was no denying that Luca had died as he had lived, but it was his friends who would not let his passing go unmarked.

Over the sound of the mourners' feet slapping the marble floor, Liz heard the sound of the workmen sealing the chamber below.

✳   ✳   ✳   ✳

The morning dawned hot and clear on the day Piero and Liz were to depart for their new life in *Firenze*.

Liz stretched her muscles and rolled onto her side to look at Piero. It was very early, and she was lying in Piero's bed with nothing but a sheet covering her nakedness. Piero was naked too, their clothes scattered around the bed, the room messy with the last of the packing still to be done.

She watched the soft rise and fall of his breathing and the dark shadows cast on his cheeks by his eyelashes. Her love for him seemed to increase with each passing day and night. Oh, the nights he gave her!

The memory of their lovemaking made her smile, and she cuddled close to him. She blew gently on his ear and nibbled at the tender skin at the base of his throat. Her persistent attempts to wake him paid off and he stirred.

"Wake up, *assonnato* (sleepyhead)," she cooed. "We have to be ready to leave. And you fell asleep after only an hour of loving me last night, so I know you've had plenty of rest."

"I didn't know you were timing me," he mumbled.

"Oh, yes, only once. I think you're beginning to tire of me." She poked him in the ribs. "That would explain why you were so easily satisfied. I remember when ..."

Her mock complaints were cut short by his mouth roughly covering hers.

"What a lovely way to start our new life," Liz remarked when he ended the kiss, and she could catch her breath.

"Let's start and end every day of our lives with a kiss," he said.

"It's a deal."

*   *   *   *

Liz dressed quickly and left Piero's room. She climbed to the topmost parapet of the city wall to have one last look, savoring every sight, every smell. The tang of the sea in the air, the sharp scent of pine from the mountains, and the yellow gorse turning golden in the morning light hinted at an early autumn. She stared at the view for a long time, impressing every last detail in her mind's eye.

She took a breakfast tray back to their rooms. Piero was up, dressed and anxious to leave.

"Are they in the courtyard yet?"

"They'll be a while longer … it's still a disorganized mess. They have our cart ready for loading. I saw Mistress Isabella in the kitchen. She is preparing a basket of food for us to take on our journey."

When they finished their breakfast, they gathered the last of their belongings. Liz picked up the Duchess's gift.

"What's that?"

"I forgot to tell you. It's a gift from the Duchess."

"What is it?"

"I don't know. She asked me to open it when we were away from the city. There's a note in it too," she said.

"When we make camp tonight, we'll open it."

"Ready?"

They hurried to the courtyard where most of their belongings had been piled next to the cart. There were Piero's crates of books and instruments, his artist's brushes and a trunk of clothing—Piero's velvets, brocades and work clothes and Liz's meager hand-me-downs.

"We'll buy you new clothes; and I have written to my mother, and she is preparing everything we will need for our new home," Piero assured Liz as they stowed their wretched possessions in the cart.

The night before their departure, Piero had received a summons from the Duke. He had been expecting it because he had petitioned for an audience to seek his permission to leave. Despite Piero's reassurances, Liz had misgivings about how the Lord of Urbino would react now that the eve of their departure was at hand. It helped considerably that the Duke was very pleased with the decoration of the chapel and had nothing but praise for Piero's work.

As it turned out, he was as generous and gracious to Piero as he had always been and presented Piero with a gift of gold Florins. The interview had gone well, and Piero decided to surprise his Elisabetta with the Duke's other gift—the two horses, *Zingaro* and *Argento*.

She lamented, on several occasions, leaving her beloved *Argento* behind.

While Piero was with the Duke, Liz sought out Mistress Isabella, and together they went to the Duchess. They found her writing letters at her desk.

"Your Grace," Liz began, "I leave in the morning for *Firenze* with Maestro Piero and Signor Lorenzo, and I wanted to thank you for all your kindnesses and tell you that I will miss you and your beautiful city. I only hope I have the good fortune to return one day."

The Duchess rose from her chair and rested her hand on the delicate rosewood desk.

The Duchess's eyes swam with tears, and Liz feared she would succumb too. She bit her lower lip to keep from weeping, lest she let her disguise slip at this late date.

"You are always welcome here, Cosimo. Wait one moment for I have a parting gift for you," the Duchess said.

Liz began to protest, but the Duchess stilled her with an upraised hand and left the room. She returned in an instant with a large package wrapped in silken fabric.

"I don't want you to open this until you are well away from the city. There is a note in there as well. I am sure you will put this gift to good use."

"Your Grace, I don't know what to say except … thank you," Liz answered, with a sniffle.

Liz clutched the package to her chest and walked slowly with Mistress Isabella toward the hall. She felt like she was riding an emotional roller coaster, but made it unscathed all the way to the door.

In the doorway, she stopped and turned to look at the Duchess one last time. She returned Liz's look, a quizzical smile on her face, before turning back to her desk.

That evening, Liz and Piero met in the second floor hallway of the artisans' building. Liz was upstairs packing and heard footsteps pounding up the stairway. She peered over the rail to see Piero's handsome face sporting a huge grin.

"How did it go with the Duke?"

"He gave me every consideration, wished me well, and gave me a money gift."

Liz looked expectantly at the small leather pouch clutched in his right hand. He hefted the bag, and Liz heard the clink of metal.

"I have not looked, but from its weight …," Piero cocked an eyebrow.

They entered Piero's room and locked the door. Then he opened the pouch and dumped the coins onto the bed. A low whistle escaped his lips at the number of Florins glittering on the coverlet.

Liz's eyes widened in surprise and she asked, "What are they?"

"Gold Florins," Piero replied, "and there must be fifty of them, I'd venture. This means we will be able to set up a very comfortable home in *Firenze*."

"How wonderful!"

Piero scooped her up in his arms and spun her around the room. They fell onto the bed laughing at the jingling sound the coins made, a delightfully musical jingle.

"I spoke with Lorenzo too, only for a moment. I think I surprised him when I asked what I would be paid for the running of the studio and managing the school, but he said he would think on it, and we would discuss it further on our trip south. So, everything is falling into place, *cara*. Are you happy?"

"Yes. Ecstatically happy. Our real life is finally beginning."

His smile faded. His serious expression darkened the bright mood of a moment ago.

"What is it? Tell me." Liz felt a chill like when a cloud passes across the sun and shade cools the skin.

He shook his head. "It's not over. The Duke warned me about deserters from Malatesta's army terrorizing the countryside. He told me to be careful and make sure Lorenzo has outriders protecting him and that our swords are at the ready. I assured him that there was strength in numbers, and if we are attacked, we would be happy to dispatch the brigands to save him the trouble. He laughed heartily at that."

"And what of a horse for our cart?" Liz asked. "We will need one that can keep up with the others." Liz thought it wouldn't do to fall behind if desperate men were waiting to pounce on stragglers.

"Lorenzo will provide us with a carthorse to carry our goods to *Borgo San Sepolcro* where I told him I would stop for a short visit with my mother before continuing on to *Firenze*."

He pulled Liz close. "He'll be surprised when I arrive in *Firenze* with a bride."

"Don't let him talk you into taking some paltry sum," Liz insisted. "And he must provide us with a decent house to live in. If it is unfurnished, that will be all the better." Liz threw her arms around his neck. "It will be such fun for us to go about *Firenze* selecting our bed and tables, pottery and such."

"You make me wish we were already there, *cara*. This is our last night in Urbino. Shall we make the most of it?"

Piero tickled her and licked at the tender skin of her throat. She giggled and tried to break free, but she was no match for him, and he easily wrestled her onto her back.

"I have a confession, *cara*."

"You? What did you do?"

"I was going to surprise you tomorrow, but I think instead I may tell you my special news now."

"What special news?"

"Maybe you should coax me to tell you."

"The hell I will. I won't kiss you if you don't tell me," she retorted brazenly.

"Yes, you will," he bragged.

CHAPTER 26

▼

When they were ready to leave, they went to the courtyard where Mistress Isabella was waiting for them with a basket of food. Liz stowed it in the cart with the Duchess's gift and a few last minute odds and ends.

She couldn't resist hugging Mistress Isabella good-bye. The good lady who had been like a mother to Liz clucked her disapproval at their departure and dabbed at her eyes with her apron before ducking back into her kitchen.

When Liz looked around for Piero, she couldn't find him. She walked around the courtyard, noisy and crowded with Lorenzo's men and carts and horses, but couldn't find him anywhere.

She finally spotted him walking up the hill from the stables leading *Argento* and *Zingaro*. She walked toward him with a lump in her throat at the thought of parting from her dear *Argento*.

"And now for my surprise. Did you forget? I told you there was a surprise, but you distracted me. The horses are gifts to us from the Duke. We are taking them with us."

Liz's hands flew to her face, and she yelped. Piero couldn't tell if she was happy or sad. She threw her arms around *Argento*'s neck and sobbed into the horse's mane.

Piero shook his head and laughed until Liz regained control of herself. She rubbed her cheek on *Argento*'s muzzle, all the while darting menacing looks at Piero.

"Why didn't you tell me? You know how unhappy I've been at leaving him," she said through her tears.

"I know. I'm sorry." He turned away before Liz could see how truly lacking in contrition he was.

They tied the horses near their cart while one of Lorenzo's men hitched a strong young horse to their cart. At last, they were ready to leave, but the column was still not ready.

"Piero, why don't we go into the chapel for one last look before we leave?"

*   *   *   *

Piero and Liz tiptoed into the chapel and made a beeline for the section of the wall where Liz's likeness stared serenely back at them. The wall appeared solid with no shimmering and no voices to disturb the deep silence of the chapel.

"It's normal, Piero, there's nothing here."

Piero touched the wall with his fingertips and then pressed the palms of both hands against it.

"Be careful," Liz cautioned.

He leaned his weight against the wall and confirmed to his satisfaction that it was solid.

"It's as solid as granite. Let's go into the crypt."

They took two candles from the stand beside the altar and descended into the cool, dark crypt. Piero led the way to the back wall and stood and said a silent prayer for the repose of Luca's soul.

"*Requiescat in pace*, Luca."

Liz whispered a fervent thank you to Luca for becoming the unwitting custodian of the fearful amulet. In so doing, he restored her peace of mind.

They climbed the stairs to the chapel. While Piero disposed of the candles, Liz gazed at the beautiful frescoes surrounding her.

"It really is the most beautiful place. It makes me sad to leave it all behind to be enjoyed by others."

"I promise you I will create more art. I should say we, because I have come to rely on you, Elisabetta. The art we create will be as beautiful, if not more beautiful, than this," he said raising his arms to encompass the whole chapel.

*   *   *   *

Minutes later, their horses tied behind the cart, they rode out of Urbino behind Lorenzo, his *contadini*, and his *cavalieri*. Liz wondered if she would ever see the city again, but she had made her choice. Her life and her future lay before her, and her heart—that belonged to Piero.

She glanced over her shoulder and saw the body of Ceva hanging from the wall of the city—a gruesome reminder of a traitor's inevitable end.

✳   ✳   ✳   ✳

They camped that evening away from the main camp beside a small stream called the *Marecchia*. After traveling at a leisurely pace all day in a westerly direction, Lorenzo had ordered the column to halt to make camp in a small rise near the source of fresh water. Piero and Liz were impatient with the slow pace, eager to get to *Borgo San Sepolcro*, but at the same time, they were thankful nothing had happened to cause them to draw their swords.

Piero's intention was to leave Lorenzo's company on the morrow when he and Liz would diverge from the group and continue further south to *Borgo San Sepolcro* while Lorenzo continued west to *Firenze*.

Despite being famished, as soon as they set up camp, they tended to the three horses before digging into Mistress Isabella's basket. The good lady had come through with a veritable feast. In addition to bread, cheese, fruit and a terrine of roast chicken, there were two small cork-topped crocks, one of wine and one containing pickled vegetables.

After they ate, Liz stored the basket of leftover food in the cart. The edge of the wrapped gift from the Duchess caught her attention, reminding her that they were going to open it that night. She carried it back to the campfire where Piero was already lounging on a blanket.

Argento and *Zingaro* and the cart horse grazed a few feet away on the last of the summer grass close to the edge of the stream where it still grew lush and green.

"Remember," she said, holding up the package, "we were going to see what this is."

Liz sat down on the blanket next to Piero and undid the fabric ties which had been cleverly cut to form strips that tied the bundle together. Inside was a folded piece of parchment sealed with red wax bearing the Montefeltro crest. It rested on top of what looked like more fabric. This fabric was an intricately woven brocade of white and gold with flowers of deep wine red.

Piero took the note, and Liz held up the fabric to reveal that it was a sumptuous gown embellished at the neck and wrists with garnets. They stared at it in amazement.

"She knew," Liz exclaimed, color rushing to her face.

"It's beautiful," Piero said fingering the fabric. "How could she know?" he mused as he opened the wax seal to read the note.

"You didn't tell her, did you?" she asked.

"Of course not."

By the light of the campfire, Piero read aloud the Duchess's tender words of affection for them. The feeling conveyed in her message made Liz feel as if the Duchess stood in front of them delivering her message in person.

> "Dear Cosimo, When you read this, I know you will be well on your way to a new life. I hope you find happiness and good fortune. Do not think that you were unsuccessful in your deception for I alone could see the halo of light surrounding you that Piero's love inspired. Think of me and your friends in Urbino when you wear this gown, and know that my thanks and my prayers go with you and with Piero. May God bless your union and make you fruitful."

It was signed "Batt. Sforza da Montefeltro" and bore the Montefeltro eagle hallmark on the parchment.

"She knew. We fooled everybody else, but not her. How did she guess?"

"I don't know, *cara*," Piero answered with a rueful smile.

"She says it was some halo of light. I suppose I was unable to hide my love for you."

When they turned in, Liz laid awake long into the night staring at the stars. While the camp slept, she was awake, still pondering the imponderable.

Piero snored softly close by on his blankets, near but not too near to arouse any suspicion from one of Lorenzo's night guard who might wander over to their campsite.

A noise crackled in the underbrush. *Zingaro*'s head came up, and he pricked his ears at the sound.

Liz sat up and heard a horse whinny from beyond the outskirts of the camp. Lorenzo's horses were on the far side in the opposite direction, so Liz crawled slowly to where Piero slept.

"Piero, wake up," she whispered as she shook him gently and pressed her hand over his mouth when he opened his mouth to answer.

"I hear intruders."

In one fluid motion, he rolled away from her and stood, grasping his sword which lay at his side.

"Go alert the others."

"I won't leave you."

"Do not argue with me. Go now," he spat, his voice a low growl.

His tone propelled Liz to run as fast as she could to the nearest sentry. In moments, the alarm was sounded, and the entire camp came to life.

Amid the uproar, she returned to their camp leading four of Lorenzo's men. She had snatched up a small sword on the way back and brandished it as she joined Piero in fighting off two attackers.

The men she brought back with her soon had the better of the men who foolishly, it turned out, had not seen the main body of the camp and thought Piero and Liz were alone and could be easily robbed.

The men threw down their swords and surrendered quickly. They were dressed in Malatesta colors and were hauled before Lorenzo who would have the task of meting out their punishment.

A sweep of the area revealed they were in no further danger. Thankfully, Piero had not been hurt.

Even though more sentries were posted, it was impossible to get back to sleep.

Piero and Liz spent the remainder of the night resting and hatching plans for their future.

With dawn a couple of hours away, they re-checked their cart and the horses and decided to leave immediately.

In going through the cart, Liz remembered the Duke's gift. She pulled on Piero's sleeve and whispered anxiously, "Where is the gold from the Duke?"

"Here safe and sound inside my tunic," Piero said, patting his side.

Liz hitched up the carthorse, secured the campsite and tied *Argento* and *Zingaro* to the back of the cart while Piero walked through the camp to find Lorenzo and say his goodbyes. He found him seated at a campfire with his *cavalieri*. Piero told him he was leaving ahead of schedule and would see him soon in *Firenze*.

"Would you like an escort from among my men?" Lorenzo asked him.

"No, *Signore*, I think it will be well enough. It is not far to *Borgo San Sepolcro*. If I leave now, I will see my mother all the sooner. Thank you, *Signore*, for your protection and company."

"Very well, Maestro Piero, all will be made ready for your arrival. I look forward to making you welcome in *Firenze*. And I think you will find me generous. It is right that you should be paid well to run the studio."

Piero's spirits soared with Lorenzo's last remark, and he returned to Liz with wings on his feet.

*   *   *   *

They stopped on a hilltop across a valley from the small city of *Borgo San Sepolcro*. Liz got her first look at the birthplace of her beloved, and her eye was drawn to the bell tower of the ancient church that sat prominently on the highest point in the town. Below it, weaving through the valley, was the *Tevere*, a small river that they had crossed farther north where it flowed past the charming little town of *Pieve San Stèfano*. The *Tevere* would continue flowing south to Rome.

Piero had insisted on riding through *Pieve San Stèfano* early in the morning where they stopped outside a merchant's shop. He admonished her to stay in the cart and darted in and returned with a bundle he threw into the cart before they continued on their way.

Liz looked over her shoulder at the bundle several times, but to her repeated inquiries, Piero shook his head and smiled to the point that Liz wanted to box his ears.

"What did you buy? Why can't I see? What took so long?"

Now, as she scanned the valley and *Borgo San Sepolcro* beyond, he clambered down from the cart, chuckling to himself in a way that vexed Liz even more. He turned the bundle over and beckoned her with his finger. She glared at him, not stirring from her seat in the cart.

"Come, *cara, mi spiace*. I won't tease you anymore. It's for you."

She climbed down from the cart slowly as if to show him that she wasn't really interested in what was in the bundle and that she wasn't going to forgive him so easily.

He twisted his mouth in a wry smile as he came from the back of the cart. When he took her in his arms, she displayed a disdainful lack of interest.

"*Cara*, did you think I would have you meet my mother dressed as a boy. She will think I have gone mad—or worse."

She felt his warm breath on her face, and smelled the maleness of his scent that she found irresistible, a combination of woodlands, smoke and something akin to turpentine that clung to him.

She looked deeply into his eyes, all the encouragement he needed. He bent his head and kissed her.

"*Cara, ti voglio bene. Ti amo, la mia tesora*," he murmured.

He released her and pushed the bundle toward her.

She tore at it and inside found a white muslin blouse with long full sleeves bordered with deep lace at the rounded neckline and wrists and a dark blue embroidered bodice with a matching blue skirt in fine light-weight wool. There were matching embroidered sleeves that could be attached to the bodice, like ladies of the court wore. Petticoats, ribbons, hose and delicate black slippers of the softest suede completed the ensemble.

"Do you like them?"

"You foolish man! What a question," she gushed.

"And I know a jeweler in *Borgo San Sepolcro* who will make our wedding rings," Piero added for good measure.

Liz hid behind the cart and used the last of their water to wash herself and then put on the new clothes.

Piero watched in admiration as the transformation took place. She brushed her hair and tied it up with the blue ribbons.

As sunlight turned her hair to gold, he promised himself he would buy her gold earbobs too for a wedding present when he bought their wedding rings.

She giggled as she tried but failed to climb into the cart with the full skirt and petticoat. "I'm going to have to get used to wearing dresses again, aren't I?"

She gripped his arm for support and landed with a thud in the cart.

For the first time, in a long time, she felt like a girl.

✳   ✳   ✳   ✳

Five days later, Liz greeted well-wishers on the steps of *Chiesa di Santa Chiara* in *Borgo San Sepolcro*, a radiant bride wearing the Duchess's gift, the white and gold brocade gown. Piero, green eyes fairly glowing and acceding to Liz's request, wore his dark green doublet and hose. Matching chaplets of ferns and flowers adorned their heads.

When they exchanged their vows with Piero's family in attendance, his mother Romana, his uncles and aunts, his cousins, Liz's thoughts turned to her own family. What should have been the happiest day of her life was tinged with sadness.

Side by side, Piero's arm protectively encircling her waist, they received the congratulations of his family and a few close friends. She pushed aside thoughts of her absent family—of her brother—lost to her forever.

Piero's family was her family now.

She wiped away unshed tears along with her sad thoughts as she reflected on her path to this moment. Rife with twists and turns, she knew through it all that the man standing next to her would bring her safely to this, her greatest happiness.

Her husband's family clustered around them. Piero's gaze sought hers, and the bright smile he gave her was full of such love and wonder that her heart nearly stopped beating.

*   *   *   *

When they first arrived in *Borgo San Sepolcro*, they had been welcomed like visiting royalty. Piero's mother was curious about the young woman who had captured her son's wayward heart. She insisted on showing them everything the women of the family had gathered for their new home in *Firenze*.

The four days leading up to the wedding passed in a blur of new faces and parties and visits from Piero's extended family who came laden with even more gifts for the bridal couple.

They hardly had a moment alone together. But Liz was cosseted and drawn into the circle of the family, and the outpouring of love and acceptance touched her deeply. She was the woman Piero had chosen, and so, they would love her as he loved her.

The morning of the wedding, Piero's aunt arrived with a beautiful veil that she had sewn from the sheerest of silk, and Piero gathered the most beautiful flowers the late summer could yield to fashion her bouquet. He tied the flowers with a wide white ribbon that he had decorated with birds, so lifelike that Liz felt she had to clutch the bouquet tightly to keep it from flying out of her hands.

*   *   *   *

They descended the steps of the church amid cheers of joy from family and friends. The throng hustled them along to the party prepared in their honor.

She smiled at him, and he stopped. He held her hand in both of his as he whispered, so only she could hear.

"And now, *Piccolina*, forever begins."

THE END

EPILOGUE

▼

Urbino, Present Day

When Lou Cummings resurfaced in the Urbino of his own time, he refused to explain where he had been. He was dirty and disheveled when found wandering by police outside the *Palazzo*. His refusal to explain his whereabouts inspired reproachful looks from the police and censure from the University officials still stinging from the disappearance of his sister.

Still, he refused to utter a word of explanation.

He bought a plane ticket and departed for home, never to return.

*　　　*　　　*　　　*

As the years passed, his memory of what transpired faded, along with his nightmares. He made peace with his parents for failing to bring Liz home.

Sometimes, he was able to convince himself it had never really happened— that it was only a bad dream. He invented explanations for himself that he could live with.

But then, a smell, or the sight of a familiar scene, or the ringing of a church bell would trigger a memory, and every detail would come flashing back as if it were yesterday.

*　　　*　　　*　　　*

Urbino, 1494

The adventure does not end with my wedding. It marked only the beginning of a glorious phase in my life. Even now, after almost twenty-five years, it continues.

In the years following our marriage, we would sometimes laugh at the memory of that couple standing on the church steps, so full of hope and promise. We sought refuge in *Firenze* from the turmoil in Urbino only to find ourselves time and time again embroiled in the political upheaval of our adopted city.

How naïve we were to think we could live a quiet life! We were inextricably tied to the fortunes of the Medici, and in particular, Lorenzo. As the power and influence of the Medici waxed and waned, it was Piero's unparalleled talent and goodness that kept us safe because he was admired and respected above all the artists in that city of great artists.

Lorenzo was true to his word. We lived a comfortable life, and Piero was incredibly busy with teaching and commissions. Artists from all over Italy—and even the north countries—journeyed to *Firenze* to see his work. They made excursions to *Arezzo* and Urbino to see his earlier works so they might learn all they could from them. Some even reported to Piero that they went to see his early works first in order to see the development of his art and understand how he had progressed, and so imitate his creative flourishes.

Through the years, every one of my girlhood dreams came true. He consulted with me before accepting any commission, and I worked with him in the studio. I was wife, lover, and helpmate, source of inspiration and mother of his children.

I bore him three children, and we were fortunate that they lived. I survived the births because I made sure I found the best midwife in the city and added to her knowledge to help me, and in so doing, she was able to help every mother she touched. She soon became renowned for the survival of her mothers and babies and tended the nobility, but would attend any mother regardless of her station.

We have two sons. The oldest is named Luca, the second is Lorenzo. The third child is my Margaretta—named after my mother. All three children have been our greatest joy.

That is not to say that our lives have been without heartache and bitter disappointments. We lost two children in the womb. And—worst of all—I have seen my beloved husband's vision slowly fail. Over the last three years, the light has gone from those green eyes that have brought me as close to heaven as I am ever likely to get.

Our son, Luca, has been his father's mainstay. He has taken over the running of the studio and helps with every aspect of his father's teaching, and has become, as a consequence, quite adept at the management of business. It is ironic that he is named after our dear old friend, the custodian of the storied object we refer to in whispers as "The Duke's Amulet."

Footsteps sound in the hall—Piero and Luca's—and the tap of my beloved's cane against the walls tells me he comes to fetch me for supper.

"Elisabetta!"

Funny, after all these years, how my heart still leaps at the sound of his voice. Love is truly forever.

Author's Notes

This is a work of fiction. However, several of the main characters are historical personages, and acknowledgment must be made to certain sources that illuminate their lives and the age in which they lived, over five hundred years in the distant past. The most notable of these sources is *The Book of the Courtier* ("Il Cortigiano") by Baldassare Castiglione, 1528 (Translated by George Bull)© 1967 Penguin Books. Castiglione's book, a seminal work that inspired courts throughout Europe, is a fly-on-the-wall look at life in Urbino, the most urbane and cultured court of the Renaissance. Indeed, many have speculated that the book was the inspiration for the flowering of medieval-renaissance court life throughout Europe. It must be stated that not all courts were as splendid and sophisticated as that in Urbino despite the model it provided. Unfortunately, there remained many princes who were unenlightened, if not venal, cruel and debauched. Their courts reflected the personalities of those who wore the royal or princely mantle.

The author also wishes to acknowledge the following:

Federico da Montefeltro and Sigismondo Malatesta: The Eagle and the Elephant, Studies in Italian Culture—Literature in History; Vol. 20: Maria Grazia Pernis and Laurie Schneider Adams, ©1996 Peter Lang.

Piero della Francesca—The Arezzo Frescoes, M. A. Michael, ©1996 Thames and Hudson, Ltd., London.

The Italian Renaissance, J. H. Plumb, The American Heritage Library ©1961, 1987 Ed. Houghton Mifflin Co.

Uppity Women of Medieval Times, Vicki Leon ©1997, MJF Books.

Uppity Women of the Renaissance, Vicki Leon ©1999, Conari Press.

*   *   *   *

Piero della Francesca *(1415?-1492)*—Not much is known of the early life of this great Italian master of the *fresco*, an art form which dates from the ancient Greeks and Romans. He was born near Arezzo in Borgo San Sepolcro, the son of a tanner and bootmaker, to a mother who was already widowed. At that time, Borgo San Sepolcro would have been part of the Papal States. His life and upbringing was dependent solely on the largesse of his mother's family, who provided him with a classical education so that he was well prepared in mathematics and Latin when he was apprenticed to local masters of the burgeoning artistic community centered in Florence. It cannot be denied that the intellectual pursuits of this clever and curious young man led him throughout his life to achieve his greatest potential, and this is solely thanks to his natural and god-given gifts. He traveled to Florence and by 1439 was working with Domenico Veneziano, a Venetian painter (hence his name), of some renown. There, he came under the influence of sculptors, like Donatello and dellaRobbia. They fueled his interest in the use of perspective, so easily achieved by the sculptor, to create paintings that fooled the eye into a multi-dimensional illusion of space and depth. He developed the use of different mediums to work in *fresco* on large expanses, such as found on church walls, which provided the ideal venue for experiments with light and color, to achieve his three-dimensional effect. His work presaged the art of daVinci and Michelangelo who most assuredly viewed della Francesca's work in Arezzo, his masterpiece frescoes (Cycle of The Legend of the True Cross, designated a World Heritage Site by the United Nations) in the Church of San Francesco. What survives of della Francesca's art—the work he did on commission from the Duke of Urbino and Sigismondo Malatesta—as well as the surviving work he executed throughout Tuscany and in Rome secures his place in the great Pantheon of the Renaissance Masters of Western Art. Sadly, as his life neared its end, this great Master was afflicted by blindness and found himself at the mercy of an unscrupulous priest named Luca Pacioli da Borgo who cared for him and later published under his own name the treatises on perspective, geometry, and mathematics penned by the great master. The truth came out—somehow it always does—and a discredited Pacioli da Borgo first suffered disgrace at the hands of his fellow Franciscans and then faded into obscurity.

*   *   *   *

Federico da Montefeltro *(1422-1482)* "The Light of Italy"—The young Federico was 22 years old when he became the Lord of Urbino. His innate talent and intelligence were recognized early on by his father, Guidantonio, who saw to it that this illegitimate son of his received every advantage to which his station entitled him. Thus, he was groomed from childhood to assume his rightful place as his father's true successor. He was heir to an ancient and aristocratic name and through cunning, diplomacy and military prowess led his family from medievalism into the age of Renaissance enlightenment. He was a scholar who compiled an extensive library with rare editions of ancient texts. He was a keen politician who forged alliances among the princely city-states to offset the prodigious power of the papacy. He was a humanist, evidenced by the fact that his Ducal Palace of 250 rooms was for the most part open to the people of Urbino who were permitted to come and go freely into all except his most private apartments. This architectural gem which exists to this day was enlarged and embellished under his guiding hand.

*   *   *   *

Battista Sforza da Montefeltro *(1446-1472)*—Federico's second wife (Gentile Brancaleoni, five years older than Federico, was his first wife) brought an alliance with the powerful Sforza family as his first marriage consolidated Brancaleoni wealth and lands in his hands. The convoluted tapestry of marriage between and among the noble houses of Italy, wherein alliances were forged and then broken and re-aligned at the death of the wife (which frequently happened due to childbirth and illness), was for the most part the political union of great wealth and power. The marriage of Federico and Battista seems to have been one of true empathy and respect, if not great passion. They were married in 1459 when Battista was 13 years old. According to the reports of historians of the time, she was well-educated and skilled in the traditional female arts. Over the course of time, she also became a shrewd administrator and conducted her husband's affairs of state in his absence. In the course of the next ten years, she produced several daughters from her eight pregnancies. She finally produced the long sought after legitimate male heir, Guidobaldo, in January 1472, but succumbed to fever at the age of 26 in July of the same year. It is a lasting testament to her memory that throughout the rest of his long life, despite the pressure to do so, Federico never remarried. Her son died childless and so the Duchy passed into the hands of the Della Rovere family, his wife's relations, who in turn were ousted by the Medici Pope Leo X who annexed Urbino and the Montefeltro lands into the Papal States and installed his nephew, Lorenzo (not Lorenzo the Magnificent) as Duke of Urbino. Lorenzo's daughter, Catherine de Medici, at fourteen years of age, married Henri de Valois, Duke of Orleans. When Henri ascended the throne, Catherine was at his side, Queen of France.

✳   ✳   ✳   ✳

The keyword of the Renaissance would have to be innovation. While the Renaissance princes and their courtiers relied heavily on the re-discovery of ancient knowledge, particularly that of the Roman and Greek civilizations, they were not afraid to build on that knowledge. Their scientists, scholars, mathematicians and philosophers revisited the monuments of those great civilizations and unearthed ancient texts which led them down new paths. The rising guilds and middle class fueled both the economy and their intense curiosity. Experimentation and exploration became the hallmarks of this New Age of Humanism and Enlightenment.

In Ross King's *Brunelleschi's Dome* (© 2000 Walker Publishing Co., Inc.), he recounts how the great work of constructing the Church of Santa Maria dei Fiore, the Duomo of Florence, especially the raising of the dome over the church, was the combined effort of hundreds, if not thousands, of craftsmen and workers. But it was the genius Brunelleschi alone who challenged the conventional wisdom of the day and designed the dome—unlike any other since ancient times—based on his study and calculations. He then envisioned and built the innovative machines and devices necessary to enable him to accomplish his goal.

The modern world can never repay the debt of gratitude to those geniuses of innovation who devised the navigational tools that Columbus and his like used to circumnavigate the globe, to the builders, composers, and artists who spurred on the human spirit to reach new heights. Without the Renaissance, would there have been an industrial revolution?

This predilection for innovation in all of the arts and sciences extended even to the culinary arts. Italy has a long tradition of occupation and assimilation by royal houses that added their customs, influence and culture into the rich panorama of Italian cuisine. When Catherine De Medici traveled from her Tuscan home to Paris (in 1533) to become the wife of King Henry II and assume the role of France's Queen, chefs trained in the Italian culinary arts were part of her entourage. Thus began the long tradition of Gallic cuisine—thanks to the innovations introduced to the French court by the Italian chefs. Two hundred years later, the *Monzù* chefs of France would return to Italy in the entourage of a Hapsburg princess, Maria Carolina of Austria, sister to Marie Antoinette, when she married the Bourbon King of Naples, Ferdinand IV.

Even today, when we walk blithely into our food markets and see the array of produce and the combinations that comprise today's bounty, we can thank that innovative Italian chef whose tradition inspires us. Because one day long ago, he or she first experimented with the humble Italian staple of pasta by marrying it to the new world tomato.

978-0-595-46217-9
0-595-46217-0

Printed in the USA
CPSIA information can be obtained
at www.ICGtesting.com
CBHW021055290924
15080CB00025B/123

9 780595 462179